MW01064778

STEEL TRAPP

THE ACADEMY

ALSO BY RIDLEY PEARSON

Kingdom Keepers—Disney After Dark
Kingdom Keepers II—Disney at Dawn
Steel Trapp—The Challenge

WITH DAVE BARRY

Blood Tide
Cave of the Dark Wind
Escape from the Carnivale
Peter and the Sword of Mercy
Peter and the Secret of Rundoon
Peter and the Shadow Thieves
Peter and the Starcatchers
Science Fair

STEEL TRAPP

THE ACADEMY

RIDLEY
PEARSON

FIC PEA
Pearson, Ridley
    Steel Trapp : the academy
T 37071

Disney • HYPERION BOOKS

New York

For Storey and Paige

Thanks to the faculty and alumni of Pomfret School, the model for Wynncliff. Peter Wormser and I traveled around in those tunnels . . . not that anyone ever knew (I hope). A portion of the proceeds from the book goes to Pomfret. Thanks also to Bobby K. for our adventures in Boston as young seventeen-year-olds. And to Marcelle, Wendy, Jessie, Jennifer, Laurel, David, Tanner, and Nancy for their help through the various drafts. (Any mistakes are all theirs!)

Copyright © 2010 Page One, Inc.
All rights reserved.
Published by Disney • Hyperion Books, an imprint of Disney Book Group.
No part of this book may be reproduced or transmitted in any form
or by any means, electronic or mechanical, including photocopying,
recording, or by any information storage and retrieval system,
without written permission from the publisher.
For information address Disney • Hyperion Books,
114 Fifth Avenue, New York, New York 10011-5690.
Printed in the United States of America
First Edition
10 9 8 7 6 5 4 3 2 1
V567-9638-5-09335

Reinforced binding

Library of Congress Cataloging-in-Publication Data on file.
ISBN 978-1-4231-1532-8

Visit www.disneybooks.com
www.ridleypearson.com

SUSTAINABLE FORESTRY INITIATIVE
Certified Fiber Sourcing
www.sfiprogram.org

THIS LABEL APPLIES TO TEXT STOCK

FIC
PEA

STEEL TRAPP

THE ACADEMY

Ingram $15.99 8/10

1.
TRESPASS

The brightly lit lower-level corridor stretched out ahead of him, impossibly long, like some kind of throat, offering no place for Steel to hide.

Steven "Steel" Trapp had walked the same corridor only once, two months earlier, while being given a guided tour by an upperclassman, a Fifth Form student—a high school junior by the name of Walker Glasscock. But he could recall with perfect clarity each door, every name on the plastic plates to the left of the doors—WRESTLING, A/V, DANCE, TRACK COACH, FOOTBALL COACH, MECHANICALS, etc.—not only the layout but the exact number of chairs in any of the rooms he'd seen on the tour. For that matter, he could remember the items on a Whiskey River dinner menu he'd chosen from two years earlier, the prices and the phone number of the restaurant, and the name—Chloe—of the waitress who'd served him that night along with his mother and father. He suspected his uncanny memory skills were responsible for his winning admission to Wynncliff Academy.

"Remember," his father had said when dropping him off, "if you don't like it, you can come home. But I want you to—"

"—give it until Thanksgiving before deciding," Steel had finished for him. "I know, Dad. You've told me that seven times."

"Seven?"

"That was the seventh, yes."

His father didn't challenge the accuracy of his son's memory. Neither did his teachers. In fact, it had been a teacher who'd given him the nickname "Steel" because young Steven "had a mind like a steel trap." He never forgot *anything*. He was something of a freak, but he'd come to live with it. He learned not to show off or misuse what his mother called "his gift." Showing off cost friendships, and lost friendships made him lonely. He'd learned the hard way.

Here at Wynncliff he would have to be careful. Other kids typically resented his ability. Teachers were intimidated by him. It wasn't going to be easy.

But presently he wasn't thinking about any of that. Because presently some big kid was chasing him, and he desperately needed a place to hide.

He didn't have to think to recall things—they were just there, always available, in the front of his mind, correcting his decisions the way eyeglasses corrected a person's vision. His recall was as fast as Google. That was why he took the fourth door on the right without reading CUSTODIAN on the plate. He quietly pulled the door shut and wedged himself behind some broom and mop handles. The closet was the size of a phone booth, a giant sink occupying nearly half of it.

He wasn't exactly sure what he'd seen, but now he didn't want to find out. Certainly not on the first day of school. He would later discover that a sign had blown over due to the strong and endless winds that streamed across the hilltop school. Northeastern Connecticut was all rolling hills and forests, broken by a few orchards and even fewer farms. It was the strangest location for a school—so far from everything. He'd already heard a rumor that the school's sports teams never played home games—only away games, as if its location were being kept secret.

A man named William Bromfield Wynncliff had

decided to build a compound of white-trimmed brick buildings in a cleared field on top of a Connecticut mountaintop, 117 years earlier. The location seemed more suitable for a wind farm than a school. And it had been the wind that had blown over a sign reading: GYM CLOSED. DO NOT ENTER. WILL REOPEN AT 12:00 P.M.

So Steel hadn't seen the sign. His objective had been to put his gym clothes into his assigned locker. It hadn't occurred to him that by arriving to the gym so early he might end up interrupting something. It hadn't occurred to him that by keying in a code on the building's security pad to gain entrance, he might be violating a school rule. The kid who had toured him around the campus on his previous visit had used the code—and Steel remembered it, just as he remembered everything. Having a security lock on the gym—and some of the other buildings— had been a curiosity to Steel at the time, but he hadn't said anything. Now, instead of going back to the administration building and asking questions, he simply let himself in, figuring this was how it was done. He'd entered the lobby and, upon hearing voices, had opened the gym doors.

What he'd seen had momentarily paralyzed him: four boys, posed down on one knee, facing four mannequins across the gym. There was a coach standing slightly behind them. All four boys were holding long stainless-steel tubes to their mouths. On the coach's cue, they fired darts at the mannequin targets.

"No!" the coach said loudly. "It's not enough to simply hit the target. These aren't spitballs! The darts must be fired with enough force to result in the injection! Without that, the effort is useless! The idea is to render your opponent unconscious."

Blowguns? Steel wondered. *How cool is that?*

He gasped, drawing attention to himself, but wasn't embarrassed to be seen: he would sign up for Blowguns 101 in a nanosecond. He had no way of knowing that because of the lighting he was only seen in silhouette; he assumed they got a good look at him. But he hoped not, as the coach shouted, "Who's there? Stay where you are!" For a moment Steel didn't process what was going on, didn't realize he was in a closed practice. Then the tension in the coach's voice registered.

When the coach spoke to the boys, saying, "Well? Go get him!" Steel stood frozen for a second as one of the boys—a *big* guy—stood and came toward him at a full sprint. At that moment he regretted using the security code to let himself in. He regretted allowing himself to be seen. More than anything, he wanted to do the right thing, given the situation.

He took off running.

The idea of an upperclassman pursuing him, on the first day of school no less, sent Steel leaping onto and sliding down the staircase's metal hand railing. He rode the next handrail to the facility's lower level. The kid hadn't tried the rail; he stayed to the stairs, buying Steel a few precious seconds.

From there he'd faced an instant decision and had gone left, because his photographic memory had delivered perfect recall of the layout from his prior tour.

A janitor closet.

He kept perfectly still inside the sour-smelling closet, his chest burning, his ears ringing, his body rigid in a giant knot.

The sound of footfalls—had he actually seen them firing *blow darts?* he wondered—sped past the door, then returned in his direction. He heard a nearby door open and close. Another. A third. Moving steadily closer. He pushed his back into the corner, the dozen broom and mop handles covering him like a lean-to shelter. He held his breath.

The door swung open.

A hand slapped the wall for a light switch, but

raked the broom handles into a noisy complaint, missing the switch. Steel did not breathe. The door shut, and the footfalls continued one door to the next.

At last, there were several long minutes of silence.

The pursuit had stopped.

He dared a peek out. An exit sign beckoned at the end of the long hall.

He ran for it and sneaked outside, taking a deep sigh, his lungs filling with the clean, crisp, hilltop air.

He was glad to be free, but more pressing was his recollection of the four boys firing darts at dummies, for he could—and did—replay it in his mind exactly as he'd seen it.

Why would a school—any school—teach kids how to fire blowguns? And why did they care if he saw it, unless it was something they weren't supposed to be doing? And if they weren't supposed to be doing it, then why had a man been coaching them? None of it made any sense.

And for once, for perhaps the first time in his life, he did not trust his own memory.

2.
DELIVERY BOYS

Brian Taddler spit the glob of gum out into his hand and smacked the side of the potted tree outside Boston's Patriot Hotel, sticking the gum on the side of the urn. He marched through the automatic doors as if he were a member of a royal family.

At fifteen, Taddler could pass for a few years older or a few years younger, depending on how he dressed. His close-cropped, nearly shaved head, and dark, brooding eyes suggested intensity if not outright menace. But Brian Taddler's smile and a missing front tooth transformed his face into youthful exuberance. This evening he wanted to look younger, and he did so in a pair of khakis and a pale blue golf shirt.

Cocktails were about to begin. There would be a

crush to get through the doors to the Paul Revere Ballroom A. He picked out the first fat woman he saw—for this was the only description Mrs. D. had given him.

Taddler drew close to this woman. In a fraction of a second, his hands could have slipped in and out of her jacket pockets. He was perfectly capable of lifting money or even removing jewelry without her being the least bit aware. But he did not. The name was wrong.

Emerson was the name of his mark. This woman's tag read *Richards*.

Taddler smiled at her, and moved on.

A moment later, near the bar, he finally spotted her. Gwen Emerson was a big woman whose wool purse didn't latch, and offered an easy target. Taddler approached her, faked a stumble as if tripping over his shoelaces, and face-planted himself into her massive chest—assuring that her purse would be the last thing on her mind. He pulled his face away and stammered an apology. At the same time he slipped a small, rectangular paper envelope from her purse into his own back pocket. A room key envelope certain to contain both the key and the room number.

"No problem," she said, embarrassed by the

contact. She stepped back and smoothed her clothing, unable to look at Taddler. She showed no sign of suspecting mischief.

The first woman he'd approached spotted Taddler's collision with Gwen Emerson, and Taddler watched as she reached into her jacket pocket and checked for her key.

She either sensed what he was about, or had spotted the grab. Either way, he realized he was in trouble when her expression turned to suspicion.

Taddler had entered the hotel's meeting room area with three possible exits in mind. He took the nearest, stepping onto the elevator just seconds before the doors were about to close.

He chastised himself for giving himself away. He should have known better. Should have made less of a scene. He'd overplayed it. Mrs. D. rewarded results, not effort. She provided Brian and a handful of others his same age with a roof over their heads. They went to school five days a week, and ate a decent dinner each night. He wasn't about to forfeit his bed at the Corinthians because of a failure to deliver.

"What floor?" a young woman asked as he stepped into the elevator.

Taddler checked the paper packet. It opened,

revealing a credit card–sized electronic room key.

"Seven," he said, offering the woman an engaging smile.

Seven-forty-six, to be exact, he thought. Handwritten in a box at the top of the card.

The young woman got off at Six. The elevator doors opened again, and he felt a sense of urgency as he followed signs to room 746. If Gwen Emerson discovered her key missing, she'd alert security. If security caught Taddler, he was toast. Mrs. D. would never come to his rescue. She'd merely replace him with another fifteen-year-old boy thrown out of a city shelter.

She would abandon him just as his parents had. He'd be sentenced to time in a juvenile detention facility—a reformatory school—the last place he wanted to be: bars on the windows, locks on the doors, mold on the food, restricted TV time, no video games, no movie over a G-rating. Taddler knew a couple of boys who had been sentenced to juvie, and he wanted to avoid it at all costs. He moved quickly down the hall, careful not to attract attention, and arrived at 746. He knocked. No one answered. He put his ear to the door: no sound, no TV, no radio. He slipped the card into the reader. A light changed to green, and the door handle chirped.

He gently tried the handle, and the door opened. He was inside.

The routine was familiar enough. He counted backward from one hundred and eighty, which would give him approximately three minutes in which to operate. He probably had more like five or ten minutes, but why push it? Hotel house detectives were not the speediest bunch, but if they received a complaint, they would follow up on it.

He reached into the left pocket of his khakis and pulled out his iPod nano and skipped to the desk.

He opened a briefcase on the desk and came out with a Dell laptop. He turned it on; as it booted, he connected a cable to his iPod and waited to connect the other end to the computer's USB port.

When it finally loaded, he searched for a particular directory and then connected the iPod. This had taken nearly the entire three minutes, and he hadn't started the download yet. He worked through some menus, allowing the computer to recognize the iPod, and then downloaded the contents of the directory.

Returning the computer to its case a moment later, he dug through the briefcase's contents, flipping through the papers he found there, looking for any account numbers, passwords, or other information that might interest Mrs. D.

Time to go.

Taddler was sweating enough to stain the armpits of the golf shirt. He considered stealing a bedside chocolate, but thought better of it.

On his way out he stopped in the bathroom to mop his face, and looked at himself in the mirror. He was a sturdy boy with wide shoulders, but at that moment he looked anything but strong. He double-checked that he had the connecting wire and the iPod. He didn't want to leave any clues to his having been there.

As he reached the door he raised to his tiptoes to peer out of the fish-eye lens.

Then he remembered to place the key card and packet back on the desk so the woman would think she'd left it behind by mistake. Mrs. D. knew all the little tricks.

As he crossed the room, he suddenly heard voices from the other side of the door. Voices interrupted by a dull electronic chirping: someone was coming into the room.

He stole another peek out of the peephole.

Two guys. *Security?*

He glanced around. Where to hide? The closet

was a sure bust. Same with the tub.

Taddler ducked behind the room's blackout curtain next to the desk chair, hoping the chair might hide his shoes. He heard the click of the door opening.

He held his breath.

"If you're hiding in here, kid," a deep voice said, "give yourself up. We plan on torturing you and beating you senseless."

Another man laughed.

For a moment Taddler considered showing himself—*had they seen him?*—but stayed put.

"Bathroom?" the first voice asked.

"Nada," said the second man.

"Closet?"

The sound of the closet doors sliding. "Zilch."

"Oh, man, check it out!" said the now-familiar voice. "What a freaking moron! The key's right here on the desk."

Taddler heard the sound of the man fooling with the key packet.

"I hate getting my chain yanked by morons like this. We're talking seventh inning, Sox down by one."

A moment later the first guy spoke into the desk phone. He was standing less that two feet from

Brian Taddler. "Key's on the desk. You want us to bring it down to her? Yeah, okay. We got it."

He hung up.

"We're delivery boys."

"Now there's something new."

"Let's go.

A moment later the door clicked shut. Taddler took that as his cue to breathe again.

3.

BLAST FROM
THE PAST

A line of four interconnected three-story brick dormitories had been built cut into the Wynncliff Academy hill so that on the east side the middle floor opened to the school's horseshoe-shaped driveway, and on the west side, the lower level led out onto athletic fields and the gym complex beyond.

Steel loved the majesty of the campus. The neo-classical brick buildings with their black slate roofs and sparkling white-painted trim reminded him of the historical buildings he'd seen in Boston and Philadelphia on family trips. The groomed lawn and magnificent old trees were reminiscent of British estates he'd seen on the Travel Channel. It was no less impressive from the back, an imposing line of handsome buildings connected by library-like faculty residences. The only thing odd about Wynncliff Academy was its isolation and anonymity. There wasn't even a sign off the farm road announcing it; a driver either knew which turn to make or missed it completely.

Anxious to get as far away from the gym as possible, Steel climbed the stairs to the middle of the dorm building's three floors, and outside. He ran smack into the sea of arriving kids, parents, and SUVs bulging with lamps, furniture, and luggage. It was a zoo out there, and he suddenly understood why his father had dropped him off so early: Steel was already unpacked, had picked and made the top bunk, shelved his clothes, and chosen a desk.

Hand on the dormitory door handle, he froze as he caught a flash of red hair among the chaos out along the entrance drive.

Can't be, he thought.

He mechanically moved toward the exit door, his heartbeat elevated, painful in his chest. His skin now prickled for an entirely different reason, and not something with which he was terribly familiar. He felt feverish. But unlike any allergy he'd ever experienced, it came on instantaneously. His mouth was suddenly bone dry and his tongue tasted salty.

He moved in a kind of trance, out the door and into the cool September breeze. A few sugar maple leaves had already turned scarlet; they clattered in the wind like broken wind chimes. Steel reached back to hold open the door and let a father and son go past carrying a desk chair. People were swarming into the dorms, moving in all directions, like in an airport or train station. Steel had lost track of the redhead, though his phenomenal memory directed him to look exactly where he'd first spotted her.

And there she was: Kaileigh.

He crossed the lawn and two walkways, dodging the throng of kids and parents carrying furniture, steamer trunks, and luggage—never taking his eyes off her. Same hair. Same height. Then he quickly convinced himself he had it all wrong: the girl wore a red-and-green-plaid skirt above black kneesocks, loafers, and a green cable sweater. Kaileigh—his Kaileigh—would never be caught dead in preppie clothes.

He saw her in profile. Again, his heart skipped painfully. It had to be. . . .

He turned sideways to avoid a collision with a bookshelf suspended between a mother and daughter, ducked beneath it, and popped up on the other side.

He was ten feet from her. He stopped where he stood. His mouth hung open to speak, but at first nothing came out. He'd never felt the heat in his face and the seizure of his chest in quite this way. What was going on? A uniformed driver was unloading pieces of luggage from a black sedan. None of the luggage matched: bags of various sizes and colors, most of it well worn.

"My parents travel a lot," she had once told him. "They're almost never home."

"Is it . . . really you?" he finally croaked out.

The red hair flew as the girl spun around, revealing her face like a curtain lifting. At first he felt like a complete moron: wrong girl. This person was refined, with a tall posture, square shoulders, and the definite body of a young woman—he didn't remember Kaileigh that way—not at all—and he reminded himself he had a perfect memory.

"Steel?"

Coughing out a laugh of astonishment, he breathed for the first time in too long.

She laughed too. And now any doubts he'd harbored vanished, for he knew that laugh without question. He moved toward her without hesitation and enveloped her in a warm hug before he considered what he was doing. She hugged him back like the friend she was, but the physical contact between them brought unexpected and not entirely unpleasant feelings for Steel. Nothing he was comfortable with. They backed away an arm's length and both erupted into blushing laughter, then talked over one another in a stream-of-consciousness blabber that had Kaileigh's driver looking on in bewilderment.

"Steel's the reason I'm here," she informed a middle-aged woman Steel hadn't seen. She introduced the woman as Miss Kay, and Steel felt he knew her. Kaileigh had told him a great deal about her governess. Miss Kay shook hands with Steel, but he sensed her disapproval.

"What do you mean, I'm the reason?" Steel asked Kaileigh.

"Your father, I should say," she informed him.

"My father . . ."

"He didn't tell you?" She studied him for some kind of crack in his veneer. Was he kidding? "It was his idea. Your father's. Wynncliff Academy. For me to go here. All my parents' money, and it took your father pulling strings to make this happen." She stepped forward and spoke in a whisper. Her breath smelled impossibly sweet—like a vanilla milk shake. "It's not your typical school, you know?"

He thought of the boys in the gym. Did she know more than he did? "I know," he said, not really knowing. "But how was my father . . . ?"

"He contacted my parents about my going here. My parents have been planning on boarding school for me since I was about six. But this place? Do you know it's not on the registry of private schools? It has like, unlisted phone numbers, no Web page. I mean . . . are you kidding me? And you don't just apply: you're *invited* to apply."

Steel knew approximately none of this. But he tried to look both unsurprised and unimpressed.

"Which is where your father came in," she said, returning him to the moment.

"Enough, Miss Kaileigh," Miss Kay said. "You'll have time for catching up later." The governess glanced overhead into the thick canopy of leaves, the branches swaying in the wind. She looked at Kaileigh thoughtfully, sympathetically, and shook her head. Clearly, beautiful campus or not, Miss Kay felt sorry for leaving her charge at such a place.

"Can I help?" Steel offered, eyeing Kaileigh's bags.

"Sure, if you want," she said.

He reached for one of the larger bags but, trying to pick it up, changed his mind and opted for one of the many smaller ones. He took two, one in each hand. To his surprise, Miss Kay hoisted the heavy one like it was nothing.

"My father?" he asked Kaileigh, still dumbfounded that he'd played a role in her attending Wynncliff. His father was full of surprises. Only recently had Steel found out that he worked for the FBI, that he wasn't the computer salesman he'd always claimed to be. He was some kind of undercover investigator. He infiltrated organized crime and ferreted out wanted criminals. It was dangerous work, and Steel had never imagined his father—*his father*—to be that kind of person.

Another thing he'd learned about his father was that he never did anything without a reason. So why had he helped Kaileigh be admitted to Wynncliff? To what purpose? To provide Steel a friend in hopes that he would like the place? He didn't put anything past his father.

"Can you believe this?" she asked excitedly, almost reading his thoughts. "Both of us here!"

No, he thought. No, I can't. But he held his tongue.

Kaileigh was smarter than he was—he knew that. She lacked his photographic memory, a condition that tricked people into thinking he was smarter than he was. She, on the other hand, had a bright intelligence and street smarts that permeated everything she did. She had a keen sense about people, and plenty of nerve. He'd met her on a train on the way to the National Science Challenge. They'd had a wild time together—had been the target of a gang with terrorist connections. Together they'd saved a kidnapped woman's life. She possessed an internal strength that Steel admired. She wasn't afraid of much, and she'd demonstrated that she could think clearly under pressure. Better than that, she was a science geek—her invention for the National Science Challenge might have won if it hadn't been stolen. And more than anything, she treated him as if he were normal. Around her, he didn't feel like the freak of nature that *everyone* else thought he was. She rarely mentioned his memory skills, and when she did it was to tease him.

He wanted to trust his father in sending her here, and yet . . . why hadn't he mentioned her coming? Why had he dropped Steel off without a word about Kaileigh?

"We're going to have fun," she said, the two of them lugging her suitcases toward the dorms.

"Yeah," he answered, outwardly agreeing with her. Internally, he couldn't help thinking: *But there's got to be more to it than that.*

4.
THE FIFTEENTH
SQUEAK

Daily school life soon absorbed the freshmen. Encouraged by teachers and advisers alike, sometimes subtly and sometimes not, Steel fell into a routine. He was awakened by his dorm master sometime after 6 a.m., was due in the common room by 7:00, in coat and tie, just ahead of breakfast in the dining hall—a chaotic, noisy assembly with smells of butter and syrup, cinnamon and chocolate, where students clambered for plates and trays while the authorities—coffee-swilling teachers assigned as heads of tables—attempted order.

Classes ran from 8:30 to 2:30, Monday through Friday, and until noon on Saturday, when at last the necktie could be left in the closet for thirty-six hours. Mandatory athletics filled the late afternoons, with a quick return to dinner that presaged the rigors of study hall.

There were tardies and truancies and disciplines meted out in the first few days, done so in a public manner so as not to be missed.

What was at first dizzying soon became comfortable, which Steel assumed was the point. He missed home, and was tempted to call, but his father had encouraged him to go at least two full weeks before doing so. Steel had made it through two weeks of science camp two summers in a row; he could make it through the first two weeks of Wynncliff.

The football and soccer teams, both varsity and JV, boys and girls, had been announced a couple of days ago, causing a stampede in the administration building. Steel had tried out for soccer but had not made the cut; he'd seen Kaileigh's name on the girls' JV list.

Wynncliff's Third Form—ninth grade classes— were harder than any he'd ever taken, and he'd been consumed by mandatory study hall until 9 p.m. five evenings a week, only to return to his room and do homework for another hour after that. He'd be lucky if he got B's.

His roommate, a stout African American kid named Verne Dundee, from New Haven, Connecticut, was a nice enough guy, but he went to sleep listening to hip-hop through a pair of leaky headphones. Steel, being a light sleeper and no fan of hip-hop, didn't appreciate the annoyance, but had yet to gather the nerve to say anything about it. He'd read in a school pamphlet—*Dorm Life for Dummies*—that the best way to be a good roommate was to allow privacy and space. He wasn't sure how noise pollution from leaky headphones fit into that agreement, but he wasn't going to push it.

As he tried to fall asleep, he heard the squeak to the door of the boys' room down the hall. It was the thirteenth squeak since Steel had entered his room for the night.

Lying there on the upper bunk, trying his best to ignore the irritating, hollow pulse from Verne's headphones, Steel awaited the fourteenth squeak—door squeaks came in pairs: entering and leaving. Sometimes that pairing was thrown off by one boy holding the door for another, but politeness was not commonplace in Lower Three. In fact, the older boys tended to torture the younger ones—hazing them and turning them into shoe-shine boys and personal butlers. More to the point, this most recent squeak of the washroom door had come on its own, nearly thirty minutes after the mandatory lights-out at 11 p.m.

He waited through one endless song squealing from Verne's headphones, and was well into a second by the time he felt his bladder suggest that a trip to the boys' room wasn't such a bad idea.

He headed down the hall in his bare feet, the cuffs of his pajamas sweeping across the polished stone floor. At night, only half the hallway ceiling's orb-shaped light fixtures were left burning, saving energy but leaving a long, dim corridor. The lavatory was located in the center of the dorm. The door squeaked as Steel entered.

The fourteenth squeak.

He fully expected to run into someone—a boy responsible for the door's thirteenth squeak, but to his surprise, the place was empty. There was no one standing at the urinals, no one taking a shower, and all three stall doors hung open. He checked the toilets just to make sure. Empty. He shrugged, decided to let it go. Clearly someone must have held the door for someone else at some point—a reasonable explanation. And though the timing of the squeaks didn't exactly fit, he pushed it out of a mind already too crowded with math and the anxiety of the following day's test.

A murmur of deep, adolescent voices approaching from the hallway sent him into a frenzy. At least two boys, it sounded like. There was no set rule that an underclassman couldn't go to the bathroom at night, but it wasn't the set rules he was worried about; it was the unwritten rules of the dominating upperclassmen. If they caught him in here alone, they were likely to force him to clean a toilet with his bare hands, or pick the hair out of a shower drain. One boy, Otis Reed, had been harassed into drinking a handful of water straight from a toilet bowl— which in turn had caused the kid to blow his dinner all over the washroom floor and had been a great source of humor for the upperclassmen of Lower Three. Steel had no desire be found.

To avoid detection, he scrambled up onto one of the toilets and pushed the stall door closed just far enough to screen him from view of the mirrors over the sinks. If one of the boys tried to use this stall, he was toast, but he took that chance.

The door squeaked—for the fifteenth time since lights-out.

The boys' voices echoed off the washroom tile, the sounds mixing with the drumming of blood past Steel's ears to where he couldn't distinguish what was being said. It seemed to have something to do with soccer practice. Somebody said something about "the program."

He waited, his heart attempting to break out of his chest, his bare feet delicately balancing on the toilet seat, fearing that if he moved even slightly, the seat might also squeak and reveal him to the boys.

Silence.

It hit him all at once. One moment he'd been staring down at the black toilet seat trying to keep from moving, the next, an eerie *drip-drip-drip* from one of the sinks.

No squeal of the door hinges having come open again. No sound of a urinal flushing, or the sinks running—beyond the slow, tortured dripping of the faucet. He waited far longer than he needed to, fearing that the boys had sensed him and were waiting to spring at him when he climbed down. But he did climb down, and there was no pounce, for there were no boys. The washroom stood empty. Completely, totally empty.

Had he, in fact, fallen asleep while trying to avoid Verne's hip-hop? Had he sleepwalked into the washroom and dreamed the rest? He reminded himself that two boys had entered the washroom. No boys had left. And yet the washroom stood empty.

He conducted a complete tour one more time just to make sure.

Empty.

Thirteen squeaks. Then fourteen. Then fifteen.

No sixteenth squeak. Again, an odd number.

A washroom where upperclassmen disappeared.

He wondered about this place, about the boys he'd seen in the gym, what his father had gotten him into—him and Kaileigh—and what, if anything, he should do about it.

5.
SIR DAVID'S
NEGATIVE SPACE

Academy assembly on Monday mornings meant an auditorium of yawning students sitting before Mr. Bradley Hastings, a thick-necked but handsome man, youthful in appearance and strong of voice. Announcements were kept brief, variations to schedules made loudly, and dismissal conducted in an orderly fashion.

Steel recorded everything about these assemblies, from curious looks between headmaster Hastings and a few of the more senior teachers, to the groupings of students.

It was during such a dismissal that Steel spotted and caught the eye of Kaileigh—though to be fair, she was already waving frantically at him from the opposite aisle.

They met in the mail room, a dismal, dimly lit warren of tiny post office pigeonholes. The mailboxes required a memorized three-letter combination, A–K, to open. Everything about Kaileigh was conspiratorial as she took Steel by the wrist and literally dragged him down two lanes of mailboxes and around the corner to a dead end, where, it was rumored, a boy had once been beaten and left for nearly three hours before discovery. It was clearly just such isolation that Kaileigh sought, or believed she required.

"Sorry," she said, seeing confusion in Steel's eyes. "But I absolutely must talk to you."

He opened his mouth to speak, but she cut him off.

"I need your help," she said.

Again, he wanted so say something, and again she interrupted before he got the chance.

"I was in . . . the little girls' room . . ." she said, blushing, "and I overheard something that absolutely needs checking out."

"The other girls in the room disappeared?" he asked, speaking quickly and forcing his words between hers.

"What?" She laughed. "Why would you say that?"

Steel had wanted to bring up the apparent disappearances from his dorm's washroom, but her ridicule prevented him from doing so. He shrugged and gestured for her to continue.

"I'm not even sure who said it," she confessed. "I don't know the other girls well enough yet to tell them apart by the sound of their voices, but it was two girls talking and not wanting to be heard. I'm certain of that. And one says to the other how she broke the no-food-or-drinks rule in the chapel. She had smuggled a cup of coffee into the chapel, when Mr. Randolph suddenly emerged from the common room, on his way home. The chapel floor had apparently been waxed, and the girl had lost her balance and dumped the decaf next to Sir David."

Sir David was a glorious Italian marble statue of a dashing knight kneeling on one knee and holding a four-foot marble sword, with a space carved out of his back and shoulders to hold the school Bible, an oversized illustrated King James edition bound in red leather.

"She panics because Randolph is a religious man—him having lost his wife and all—and maybe he was not heading home but to the chapel for a few prayers before dinner, or maybe to play the chapel organ or something. He does that almost every night, supposedly. And there's her decaf, in a puddle at the foot of Sir David. So she goes to mop it up, seeing how much of it she can contain with a napkin, and to her surprise, it all comes up. One napkin. An entire cup of coffee."

"So she was okay," Steel said purposely, wondering why he was using what little free time he had to listen to her, when he could have been doing something important, like playing PlayStation.

"Earth to Steel! Have you ever used a school napkin? They're the size of half a Kleenex. There is no way it could have absorbed a full cup of coffee. Which is the whole point."

"A napkin is the point?" he said, deciding to keep his editorials to himself.

She jutted her chin out, then arched her eyebrows. She did everything except say, "How stupid can you be?"

"The coffee disappeared beneath Sir David," she said. "That's the only explanation."

He kept quiet, still not getting it.

"I take it you've studied fluids and liquids," she prompted.

"Some."

"Sir David has to be a half ton of marble sitting atop a marble floor. There is no way a cup of coffee could fit in the space between the marble of his pedestal and the marble of the floor. The only logical conclusion—and this is the *same* conclusion the two girls had—is that there is negative space beneath Sir David."

"Negative space." It blurted out of him.

"Are you thinking what I'm thinking?" she pressed.

"I doubt it, but it's possible. A crypt?"

"Yes. Or an underground burial ground or tomb, or something! It's like *National Treasure Three* is what it is. And we're like Nicolas Cage."

He debated telling her about the fifteenth squeak.

"What?" she asked. He hated the way she could read his mind. It wasn't the first time.

"I wouldn't be so sure it's a crypt," he said.

"Why not?"

And so he told her about the boys disappearing from the dormitory washroom. He finished by saying, "It's a little harder to make upperclassmen disappear than a cup of coffee."

"You're thinking they went into some kind of hidden staircase or tunnel?" she said.

"I wasn't exactly thinking that," he said. "Not until you came along."

"Like a network of tunnels or something under the school?"

"Let's not get ahead of ourselves. But it might be

worth checking out. Sir David. Tonight."

"But we could be expelled," she said.

"But now that you've told me, I have to know," he said.

"No you don't."

"I do. It's just the way I am. And besides, they're not going to expel us if we turn up some ancient tomb that goes back to 1660. That's when the chapel was built, you know?"

"That's impossible," she said. "The school was founded in the late eighteen hundreds."

"Yeah, but the chapel was built in 1660 in *England*, Kaileigh. It was taken down, shipped across the Atlantic, stone by stone, and reconstructed here in 1881, soon after the founding of the school, which was then a priory."

She looked at him, impressed.

"So I read that pamphlet they gave us at orientation."

"And remembered every word."

"My curse."

"But a priory! That's monks, right? Monks loved tunnels and crypts. And I heard the school has a history of secret societies and clubs."

"From whom?" he asked. He'd not heard any such rumors, but the idea of secret societies appealed to him. He thought of the boys with the blowguns. He thought about his father having worked to get Kaileigh accepted.

"What did you mean by 'They're not going to expel *us*'?" she asked.

"You're going to let me do this alone?" he said.

Her eyes pleaded with him. She didn't want to be dragged into this.

Steel said, "The first day of school, right before I met you?"

"Yeah?"

"I saw some guys. It was so freaky, I haven't mentioned it to anyone."

"Freaky, how?"

"Maximum freakiness," he said. "I missed a sign saying the gym was closed, and I kind of *let myself in*, and I saw these guys—upperclassmen, I think . . ." He paused, realizing how stupid this would sound. "Ahh . . . using . . . blowguns in the gym."

"Blowguns . . ."

"I know how it sounds, but I'm serious: they were shooting at mannequins."

"Mannequins . . ."

"And the coach was telling them to shoot harder if they wanted the darts to work."

"Darts . . ."

"Yeah . . ." He felt about an inch tall.

"So you're saying this is a weird school," she said. "Tell me something I don't know."

"No, I'm saying these guys . . . I mean, they're obviously *different*. Right? I mean, you think Blowguns 101 is on everyone's elective list? They're different like . . . I'm different," Steel said.

"And where do I fit in?" Kaileigh sounded like she was ashamed of not being a freak of nature.

He avoided answering her. "So if there's a tomb beneath the chapel, or if there's a bunch of tunnels or something," Steel said. "Or if there's a group of students doing something in secret, I've got to know about it."

"Because of the way you are," she mocked.

"Don't, okay?" he said. "We've both seen the stories on the news about boys doing stupid things in secret at schools. It doesn't usually turn out so great for the other students. I need to know what's going on, and I need to know from you if you're in or out. I'm going to check out the chapel. You can do what you want."

She pursed her lips, deep in concentration. "If I get kicked out of here, your father will not be pleased," she said.

"So let's not get caught," Steel said.

"Right," she said sarcastically, shaking her head, but allowing a small smile to reveal itself. "Good idea."

6.
THE BOATHOUSE

The cloud cover over Boston held the threat of rain like a fist wrapped around a sponge. Some people on the streets carried umbrellas, while others wore trench coats in preparation, everyone walking with hunched shoulders as if the rain were already falling. On the bank of the Charles River loomed an imposing structure. From the outside it looked like a cross between a stone library and a church. It was situated on a small weedy patch of mostly brown grass populated by a few withered and struggling trees that had once been mighty. A pair of resident squirrels skittered between the trees—trees that had outlived generations of Bostonians who had used this place.

The sounds were many: cars and trucks on

Commonwealth Avenue, not far away; the insectlike buzz of an outboard motor spilling up from the Charles, interrupted occasionally by the rhythmic chanting of a coxswain; the whine of a jet aircraft on final approach to Logan Airport.

The building had seen many lives, many uses: for twenty years it had been a fraternity house for a famous university. For six years, a storage place for rowing sculls—owing to the property's relationship to the Charles River. For one brief moment of glory it had served as campaign headquarters for a failed politician, draped in bunting with red-white-and-blue signs planted on the lawn.

Now, considered abandoned by most who drove past, it was commonly referred to as the boathouse, and it fell under the protection of the Boston Commission for Historic Restoration and Preservation, a pet project of a former mayor, a man determined to preserve nineteenth century architecture. The building was considered too beautiful to tear down, too far in disrepair to receive funding to rehabilitate, and so it languished in the shadows of more practical, if less satisfying, buildings that served as its neighbors. It was also known by some as the Corinthians because of the four stone columns that supported a false gable carrying a gorgeous frieze depicting Paul

Revere's famous ride. Some Boston blue bloods believed it haunted.

A small squirrel made its way along a narrow, well-traveled line in the grass where the unkempt and weed-ridden lawn met the building's stone foundation. The squirrel's tiny ears twitched at the onset of unfamiliar sounds, and it scurried more quickly, darting down the path with the erratic stop and start of an animal that believed it was being stalked. The squirrel reared onto its hind legs and sniffed the air as it reached the rusted stub of a decayed iron pipe that was layered with globs of cracked concrete where the pipe protruded from one of the stone columns. Hesitating for only one quick squirrel heartbeat, the creature leaped effortlessly and disappeared into the darkness, lifting its feet daintily to avoid the stagnant and foul-smelling water that had festered for years, decades perhaps, in the bottom of the pipe. If a squirrel could hold its nose, this one would have.

It raced blindly through a number of intersections, turning first left, then sharply right, then left again, the route committed to memory from a hundred other visits. Finally a faint glow appeared as the pitch-black melted into a gray fog. The squirrel reached a dead end and jumped straight up, its little feet scratching at the rim of a pipe flush with a wooden floor in a small room that echoed with the sound of dripping water. Across the floor, up a slanting board that had dislodged from the ceiling, the squirrel scampered and sprang into flight, traveling a full six feet into the air before reaching a dangling light fixture that swung first forward, then back, then forward again, the squirrel using the momentum to launch toward the next fixture. Its tiny claws on its equally tiny feet scratched across the floor above a ceiling as it danced from one room to the next, knowing little of the area below.

"You hear that?" a boy of fourteen said from where he sat on two stacked car tires directly below the route of the squirrel.

"Rats," said another boy, who wore his nearly orange hair over his ears and down to his shirt collar in the back.

In the room were were six of the currently nine boys at Corinthians, varying in age from twelve to seventeen. They sat on secondhand lawn furniture: pool chairs and a chaise lounge or two, some without all the original plastic straps. There were nine cots spread between two rooms, with fresh linens and towels provided once a week. (One of the boys held a job at a Laundromat.) A bench seat was pushed against one wall—the middle row from an SUV, complete with cup holders. The bench was occupied by Brian Taddler, who had made a point of lying down so that no one would attempt to share it with him. Taddler sometimes slept on the bench seat as well, and he farted a lot, clouding the surrounding area with rancid odors that would not go away.

"Squirrels," Taddler said. "It's squirrels." He stated this absolutely, though he had no idea if he was right. He did this primarily to convince himself of it, for he was terrified of rats and found it hard to sleep if he pictured the rodents running around. A mental image of a cute little squirrel was altogether different, though he would never ever use a word like "cute" around this lot.

They were tough boys, each and every one. Not as tough as Brian Taddler, or so he convinced himself. He did not want to test the theory.

"I've seen the little black *rice* they leave behind," Johnny said. "And squirrels don't poop no black rice. Their stuff is more like pellets."

"Well, I've seen plenty of pellets around."

"So maybe it's both," Johnny said, not wanting to pick a fight. He was an okay boy who might have once played on a Pop Warner football team had he been dealt a better hand. He had wide shoulders and a thick, brutish chest. But his face was cherubic, his cheeks a constant violent red, and his voice had not yet broken, providing him a high tenor that was a good imitation of Alvin the chipmunk.

His mother and father took turns testing the physical limits of alcohol abuse. He'd run away in his fifteenth year, and had been briefly in residence in a city shelter, the same as Taddler and most of the others.

The boys spent a good deal of time in this particular room because its skylight was intact, and because a large hole in the plaster of the far wall offered access to a complex escape route that eventually led outside—an escape route that required one to be shorter than five foot four and less than one hundred and forty pounds, meaning if discovered by adults, the boys had a viable exit strategy. It was also a room that, in winter months, when the steam heat failed, as it often did, was small enough to retain some collective body heat.

Over near the hole in the wall, a group of car batteries had collected, all but one dead. A braid of wires ran from the live battery's stubby terminals, including two that disappeared up through another hole in the ceiling, eventually reaching the roof, where they had been connected to a solar panel purchased through Amazon.com. The solar panel trickle-charged the car battery, filling it with power by day, so the boys could drain it at night with lights, PSPs, and iPods.

The other wires powered such luxuries as a seven-watt compact fluorescent bulb and a variety of improvised security devices, each installed at an entrance and collectively wired to a red taillight stolen off a motor scooter.

Presently, the taillight flashed once and stayed red for a count of three. Then it went dark. All six boys moved silently toward the escape hole, their eyes trained on the warning light. It illuminated once again for a count of three, then went dark.

The boys relaxed noticeably. That was the sign for "all clear."

"I'll check," Johnny said. He headed out the door and through a maze of interconnected hallways and eventually into the building's central gallery, a circular space holding what looked like a stone altar, and surrounded on three sides by smaller Corinthian columns. Stories about the altar included a human virgin sacrifice and the speculation that it was a pedestal for a missing statue, all part of the boys' late-night entertainment, which also included ghost stories about bodies buried beneath the building.

Lending to the stories had been the discovery of

six peepholes throughout the building, which afforded spying on adjacent rooms. In each case, a small slit had been cut into a wall, offering a vantage point, sometimes into a hallway, sometimes a meeting room, or into the central gallery, where Johnny now trained an eye.

A woman entered. Well dressed, like a librarian or schoolteacher, she moved comfortably and confidently in the dim room, waving directly at Johnny's peephole. Johnny waved back, though his effort went unseen because of the wall separating them.

"It's her," Johnny confirmed, reentering the small smelly room.

Each of the boys shifted uncomfortably, trying to sit up straight.

"Was she bringing—"

"Yeah. Of course," Johnny answered.

As the woman entered, Taddler wondered how a person could look so unremarkable. She had a plain yet somehow expensive look about her, which Taddler saw even if the other boys did not. Derek, one of the older boys, had claimed she was a parole officer. Taddler didn't think so. A preacher's wife, he thought. Or a single woman who took care of her aging mother by night and tended to a handful of young teenage boys by day.

Whatever the case, the woman had saved each of the boys, one by one, from a life on the street, and though they held their gratitude in check, it leaked out in small ways—radiant smiles, penetrating looks, and the occasional kind offer of a chair, or moving the room's single light closer to her. The charitable Mrs. D. had put a roof over their heads and food in their stomachs. She arrived at the Corinthians each evening about the same time, bearing grocery bags of canned and preserved foods. Maybe she bought the food. Maybe she borrowed it from a shelter. Taddler didn't care. She helped the boys earn small amounts of money, rewarded good behavior, provided them with food and clothing, and looked to place them either in schools, private homes, or other institutions. For now, the food was all that mattered.

She carefully set down the grocery bags. The boys knew better than to even touch them while in her presence. She demanded and won their full attention.

"Collection? Derek, it's your turn, I believe."

"Yes, ma'am," Derek said, his tone softer than what he used on his friends.

"Sixty-seven dollars, ma'am." He passed her the cash.

She accepted it, saying, "Very good. Not bad at all. That should buy you all enough food to see you through the weekend." She stuffed the money into her purse without counting it.

The purse was real leather with a shiny interior. Inside was a fat, purple, leather wallet, a fancy pen, and some sunglasses. Taddler found everything about Mrs. D. intriguing. Her actions seemed genuine, though her purpose clouded. She claimed to want the best for them. He wasn't so sure.

"There's a job to do. There are papers in a guest's room at the Haymarket," she said. "Each room has a printer/copier, so all we have to do is find the papers and copy them."

"And get out," Johnny said, causing the other boys to chuckle. Not Mrs. D. She'd given them only the small piece of her name, just as she'd given them only a small piece of anything to do with her. Even the boys who'd been there more than a year knew precious little about her.

"There's ten dollars in it," she said, drawing a ten from her purse and waving the bill like a small flag.

Johnny sprang for it, and she snatched it back.

"The papers are personal letters addressed to a Mr. Ron Ungerman. They are printed on stationery bearing the emblem for the United States Department of Labor. You need to copy only those letters bearing the emblem. When the job is complete, John," she said, "and I have the copies, you will be paid. Room 1426 at the Haymarket, arriving tomorrow night, departing the next day. He works out mornings from seven to seven forty-five, give or take a few minutes. Do you know what that means, John?"

"I want to arrive a little after seven," John said, squinting his yellowish eyes, "and be out of the room no later than seven thirty."

"Precisely."

"Brian will accompany you," she instructed. No one ever argued with Mrs. D. If Taddler objected to being assigned to the job, his residence at the Corinthians would be canceled.

And then what?

She handed Taddler a room card for the Haymarket. No more was said. He understood that this card would not open room 1426, but it would serve an important purpose. Mrs. D. had chosen him because he, of all the boys, was the most skilled pickpocket. She'd chosen him to join Johnny—a fast runner and smooth talker.

She seemed to be always assigning the boys these special jobs. Paying jobs. Sometimes it felt as if the other assignments—the panhandling, or playing music in the subway, or putting fliers on parked cars, or handing out giveaways at intersections—

HARPETH HALL SCHOOL LIBRARY

were nothing more than training runs to sharpen and hone their various skills. Travis was the boy who handled the computer work—copying the contents of a thumb drive, or burning a bunch of files to a DVD. They rarely were asked to steal electronics—only the *contents* of the electronics: a download from a phone, a PDA, or a laptop.

Maybe she was some kind of spy.

That would make Taddler a secret agent, which was fine with him.

"We have something big coming up," she reported. "I need you all well rested and at your best." She handed out passes to the Boys' Club. They could swim and shower there. They did this twice a week, and it was a highlight for the boys because she also gave out gift certificates, as she did now, to McDonald's, or Wendy's, or on rare occasions California Pizza Kitchen, a favorite. The gift certificates were for Pizza Hut, which was right up there with CPK.

"How many of us?" Johnny asked, inquiring about her reference to "something big."

"All of you."

For a moment there was no sound in the room except a vague humming from the battery.

"All of us," Johnny repeated.

There had never, ever been a job that required more than three boys at once.

"All nine of us?" Taddler said.

"Clean, well fed, and well rested," she said. "There will be no room for mistakes. No tolerance if mistakes are made."

The comment put the boys on notice. Wilhem had been advised of the no-tolerance policy, and no one had seen Wilhem in over a month.

"Enjoy your dinner," she said, snapping her purse shut with a firm click. "And you keep your eye on that red light. This is no time to be caught."

"Are they looking for us?" said Johnny, his tone a little too close to hopeful. Johnny was from Minnesota. He'd run away over a year ago and had wondered privately to Taddler several times why no one had ever come looking for him.

"Maybe they are looking for you," Taddler had answered him. "Just in the wrong place." But for now Taddler kept his mouth shut, afraid of the grim expression that had stolen onto Mrs. D.'s pasty face.

She pursed her lips, turned, and walked out, leaving several of the boys diving for the grocery bags, while Johnny sat back from the others, taking a moment to speculate on the unnamed mission yet to come.

7.
GARGOYLES AND SHADOWS

The snap of the school flag caused Kaileigh to jump. There was no wind to speak of, just sudden gusts and bursts overhead that rustled the leaves of the sugar maples and black oaks, sounding like pebbles striking a car windshield.

She and Steel had snuck out of their dorms and followed tree shadows to reach the side of the chapel.

"Has it occurred to you how stupid it is to do this?" she asked. "I don't know about you, but I'd rather not get expelled. I just got here, and I kinda like it."

"But you miss home," he said.

"Me? No. Not so much. My home is bascially Miss Kay and me. She's nice and everything, but to

54

be honest, this place is more fun than being at home with her."

Steel set his wristwatch back an hour. He told Kaileigh to do the same. "We're both from the Midwest," he said. "If we tell 'em we never changed our watches, then . . ."

"We're an hour behind," she said, obviously impressed. "You're devious."

"Practical," he said.

"We won't need the watches," she said.

"Because?"

"Because all you have to do is kiss me."

"What . . . ?" He cleared his throat.

"If we hear someone coming . . . if we think we're about to be caught . . . then you kiss me. We make out. We're caught making out, not spying on the chapel. My roommate, Cassandra, was telling me how they hardly ever do anything to kids caught making out. Especially the first couple of times."

"The first *couple of* times?" he muttered.

"Some extra study hall for a while. That's about it."

"Is that right?" He wasn't hearing everything she said because his ears were ringing. He was stuck back on the idea that he was just supposed to start making out with her.

"That's it." She turned to face him, the shadow so thick he could barely see her. "Is that a problem? It's not like it means anything. Don't get any stupid ideas. It's not like I *want* to kiss you, or whatever. I'm just saying . . . if it comes to that, then that's what we do."

"I . . . get . . . it," he said. He felt like he might puke, he was so nervous. He considered reminding her that she'd already kissed him once. But he didn't. It had only been a peck on the cheek, not making out, but it was technically a kiss, and he had not forgotten it. Nor could he.

"You ready?" she asked.

He wasn't sure exactly what she was asking: did she want him to practice kissing her, or was he ready to enter the chapel?

"Set your watch back an hour," he said, reminding her.

She smiled widely, reaching for her wrist and doing as he'd said. "Yeah. Okay. That's what I like about you: you're practical."

"The side door," he said, blushing in the darkness.

"What?"

"There's a side door. It was in a photograph in a pamphlet they sent us. Red ivy on stone. Do you remember that? The stones. These stones," he said, placing his hands on the chapel. "I recognize them from that photo. The rest of the buildings are all brick. This is the only one made of stone."

"You are a freak of nature. You know that?"

"You're not the first to say that, but it's not my favorite thing to be called, if that's what you're asking."

"You remember a photo from a pamphlet that we all got in the mail . . . what . . . in July? Are you kidding me?"

"I'm kinda of stuck with it," he said.

"I wouldn't complain if I were you," she said.

That's what you think, he thought.

"You lead," she said.

Steel avoided the lighted paths and headed around back of the towering stone edifice, beneath the spreading canopy of a silver ash tree that had a trunk four feet in diameter. It didn't escape Steel that the tree had likely been there for several hundred years. Something about that sense of history touched him, and for a moment he paused, looking up into the dark tangle of majestic branches.

It proved impossible to move through the fallen leaves without crunching. For this reason they took their time, ducking into shadows periodically and catching their breaths, frantic from nerves.

"Exactly why are we doing this again?" Kaileigh asked in a harsh whisper.

"If something is going on, something secret or against the rules, then we need to know about it," he answered. "What if there are a bunch of weirdos planning something . . . You know, like those shootings in schools that are always on the news? What if we can stop something like that?"

Kaileigh clearly hadn't considered that possibility. "You think?" she gasped as she hugged him from behind. Steel went rigid with surprise. Was she going to try to kiss him? Then he heard her sigh, and looked back in the gloom to see her looking up. He followed her gaze: the grotesque face of a stone gargoyle crafted as a rainspout looked down on them, devilish and twisted. It was but one of many such griffins up there.

"Relax, the griffin is just the school mascot," he whispered, patting her hands locked around his belly. She released him and they moved on.

They rounded another corner—the chapel was designed in the shape of a cross—and approached a door that looked, in the gray muddled light, exactly as it had in the school brochure. Crafted of ancient, heavy, dark wood, it was framed by the large chiseled stones that formed the chapel walls, the doorway wrapped in ribbons of creeping ivy.

Steel grabbed hold of the oversized cold iron doorknob and twisted. There came no cry of old hinges or horror-movie squeaks. The door swung open silently, and they were met with the sweet smell of cedar mixed with the slightly musty odor that came with the structure's old age.

Open cedar armoires occupied three of the four walls, holding robes for the choir. Black music stands stood in front of empty chairs formed around an upright piano littered with sheet music. Diagonally across the choir room from them, a closed door invited their curiosity. Steel hurried over to it. Kaileigh followed. The door had a heavy iron ring in place of a doorknob, and Steel lifted and twisted it, drawing the door open a crack. Standing alongside the chapel organ to their right, they faced the chancel, and across an expanse of marble flooring, the choir pews. The chapel altar rose to their left. The pipe organ itself was very large, with four tiers of keys and multiple rows of labeled stops.

The once Episcopal church had a unique design. The pews ran parallel to the nave—rows facing each other with the wide nave in between.

"Sir David," Kaileigh hissed, pointing to the back of the life-sized knight kneeling just below a single step that led down from the transept. Kaileigh's whisper echoed through the hall. The lofted roof's heavy crossbeams towered nearly forty feet overhead.

They had taken three steps toward Sir David when they were stopped by a sharp click and the rough sound of scraping wood.

Steel took Kaileigh's hand and pulled her into a cramped hiding place atop the pipe organ's foot pedals. His heart lodged in this throat; they could ill afford to be caught.

Muffled voices echoed off the stone walls and raced through the eaves.

He and Kaileigh sat facing each other, toe to toe, their legs balled up, arms wrapped tightly around their shins, fingers laced. The foot pedals were long pieces of maple wood. The sides of the instrument created a small cave, and they huddled within it. Kaileigh caught Steel's eyes and pursed her lips into a kissing pucker, reminding him of her plan. He shook his head "no." She nodded "yes" back at him.

A second pop rang through the cavernous chamber, and the voices were no longer muted but present. More voices than just moments earlier, now whispering low and conspiratorially. The shuffle and squeak of rubber soles cried against the marble.

Four boys passed within a matter of inches of the

pipe organ and headed into the choir room. The last stopped and turned. Steel couldn't see above the boy's waist, but he pictured him raising his head and taking a long suspicious look into the chapel. He'd sensed them.

Thankfully, the boy didn't look down. But he did take a step back, and in that instant, Steel got a good look at him.

He had a square jaw, wide nose, and a dimpled chin. Red hair, perhaps, or blond—the light was poor. He had a strong build, with broad shoulders and a thick neck. Definitely an upperclassman. Maybe even one of the four he'd seen that day in the gym. Steel couldn't be absolutely sure, but he thought he recognized him from the dorm. Could he be one of the boys who'd disappeared from inside the washroom on Sunday night?

"You checked?" the boy said. "Before we—?"

"Yes. Of course," answered another voice from within the choir room.

The upperclassman took one last inquisitive look around, and then entered the choir room, drawing the door shut behind him. A moment later, silence.

Steel heaved a sigh of relief.

"I'm out of here," Kaileigh whispered. "No more for me."

"But we're here," Steel protested. "Sir David. Please?"

"Not me," she whispered. "Not now. I'm out of here."

"Wait for me by the ash tree, then," he said.

She didn't acknowledge him. Instead she stood, looked around, and was gone.

Steel unfolded himself and walked out past Sir David and into the nave. The four boys had not come through the main door; he would have heard that. They had not come through the only other door—the door to the choir room.

So how had they just suddenly appeared? he wondered.

He pushed and pulled Sir David, but to no avail. It didn't budge in the least. It had to weigh a ton or more. He couldn't imagine anyone—even four upperclassmen—moving it. No, if there was a secret entrance to the chapel, it would involve the dark wood paneling, intricately carved and decorated with many moldings that arched over each of the back bench seats. Any one of these might conceal a secret door, released somehow—some piece of wood-work moved, or a hidden lever tripped. A sixteenth century monastery must come with some secret passages.

If there was a secret passage, Steel would need hours to pound on the paneling, listening for hollow spaces and searching for a release. He left the chapel feeling defeated.

He and Kaileigh met up under the ash tree. They were heading back toward the dorms when she stopped and turned to face Steel beneath the gloomy shadow of a towering sugar maple.

"If we make a plan," she said, "we have to stick with it."

"What plan?"

"You know," she said. "*The* plan." She puckered up.

"I didn't agree to any plan," Steel objected. "It was your idea."

"Same thing," she said. "I didn't hear you complaining. It wouldn't be so awful . . . kissing you. People do it all the time."

Thankfully, she turned and left him before Steel was required to come up with some kind of answer. But he stood there watching her move through the shadows, and he wondered if he'd missed a chance at something he might regret.

8.
VIGILANCE

Steel considered his options in order to reach his room without being caught. Upperclassmen—Fifth and Sixth Forms—still roamed the campus, primarily moving between the dorms and the athletic center's student lounge, or the library. The movement of these students provided him with some cover—he wasn't entirely alone and therefore sticking out—but it also meant there were many eyes to see him. He'd been warned of upperclassmen torturing younger students caught after hours: spraying them with hoses, stripping them naked and making them run to their rooms across the junior varsity soccer field—right in front of one of the girls' dorms.

All because if a Third or Fourth Form student was

caught violating curfew, they impacted the liberties and freedoms of the upperclassmen. In this way, the school had created a polarized environment where the older students monitored the younger students, if for no other reason than to protect their rights to a later curfew.

Given the uniform of coat and tie, most of the guys looked alike from a distance. It was only Steel's height and boyish face that might have given him away as a younger student. The secret, Steel thought, was to stand as tall as possible, and to walk with confidence.

Above all, he could not allow himself to be caught. He spotted a shortcut. He could climb into the breezeway and cut through to the lower dorms, avoiding the administration building altogether.

He stayed in shadows, heading for the breezeway. Halfway there, he heard voices and stopped short. Looked around again. Still no one . . . Then he placed the voices. They were coming from his left, from one of the basement classrooms in the administration building. These windows—there were eight in all—were below the level of the grass, in dug-out bays.

He might have continued on—the breezeway was so close now—but he recognized one of the voices, knew without any doubt it was the same voice he'd just heard in the chapel—the same upperclassman.

What was he doing over here?

Remaining in shadow, he moved toward the concrete semicircle dug down into the ground, which contained the glowing window from a basement classroom. Dropping to his knees, he crawled the final few feet.

The window shade was drawn three quarters of the way down, the window open a gap. Steel had a view of six pant legs and three pairs of shoes, and three silhouettes were projected onto the shade like shadow puppets. Of the three, one was considerably taller than the other two; this person wore proper trousers and shined shoes—a teacher. The other two wore blue jeans and leather boat shoes.

"The problem is . . . *identification*," said a deep voice in a British accent.

Steel knew of two teachers with British accents: a math teacher named Randolph and a chemistry teacher known to the kids as Munch.

"But if it's true . . ." said the voice of the upperclassman from the chapel. He said something else, but Steel missed it. Only his final words, ". . . all in trouble," came through distinctly.

Trouble?

"Agreed," said the British accent.

"And how . . . find . . . ?" said the third person. His voice was younger. Steel desperately wanted to determine who he was. He edged slightly closer, his hands now touching the curving concrete wall that formed the window well.

Movement flashed in the corner of his eye, and he pivoted his head slowly to look in that direction.

Benny the Bulb, the JV football coach, was walking toward him. Instinctively, Steel slipped over the edge of the concrete retaining wall, hanging by his fingers, his back facing the window.

"What was that?" came the British accent from behind him, the words clear. "Have a look."

Steel pressed his cheek to the cool concrete—it smelled like chalk—and remained stone still. Light flooded the dugout out as someone peered out the side of the shade. Steel held his breath.

The light reduced as the shade was released. Whoever had peered out had looked right past him. Steel took it as a sign: he was not to be caught.

"Benny the . . . It's Mr. Morgan, sir, doing his rounds," said the upperclassman's voice.

"We can't be seen together," said the British accent. "Not this time of night. Too much explanation required. Remember what I said."

"Yes, sir."

"Vigilance!"

"Yes, sir."

"It's paramount this be resolved in a timely fashion. Immediately, if not sooner."

"Understood."

"Go then. And hurry. We don't need Ben asking questions."

The muted sounds of a door opening and shutting came next. At the same time Steel heard Benny the Bulb enter the building through a nearby door.

Steel's fingers were bloodless and about to fall off.

The light went off behind him. He heard the click of the classroom door.

He tugged and pulled himself up and out, the soles of his shoes slippery on the concrete. At last he was lying in the grass, panting. He'd broken out into a full sweat.

Two figures crossed the breezeway, heading from the administration building to the dorm—he was willing to bet it was the upperclassman and the other student who'd just been talking to the teacher with the British accent. He lifted his head, trying to get a good look at their faces, but failed to identify them.

He had to hurry: Benny the Bulb wouldn't be far behind them.

He scrambled to the breezeway, climbed through one of the open-air windows created by the arches, and dropped down. He hurried for the stairs.

"Who goes there?" The British voice was immediately behind him.

Where had he come from?

Steel had the choice of staying and being caught in a curfew violation, or taking off. Leaping three stairs at a time, he reached the lower level at a full run.

"Hey, there!" the British man said. He cried out sharply for Steel to stop.

Steel hugged the backside of the lower level dorms, racing for the doorway to Lower Three, ducking beneath one dorm room window after another. He looked left: no one was currently coming from the gym.

But was the teacher following him?

He ducked through the door, flew up three stairs and turned right, entering Lower Three. Several boys were walking the hall in nothing but towels. He knew two of them, though not by name.

He reached his room just as he heard the hallway door open . . . *The teacher with the British accent?* he wondered.

Coming into his room, Steel pivoted immediately and eased the door shut.

He slowly turned around, short of breath and sweating profusely.

Sitting up in bed with a paralyzed look, Verne opened his eyes widely and looked left.

And there, in Steel's desk chair, was a man in a coat and tie, dark trousers, and polished black shoes.

"Mr. Trapp, is it?" asked the man—a teacher, familiar by face—turning his wrist to mark the time.

9.
AN UNEXPECTED
VISITOR

The man had a pinched face, tightly set blazing blue eyes, a high forehead, and a stubble of short cropped hair, absolutely flat on top. He possessed a look of fierce intensity, his mouth too small to have ever smiled.

Steel stood stone still. A bead of sweat dripped into and stung one eye. He reached up and rubbed it, making it worse, then dragged the sleeve of his school blazer across his face, mopping up.

"Do you happen to know what time it is, Mr. Trapp?" The man's voice was somewhat hoarse, but not lacking in authority.

"Five of ten, sir," Steel said.

The man on the bed pointed to a desktop clock radio belonging to Steel's roommate. 10:55, the display read.

Steel glanced at his watch. "But . . ."

"Step over here," the man instructed.

Steel did as he was told.

The man reached out and took Steel by the wrist. As he started to twist Steel's arm, Steel thought he intended to hurt him—but it was only to get a better look at his wristwatch. Noting the time on Steel's watch: 9:56, he said, "I'm willing to give you the benefit of the doubt, although it is beyond me how, with the incorrect time on your watch, you could make dinner or classes, and yet fail to meet curfew." He looked directly at Steel, his eyes like lasers. "Nice try, Mr. Trapp. An *A* for effort. But I wouldn't try it again."

Steel knew better than to attempt to talk back to a teacher. He kept his mouth shut, wondering what this guy wanted with him. It should have been his dorm master, Mr. Roare, checking up on curfew. Now that his anxiety had lessened, his memory kicked in and he recalled everything about this man from the *Third Form Handbook, An Introduction to the Wynncliff Faculty.*

"Allow me to introduce myself," he said. "I'm—"

"Walter Hinchman. Forty-seven years old. A graduate of Williams College, with a master's from Columbia. You teach Fourth Form English Literature, a Fifth Form course called Chaucer and Shakespeare: The Power of Poetry, and Sixth Formers, The Mystery of Myth."

Hinchman nodded thoughtfully, either impressed or annoyed, Steel wasn't sure.

"Sit down, Mr. Trapp." He indicated for Steel to sit across from him on the edge of Verne's bed.

Steel obeyed, though reluctantly. Verne squirmed and moved over.

"I've heard of this remarkable memory of yours," Walter Hinchman said. "Quite an impressive display, just now, though I think you could put it to better use than showing off."

"Yes, sir."

"Have you heard of ga-ga, Mr. Trapp?"

Steel's heart fluttered. Was he actually going to get off without punishment? "Well . . . yes, sir. I have."

"Ever seen it played?"

"I've seen some of the upperclassmen playing, sir. From a distance."

"Did you know your father played?"

"My dad?"

Hinchman nodded. And to Steel's surprise, his small mouth did know how to smile. It was a strange smile, as if a line had been cut into a piece of paper; his lips barely parted.

"He was on the Spartan Club championship team, three years running. I played *against* him in the finals. And lost."

"He's never mentioned it," Steel said. The more he learned about his father, the less he felt he knew him.

"Do you know anything about the game?"

"Not much." Steel knew that club-level ga-ga was considered the elite sport at the school, but he pretended otherwise. He wasn't sure what Hinchman was getting at.

"It's a year-long sport that you play in addition to whatever seasonal sport you've signed up for, so it requires excellent grades because of the extra load. You must maintain a B average, a 3.0. It's played inside during the winter term—we share the wrestling room—and outside in spring and fall. There are four clubs—Corinth, represented by the Minotaur; Sparta, by Medusa; Argos, by Apollo; and Megera, by Poseidon—that compete for school championship. You *never* refer to a club by its symbol, only its ancient city. The winning club then advances to represent the school in an interconference tournament in the spring. Each of the club teams consists of five starters—three boys and two girls—and two substitutes—one boy and one girl. Seven students per team. Twenty-eight students altogether out of a student body of three hundred eighty-five. It is among the highest honors at the school to play club-level ga-ga, and typically ensures the student athlete the offer of a scholarship at one of the Ivy League colleges.

"It's a game of quick reactions, endurance, teamwork, and mathematics—geometry, to be specific. I see on your test scores that your math, specifically your geometry, is quite good."

Steel had never had a grade lower than an A+ in any course. Photographic memory went a long way toward preparing for tests and completing homework. He never forgot what he read; never forgot what a teacher said. The other kids considered him ridiculously smart, but he didn't think of himself that way. It was more magic trick than brains. Sometimes he felt like one of those birds that could speak phrases in English, yet had no idea what it was saying.

"I suppose," Steel said modestly. He didn't want his roommate thinking of him as some kind of brainiac nerd, ace student. That was a label certain to ruin any chance of finding decent friends.

"In particular," Hinchman said, "your memory

skills intrigue me. Did you know that athletes, like all humans, are pattern oriented? We tend to do things the same way. Take drying yourself off after a shower. Keep track of it sometime. You tend to do it the same way each time. One person might start with his hair or his face, then shoulders, or the back, or arms—but he'll do it the same way, the same pattern, nine out of ten times. A man shaving his face—same thing. The order in which we dress, or button a shirt. The direction in which we lick an envelope. A million different patterns that become the behavioral skeleton of who we are. The same is true of athletics. We actually strive, in athletics, to repeat ourselves. To serve a tennis ball the exact same way each time. Or throw a football. Or dribble a soccer ball. We are, in fact, *trained* to repeat ourselves so that our mechanics become flawless, so that we become as efficient as possible."

"I hadn't thought of it, exactly," Steel said. This guy was *weird*.

"Ga-ga is no different, Mr. Trapp. Split-second timing and reactions. Key to the game. Speed, agility, and decision making. Do you see where I'm going with this?"

"Not exactly."

"Well . . . maybe a facile memory isn't everything,"

Hinchman said. "I'm inviting you to try out for the team."

"Me?"

"I coach the Spartans, Mr. Trapp. Three club championships in nine years. We went to state twice. We have not won that honor . . . yet, but the Spartans have a promising team this year. Much stronger, in my opinion, than the Megerians or Argives. More promising by the minute, I might add."

"I'm an underclassman," Steel reminded. "Third Form. I thought—"

"Exceptions can be made." He stood. "I'm not suggesting you'll qualify, Mr. Trapp, only that an opportunity is there. It's only a tryout, after all."

"But I don't know anything about ga-ga."

"I've just told you: I coach. Coaches teach, Mr. Trapp. You will meet me in the ga-ga pit at six a.m. each morning for the next week. Tryouts begin the twenty-seventh. Competition will be fierce. It won't be easy. Might not even be possible. But I'm offering you my services, my experience. And it would be foolish of you to refuse, so I will not offer that option. Athletic shoes, sweats, and long sleeves. Six a.m. tomorrow."

He moved toward the door, where he paused and

looked at Steel with his sharp eyes over a severe Roman nose.

"Curfew violations result in any club athlete losing that distinction. He or she is immediately off the team. I'd get my watch fixed, if I were you. Do we understand each other?"

Verne, sitting up in bed, watched the exchange with barely contained excitement, stunned to hear of the invitation for Steel to tryout for the Spartans.

"Well, *answer* him!" Verne said, prodding Steel.

Steel's head was spinning. He'd gone from expecting to be punished for skipping curfew to an invitation to try out for a sport he knew nothing about. His voice was too tight to speak, so he simply nodded.

"You've made the right decision," Hinchman said. "Do not be late, Mr. Trapp, or the invitation will be withdrawn."

10.
ROOM 1426

Taddler, dressed in stay-pressed khakis, had added a navy blue sweater he kept clean for special missions. He'd combed his hair and brushed his teeth and had spent several minutes wiping off his running shoes to make them as presentable as possible—although their ratty condition was a bit of a giveaway. Johnny, wide-eyed and rosy-cheeked, waited for the signal from a bench across the street. He wore blue jeans and a dark sports coat, looking like a preppie, and prepared to play the part. Both boys carried small two-way radios that fit easily into a pants pocket.

At 6:45 a.m. Taddler approached the hotel entrance on foot, carrying a Health Mart shopping bag.

"Hey, how you doing?" said the doorman.

"Better than my mother," Taddler said, hoisting the bag.

"You mind if I see your room card?" the doorman asked. If it had been noon, Taddler wouldn't have been questioned, but the early hour raised some eyebrows. Mrs. D. had been warning them for weeks that the hotels had increased security. How she knew this stuff was unclear, but the boys took her word on it. She was a smart lady, and no one was going to bite the hand that literally fed them.

Taddler flashed him the card and stuffed it into his pants, wanting to appear slightly annoyed at being bothered.

"Thanks," the doorman said, setting the revolving door spinning.

Taddler stepped into the moving wedge and pushed the door around to the other side, where he was greeted by the soft sound of classical music, the smell of coffee, and a group of friendly faces, from the bellman to two women behind the registration desk. The atmosphere was so far from that of the Corinthians that each time Taddler did one of these missions he felt it had to be some kind of dream. The wealth and privilege of the people in these hotels was otherworldly, as was the general acceptance that this was somehow normal. They seemed so accustomed to it, and he had to wonder what that was like—to live the way the guests did, or even to have a job in a place like this. He wondered if he might ever stay a single night in such a place, and imagined how exceptional a night that would be for him.

With experience as his guide, he headed for the elevators. He rode up four flights to bypass the mezzanine and conference floors. He hung the Health Mart bag on the handle of the service stairs to be temporarily rid of it, and stepped into the hall. He waited, standing on the landing marked Four, waiting for the scuffle of shoes on concrete.

They came from above, and he could tell by the rattle that it was food service—exactly as he wanted. He started up the stairs, and soon saw a woman wearing a uniform on her way down, carrying a spent room-service tray. He purposely took up a little too much space on his side of the stairs. As she slowed to pass him, he spoke loudly.

"The elevators are a nightmare."

"Tell me about it," she said.

He gently nudged her, sending the tray off balance.

"Sorry!" he called out. He intentionally overreacted and reached out to stabilize the tray.

The all-access room card was most often carried in the small apron that the women wore. It was a tricky area to access; he had to make sure he kept the pressure away from her body. As his left hand grabbed the tray, his right slipped into the apron's front pouch and touched the cool plastic. He deftly deposited the card given to him by Mrs. D. and withdrew the card belonging to the waitress. All in less time than it takes a frog's tongue to catch a fly.

With the tray kept from falling, he apologized again and hurried up the stairs.

He'd needed both hands free to accomplish the switch, which was why he'd left the drugstore bag behind.

What he didn't know was that a hotel detective had found the bag only minutes after he'd left it, that the detective had called it in, and one of the doormen remembered a kid with a similar bag. As Taddler reached the seventh floor and pulled out the two-way radio, he had no idea that they were already looking for him.

"Johnny?" he said.

"Yeah?"

"I'm on Seven."

"Got it."

Five minutes later the elevator on Seven opened,

and Johnny and Taddler crossed paths, switching places. As they did, without any acknowledgment of the other, their hands barely brushed. The all-access card passed from Taddler to Johnny in a move so practiced, even a cop wouldn't have spotted it.

Taddler rode the elevator down to the second floor, to the health club.

He avoided the business breakfasts in the private dining rooms and headed straight to the club. He approached the desk to ask a question about services, but his eyes were on the sign-in sheet on a clipboard next to the stack of towels.

R. Ungerman had signed in at 7:07.

Taddler reached into his pocket and pushed the radio's call button twice, sending two clicks and signaling Johnny that the room was empty.

Then Taddler explained that his mother was wondering if they offered something called a Chinese Oil Massage.

The woman smiled and handed him a price sheet.

He thanked the woman and left; mission accomplished. Any minute, Johnny would be on his way inside.

Grover Cleveland IV, a direct descendant of the U.S. President, and currently director of security for the

Haymarket Hotel, had the habit of pinching his chin and rubbing his goatee when something interested or annoyed him. His employees knew better than to interrupt him when they saw the gesture coming, as they did now. Due to his ancestry, Cleveland held an overinflated opinion of himself. Being a hotel detective was not exactly the same as being president of the United States, but don't tell Grover Cleveland IV that.

Two weeks earlier, he and every other hotel director of security in the city had been notified of a ring of petty thieves operating in area hotels. Sometimes money was taken; other times information. It seemed to be highly organized and possibly involved teen youth. The Organized Crime Bureau in the Boston Police Department had assigned Detective Mark Ulrich to the investigation. Ulrich was to be notified if anyone had information.

Grover Cleveland picked up the phone and then hung up before speaking. He stroked his goatee, his beady eyes dancing side to side. He didn't want to make a fool of himself with the Boston police; on the contrary, he hoped to impress them.

The mention of the suspicious shopping bag, and the doorman connecting it to a male youth entering the building, raised the hackles on the back of

Cleveland's hairy neck. He directed Howard Lightfoot to use security camera footage to identify the boy who had entered the hotel, and then "follow" him by moving from one camera to the next.

The trouble with the plan was that it proved too time consuming. It took Lightfoot five minutes to find the images of the boy entering the hotel, and another two minutes to pick up sight of him in the lobby. Too long.

"Keep working on it," Cleveland said, thoughts grinding like gears in his tired head. He'd stayed up late the night before watching a DVD of *24*, and all the coffee in the world couldn't help him right now.

"If I could make a suggestion," Lightfoot said from his chair in front of the video control board. He was a big man with pitch-black hair and angular features.

"Go ahead," Cleveland said.

"I can bring up all the hallway views on monitors two through six. Rotate through them in five-second intervals." He did this as he spoke. Images of the hallways appeared. "If there are any kids— teenage boys—walking around, we'll identify them." He took a deep breath and waited for Cleveland to either explode or claim that this was his intention all along: both of which Cleveland was known to do. Cleveland only stroked his chin, which Lightfoot took as a good sign. "If we were then to post Kreutz in the lobby, and you were to take the arcade exit . . ." Another pause. "I don't think anyone could *leave* the hotel without our knowledge. Not unless they used one of the service exits, loading docks, or the kitchen access. They'd have to know their stuff to use any of those."

"There are twelve ground-floor exits to the hotel," Cleveland reminded him. "Sixteen fire escapes and five garage levels. We have only the three of us at the moment: you, me, and Kreutz."

Again he reached for his phone. But again he decided against calling the police. It would be too embarrassing if it proved to be for nothing.

Lightfoot had forgotten about the garage levels. He wasn't sure what to say.

"What I would suggest," Cleveland said, "is that you monitor the video. Assign Kreutz to the lobby. I'll take the arcade entrance." He made it sound like he'd just thought of this all by himself. "We'll stop any teenage boy and make sure we connect him to a reservation and an adult." He paused. "What do you think about that plan, Lightfoot?"

Howard Lightfoot rolled his eyes. It was a good thing he was facing the bank of computer screens and not his boss.

Cleveland puffed out his chest imperially and charged out of the small basement office like the military commander he wished he was.

Johnny used the room-service key card to gain entrance to 1426. He didn't knock. If it turned out someone was in the room, he would look confused and mumble something like, "How come the stupid key worked?" and then leave as quickly as he'd come. He had a real gift when it came to lying.

No one was in the room: Taddler had done everything right.

Johnny moved quickly to the other side of a handsome desk. There was a leather briefcase on the floor. He opened it and concentrated as he flipped through the contents, needing to remember the exact order he found things in. He used the notepad by the phone, writing down the sequence of what he discovered: a *Time* magazine, a printout of an Internet map page, two Netflix DVDs, and a manila folder.

Inside the manila folder he found the letters Mrs. D. had mentioned. He jumped up and fed the letters one by one into the printer/fax/copier. Before he pressed the START button, he counted the number of blank sheets of paper in the feeder: *seven*.

He counted eleven letters to copy.

He slipped out an oversized mailer from where it was tucked into his back beneath his shirt, and counted out eleven sheets of blank paper and fed them into the feeder.

He hit START.

The copier was incredibly slow. Each sheet took five or ten seconds. It seemed an eternity.

His radio clicked three times. *Pause*. Three more clicks.

He was to talk if able.

"Yeah?" he spoke into the radio.

"I'm looking down from the mezzanine into the lobby. Looks like they maybe put a guy on the door."

"No way." Johnny leaned over the printer/copier, wondering how it could take so long. There were still six letters to go.

"We could try the entrance to the shops, but I gotta think we have problems." Taddler was holding the radio like a cell phone, and he had the volume turned way down so that only he could hear, but he still felt as if he stuck out, being the only kid for a million miles. "I'm not sure what to do," he admitted.

Five letters to go. The machine was taking forever.

"You there?" Taddler asked.

"Yeah," Johnny answered. "This thing is pathetically slow. I can't believe it."

"I think you should abort."

"I'm so close."

"Yeah, but . . . I still think—"

"Okay. I'm almost done," Johnny replied, his transmission interrupting Taddler's.

In the basement security office, Howard Lightfoot caught something out of the corner of his eye. It was not easy watching four monitors that covered seventeen floors, each image changing in five-second intervals. He froze all the images and then reversed the playback on screen four.

A kid entered the frame, walked to a room, and entered.

Lightfoot counted the doors.

"1425 or 26," he spoke into the hotel radio. "A kid entered. A boy."

"I'm on my way," Cleveland replied. "Stay with him, Howard. Monitor his every move."

"I'm on him," Lightfoot answered. He kept the other screens on PAUSE, the one screen now the center of his attention.

Taddler saw the man he believed to be a house detective move toward the bank of elevators, his finger pressed to his ear.

Taddler hurried down the escalator and then controlled his urge to run, and instead moved calmly toward the revolving door while only yards from the house detective, whose face was presently turned away from him.

It looked as if the guy had heard something over the radio, and had moved toward the elevators as a result.

Taddler hoped that didn't involve Johnny.

"Hey!" he heard a voice from behind.

The house detective.

Taddler took off running.

"Stop!" the man shouted.

Taddler hit the revolving door and pushed hard, the big doors easing forward. Reaching the other side, he turned to see the man coming toward him at a full run.

There was no way he was going to outrun this guy.

He looked down. A big pink concrete urn held a small evergreen tree. He leaned his weight into it, raised it up on its edge, and was able to rotate it so that it wheeled toward the revolving door. He moved it into the path of the door by a good six inches, then turned and ran.

He heard the collision as the detective hit the

revolving door hard, and the door advanced, colliding with the urn. Refusing to move.

It bought Taddler the time he needed. He ran to his left, then left again down an alley along the side of the hotel. Another block and he'd have his choice of a bus or the Red Line.

He had the radio out and in hand. "Bail! Bail!" he shouted. "Mayday! They're after us!"

He hoped like mad that Johnny had heard.

Johnny slipped the manila envelope containing the copied documents along the small of his back and covered it by tucking in his shirt.

Taddler's words, *"They're after us!"* swirled in his head. To be caught would not only mean the police, but would also be an end to the Corinthians for him. It was unthinkable: the Corinthians was as close to a family as Johnny had—discounting those people in Minnesota.

He returned the originals to the briefcase just as he'd found them, and hurried to the door. Cracking the door just a fraction of an inch, he peered out.

A man holding a radio was coming down the hall toward him.

Johnny knew about hotel security. He knew he was outnumbered. For a moment he froze, unable to think what to do. It's not as if there were lots of places to hide. He could make a run for it, but what chance did he have against such odds?

He heard a knock on the door of the next room over: the house detective had picked the wrong room. Then he heard the door open.

If he had any chance, it was now.

He peered out of the fish-eye peephole: an exit sign over an unmarked door to his left. *A stairway.* He gently pushed down on the room door lever and opened it as quietly as possible. He didn't dare shut it for the loud click it would make, but he pulled it nearly closed. Then he sprinted for the exit.

As expected, he found himself in an echoey, concrete stairway.

They would expect him to go down.

He took off up the stairs. As he climbed, he looked for any sign of security cameras. *There!* He spotted a black plastic bubble in the far corner of the landing as he arrived.

He heard the door below blow open and the furiously fast footfalls of the house detective *descending* in pursuit of him.

Johnny lowered his head, keeping his face off the security cameras, and pulled open the door to floor Fifteen, realizing he might already have been spotted.

Elevators to his left. He couldn't take the stairs.

By now the house detective would know that Johnny had headed up, not down. By now they probably knew he was on Fifteen.

He could barely breathe.

A maid's cart to his right.

A black plastic bubble on the edge of the hallway, nearly directly overhead.

Maybe . . .

He hurried to the cart and peered into a room. The maid was cleaning in the bathroom, the bathroom door nearly closed.

He grabbed a can of window cleaner from the cart, raced back down the hall, and shot a spray of CleanVu up at the camera until it was speckled with a sudsy slime. The view from the camera would be like looking out a car windshield in a carwash. Placing the spray can back on the cart, he checked once again that the maid was in the bathroom. He heard her clanking around in there, gathered his courage, and slipped through the door and into the open closet. He sat down and carefully, quietly, shut the sliding door, leaving only a crack to peer through.

He switched off his radio, not wanting any sounds to give him away.

He held his breath when, a minute later, a beefy woman who reminded him of a shelter nurse mopped her way backward out of the bathroom. She put some stuff on her cart, removed the rubber wedge that held open the door—the top of her head coming within inches of Johnny's eyes—and pulled the door shut behind her.

Johnny threw his head back and released a long but nearly silent sigh.

He would wait an hour and then make a mad dash down the stairwell. By then security would assume he was long gone.

11.
GOING GA-GA

A chilly mist hovered above the soccer field like a veil of gauze, masking any view of the gymnasium and natatorium beyond. A murder of crows flew in and out of the smoky layers, their *caws* piercing the still, mud-scented morning air and echoing off the dormitory's ivy-covered brick walls. As Steel crossed the adjacent field, the mist swirled around him, looking sometimes like long fingers attempting to grab him, or animal faces, or, at last, like a gray stone archway leading directly to the ga-ga pit and the silhouetted figure that awaited him there.

Mr. Hinchman had a military demeanor: he carried his shoulders square, his back stiff and straight. His small mouth failed to reveal any emotion. Only his steely eyes gave hint of the man's personality, which could scarcely be considered anything but severe and intense.

"Are you ready, Mr. Trapp?"

Steel nodded, though somewhat reluctantly.

"Ga-ga is a game of reaction, agility, split-second timing, and most of all, deception. On the surface it is the picture of simplicity: don't get hit by the ball. But nothing is as simple as it appears." The glare of his eyes seemed to penetrate Steel; he was trying to convey much more than his words afforded.

The pit itself was a space defined by ten-foot, waist-high, octagonal walls, the floor of which was hard-packed sand and dirt.

"There are a few basic rules, as you may or may not know. The idea is to hit the other person with the ball, below the knees. This strike puts him out of the game. You must only slap the ball. If you catch it after it hits the ground or a wall, you're out. If you scoop or 'carry' it"—he demonstrated palming the ball—"you are disqualified and ejected. You may not leave the pit or use the walls to jump. You may not touch the ball twice in a row, though you can use the walls to pass it to yourself—called dribbling.

"As I explained, we typically play with two five-person teams. Players are eliminated in the ways I've just explained. Teammates may pass the ball. However, if the ball should strike a teammate at or below the knees, he too is out, regardless of who hit it."

"Sounds easy enough," Steel said.

Hinchman raised an eyebrow and scowled. "Yes, it does, doesn't it?" He waved Steel over the wall and into the pit to join him. "We play the game with a slightly undersized volleyball that we call the 'spud.' It is a very fast ball, the strikes often sting, and it can be dribbled and passed quickly due to its small size and firm inflation. It bounces out of control easily and therefore requires the striker to demonstrate the utmost precision."

The way Hinchman spoke, he made ga-ga sound like it was a religious experience instead of a game. Briefly, Steel considered opting out, telling Hinchman he wasn't up for this. But the man's fiery look told him that to do so would condemn him in this man's opinion and, if word got out, the opinions of many others. He'd been offered what would be considered an honor, and he knew he would be stupid to turn it down.

Practice began. Steel stooped over and protected his legs with open palms to deflect the "spud." Hinchman hit him with the ball time and time again, first with direct shots, and then, as Steel became more practiced, from ricochets angled off the walls.

"You're good at this," Steel said, while they continued to play. In thirty minutes of practice, Steel had managed to hit Hinchman only once. He was learning that there was as much skill involved in dodging or avoiding a hit as there was in striking or deflecting the ball. It was part dodgeball, part billiards.

"I was on the runner-up team my Fifth and Sixth Form years. I want you to focus on—"

"The angles," Steel interrupted.

"Yes. Exactly. And patterns. Use your memory skills. Study my play. Learn to anticipate my next move."

Hinchman struck Steel three times in a row. He stopped the play and gave instruction.

"Angle of incidence equals the angle of reflection. Whatever critical angle the ball strikes the wall will be the same angle it will leave the wall, meaning its course is entirely predictable. You must learn to never take your eye off the ball, to mentally measure how it comes off a striker's hand or wall. This gives you a split-second advantage over its trajectory, the chance to anticipate its destination, and therefore the opportunity to avoid being hit."

He hit a ball slowly off the wall at Steel.

Steel suddenly saw things as if a transparency sheet had been overlaid with the mathematics drawn out in colored dashes and arrows. He jumped, and the ball passed beneath him. Hinchman found it in him to grin, though only slightly. He hit the spud again, and again Steel avoided a shot that earlier would have hit him.

"Excellent!" Hinchman called out proudly. "You can *see* it now, can't you?"

"I *can*!"

"Any patterns?" Hinchman asked.

"When your right foot goes back, you're about to strike. If you lift your head, it's a wall shot. Chin down, it's straight at me."

"Impressive!"

The play continued. Steel nimbly avoided any hits, while quickly developing a shot that involved deflecting a ball on the move rather than stopping the ball and striking it fresh.

He hit Hinchman twice with the deflected strike. It was all a matter of measuring angles, something he found incredibly easy to do.

"You have a unique shot, Mr. Trapp," Hinchman said after the second strike landed. He had stopped the ball. He stood tall, breathing rapidly. "These are the skills we will build upon. With time and practice and patience, we will see how far your abilities will carry you."

"What's this?" It was Kaileigh.

Steel had no idea how long she'd been standing there, watching. He looked around: students were heading to breakfast in their uniforms. He checked the clock tower on the administration building. He was absurdly late; he'd be lucky to eat this morning.

"Ga-ga," Steel answered.

"Isn't that a sound a baby makes?"

"It is anything but a child's game, Miss Augustine," Hinchman said. "You will be introduced to it in gym class. Perhaps you'll find it interests you. We can always use skilled players."

Hinchman knew Kaileigh's last name. Steel wondered if he knew all the students in such detail. And if not, why her?

"Mr. Hinchman is the *Spartans'* coach," Steel said.

This had the effect he'd hoped for: Kaileigh's jaw dropped.

"But you're Third Form."

"It's only a tryout, Miss Augustine," Hinchman said. "Some coaching. We don't want this getting around school just yet."

Steel wiggled his eyebrows at her.

"A little late for that," came a deep-throated voice. "Third Formers should know their place."

"Ah!" said Hinchman. "Mr. DesConte."

"Mr. Trapp, meet the reigning school champion, Victor DesConte."

"Dez," said the deep voice, introducing himself.

Steel turned, already extending his hand to greet the boy behind him.

He stood face-to-face with the square-jawed boy he'd seen in the chapel the night before. The boy he'd overheard meeting secretly with a British-accented teacher.

"Nice to meet you," Steel said. He heard Kaileigh gasp from behind him. She mumbled something about breakfast, and headed off in the direction of the dining hall.

Victor DesConte shook Steel's hand, sparing him no strength.

"Mr. Trapp is a legacy," Hinchman said.

"Interesting," DesConte said.

"Mr. DesConte is a legacy as well, Mr. Trapp. Your fathers may have very well known each other. Victor is a second-year Argive. Academy champions last year."

"And this year too, with any luck," DesConte

said. This seemed a direct challenge to Hinchman.

"I'm offering Mr. Trapp a chance to try out for Sparta," Hinchman explained.

DesConte took a step back, anything but pleased. "But he's—"

"Trying out, is all," Hinchman said. "Some practice work. Nothing more for now. We'll see how far we get."

"Indeed we will," said DesConte, his voice raspy and displeased. He towered over Steel. "Good luck." He didn't mean it.

"That's the second time you've mentioned luck," Steel said. "I thought it was more a game of skill."

His comment caused Hinchman to bite back a smirk of satisfaction.

"I kinda hope you make the team," DesConte said, walking away.

"Don't mind him," Hinchman said, once DesConte was well out of hearing range.

"Hard not to," Steel said, deciding right then and there to devote himself to the game.

12.
NO PLACE LIKE HOME

A week of early morning ga-ga training and loads of homework left Steel as tired as he'd ever been. With the fatigue came a change in mood: he felt determined to make the team, and even more determined to find out what he'd become a part of.

Despite Steel's appeal for a cell phone, his dad had given him a telephone calling card instead. He put it to use on a Friday evening after study hall. Finding his way to the converted basement of the administration building, he waited for one of the six payphone booths to free up, and called home.

"Hi, Mom," he said, as she picked up.

"Sweetheart! How wonderful!" Her voice was bright and cheery as always.

He felt his pulse rise at just the sound of her voice.

"Honey?" She called out loudly away from the receiver, "It's Steel!" When she next spoke, her voice was measured. "How are you, sweetie? Is everything going okay?"

"Terrific." Offered with plenty of sarcasm.

"Do you like it there?"

"I love it."

"Miss home?"

"I suppose. But I'm not calling 'cause I'm homesick. I want to talk to Dad about something."

There was a click on the line: his father had joined the call.

"Steven?" His father. Mr. Wynncliff himself, apparently.

"Hi, Dad."

"I understand you've met Walt Hinchman."

"Yeah." He wondered both how and why his father knew this. "That's kind of why I called."

"What do you think of ga-ga? I hear you're a natural."

"It's great. I try out on Monday."

"I wish I could be there," his father said. "Being invited to try out for a club team, son," his father said, "and in the Third Form, no less, is quite the honor. And the Spartans, of all teams."

"What's going on, Dad?"

There was a pause on the other end of the line. "What do you mean?"

It was as if his mother had left the call. She was like that around Steel's dad. When he was home, or driving the car, or on a phone call, she kind of disappeared, as she had now.

"Wynncliff," Steel said. "Why Wynncliff?"

"It's a good school," his father said, clearly intending to say more, but Steel cut him off.

"And why Kaileigh?"

"What about Kaileigh?" his mother asked, when the silence built to where no one was sure if the line was still open.

"Kaileigh's here, Mom. Dad arranged it."

"Sweetheart?" This was directed to her husband.

"She's a smart girl," his father said defensively. "Very smart. Why not Wynncliff?"

"Her father could *buy* Wynncliff," Steel said. "He could get her into any private school she wanted. But she ends up here at Wynncliff. How did you manage that, Dad? How did you convince her parents it should be here instead of Andover or Choate or Exeter?"

Steel heard his mother breathing heavily into the phone. He knew she was upset, and assumed this was news to her.

"I thought you liked Kaileigh," his father said.

"That's not the issue."

"Don't talk to me with that tone of voice, son."

"Don't try to avoid the question."

"This conversation is over if you continue with that tone."

"So far this isn't a conversation," Steel said, "because you won't answer the question."

"You have to give it time," his father said.

"Give *what* time?"

"The school."

"It's a pretty simple question, Dad. Why Kaileigh? You hardly know her. She's a runaway, a stowaway who I meet on a train, and you decide she's Wynncliff material?"

There was a long vacant moment, only the sound of his mother's desperate breathing filling the line.

"I can't answer that, Steven. Not now. Not yet."

"Can't, or won't?"

"Won't."

"Because?"

"You're at that school for a reason, Steven. So is Kaileigh. It's a special school."

"It's a weird school," Steel said. "There are things going on here—"

"You see how perceptive you are? That's a big part

of the reason you're there. Why you were invited."

"Invited?" Kaileigh had mentioned the same thing.

"Well . . . yes. Invited. They don't ask just anyone."

"And was Kaileigh invited?"

"Obviously," his father said.

"I don't get it."

"Not yet, no. But you will. I think you will," he added, somewhat as an afterthought. "This isn't easy for me."

"For *you*?"

"For any of us. All I ask is that you give it more time. By Thanksgiving it will sort itself out or not. I promise you that if we can speak in confidence, I'll explain as much of it as possible at that time."

"Do you ever tell the truth, Dad?" he blurted, regretting it immediately. But the fact was that his father had claimed to be a salesman all of Steel's life, until it turned out he was a special agent for the FBI. Steel no longer trusted him.

"Was I invited because I'm your son?" Steel asked. "That's why I was asked to tryout for ga-ga, wasn't it? They call it a legacy—the son or daughter of someone who went here. So I'm a legacy. And I didn't even know that. How come you never told me about Wynncliff, or ga-ga, or that you were school champion, or whatever you were?"

"It was long time ago."

"Yeah, but coming here . . . that wasn't my idea. Not really. It was yours."

"It was your decision, not mine," his father protested.

"You know the answer to that," his mother said, speaking up for the first time in several minutes. "The public schools here, Steel. A child of your aptitude . . ."

He'd been hearing nothing but "potential" and "aptitude" from his parents and teachers forever.

"I admit I have a weird memory," he said, "but that doesn't make me a boy genius or something. I just happen to remember stuff."

"But that's how they often measure genius, son," his father said. "We've discussed this often enough."

"Yeah? Well, they should find another way."

"You're a good fit at the school, Steven. You'll find that out soon enough."

"Because I'm good at ga-ga? What about Kaileigh? What's she so good at?"

"We're doing this for you, Steel," his mother added.

"If it's for me, then why won't Dad answer my questions?"

"All will become apparent as you get farther into the semester. Certainly by Christmas."

"I thought you said Thanksgiving," Steel said, objecting.

"I think we should make it Christmas break."

"Then there is stuff to explain," Steel said. "So why not just explain now?

It had only been after getting himself into the trouble at the National Science Challenge that Steel had learned the truth about his father. He didn't know now if his father was just saying stuff to string him along, or if, in fact, there was really some other reason for his being at Wynncliff.

"What's going to become so apparent?" Steel asked.

"I shouldn't have said anything. You've got to promise me you won't say anything to anyone about what I've just said. That's all I'm going to say."

Steel knew that tone of voice. His father wasn't going to answer anything.

A knock on the door startled Steel.

He turned: Victor DesConte filled the narrow window of the phone booth.

He tapped his wristwatch.

Steel pointed to the empty phone booth next to him.

DesConte shook his head. He wanted this phone booth.

"I guess I gotta go," Steel said to his parents. He hung up after a few hasty good-byes.

He swung open the door. "There are other phones," he said.

"So use 'em. This is my phone booth," DesConte said. His low voice was forced, like he wanted to sound older than he was.

"There you are!" It was Kaileigh.

Victor DesConte pivoted around and looked back and forth between Kaileigh and Steel.

"Get out of here," he said. "Curfew's in like twenty minutes."

Steel felt reluctant to obey this guy. On the other hand, Dez was about twice as big as Steel, and an upperclassman. He also sounded like he actually cared that Steel met curfew. So Steel did as he was told.

Kaileigh led him out of the admin building and across the back field.

"What's up?" Steel asked.

"We're not going to miss curfew, I promise, but if we're not over there in the next ten minutes, we're going to miss it."

"Miss what?" Steel asked, lowering his voice, as Kaileigh just had. "Over where?"

"I'll explain on the way," she said. "Are you coming or not?"

"Wait a second," he protested. "How'd you find me? How'd you know I was here?"

"That's the point, stupid." She glanced around furtively, obviously concerned that someone might be listening. "Are you coming or not?" she whispered. "If you don't want to, that's okay."

But it wasn't okay. She sounded disappointed and her shoulders slumped.

"I'm coming," he said.

Her face brightened. Her entire demeanor changed. It had all been an act.

Drama queen, he felt like saying. He knew he was in trouble—knew it had nothing whatsoever to do with the chapel, and everything to do with this girl.

13.
PENNY

Kaileigh led him toward the arts and sciences building, a neoclassic two-story brick building with white trim and double chimneys. This differed from the science lab, an ugly structure erected in the 1950s that was all glass turquoise and salmon panels. Thankfully the lab had been hidden slightly down the hill, beneath the school library. The arts and sciences building stood just behind the administration building in a field of mowed grass adjacent to the JV football field, and not far from the gymnasium/natatorium.

Steel listened to Kaileigh, amazed by her abundance of energy and her ability to make anything sound as if the fate of the free world hung in the balance.

"Have you met Pennington?"

"Pennington Cardwell the Third?" Steel asked, unable to contain the disdain he felt for the boy.

"You don't have to sound so thrilled about it."

"It's just . . . he's so *preppie*, you know? I mean what's with 'the Third' and all that?"

"It's his name, Steel. In fact, Steel isn't even your name, is it? It's Steven. So who's calling the kettle bleak?"

"It's *black*," Steel corrected. "The pot calling the kettle black? It's irony, Kaileigh: they're both black."

"Which is exactly my point: my parents don't want me, Pennington's ancestors probably came over on the *Mayflower* or something, and you're some freak of nature. It's not as if any of us in this place are exactly normal, you know."

"Yeah, yeah. Whatever. None of us are ordinary."

"*Is.*"

"What?"

"Forget it."

"What's with you, anyway?" she asked.

"What do you mean?"

"You're all angry, like."

"I'm having a bad day," he stated. He didn't really feel like he was having a bad day, but it seemed the easiest way to stop the conversation. "So what about Pennington Cardwell the Third?"

"Well, if you wouldn't interrupt all the time." She slowed as they approached the building, finally stopping as they reached the twin white doors. "Penny's a computer nerd. Computers and photography. Fourth Form." She sounded impressed.

"So?"

"So when he was twelve he was arrested for hacking traffic cams. They had these cameras at the tollbooths on the highway meant to take pictures of license plates of cars that ran the tolls. His father got this summons or something, saying he owed like thousands of dollars for running tolls. His father is a banker. He rides a *bike* to work in Boston. It was totally messed up. But the court made him pay or lose his license. So Pennington takes a digital picture of the judge's license plate and then hacks the system and makes it so the judge has run like fifty tolls going back two years. Just to show that it could be done, and that it had been done to his father. Only there were people who didn't appreciate it, and Penny got busted, and eventually, a couple years later, he ended up here at Wynncliff."

Steel was indeed impressed, but for some reason he didn't want Kaileigh knowing this. "So?"

"So, you've got to admit, that's pretty cool. Just that he could do something like that."

"I guess."

"You really are having a bad day," she said. "Is everything okay?"

"Fine."

"So anyway, Penny . . . well . . . I guess I should let him tell you." She swung open the heavy door. The inside of the arts and sciences building felt new. All the paint—white paint—glistened, and the brass hardware sparkled. It reminded Steel of a dentist's office or a new office building: the smell of the paint and new carpet, the gentle hum of air-conditioning, and the way that as the doors closed, they shut out all sound. They hurried up a flight of stairs. Kaileigh moved with a sense of urgency. Steel wondered what was going on. He found her excitement contagious.

She knocked once on the computer lab's blue door and swung it open.

Pennington Cardwell III looked like a banker. He had a tight small mouth and a severe posture. He stood up from a chair in front of three computer monitors—all of them showing different Sudoku games—and he was all of five feet tall. Smaller than Kaileigh. His hair was trimmed short, above his ears and in a straight line at the back. He had gray eyes, a sharp nose, and a face that looked smart and much older than he actually was. Steel got the sense that Penny Cardwell III was sizing him up, the way he took a step back after shaking hands.

"You sure?" Cardwell's eyes narrowed as he looked over at Kaileigh.

She nodded.

"Sudoku?" Steel asked. He glanced at the wall clock. He had homework to do. He'd heard of a Sudoku club, but had zero interest in it.

"It's just a pastime," Penny Cardwell III said.

"You have time for pastimes? I'm impressed."

"Third Form takes some getting used to," the boy said. "The homework."

"Tell me about it," Steel said.

"But it's weird: I think Fourth Form is actually a little easier. I mean, there's more work, but somehow it gets done quicker."

"We're like trained dogs," Kaileigh said. The three of them laughed—Steel out of nervousness. There was an electrical charge in the air. Pennington Cardwell III gave off a deep calm, a brainiac thing that Steel found disconcerting.

"Kaileigh mentioned that you and her . . . you've discovered that not everything at Wynncliff Academy is what you might call explainable."

Steel flashed Kaileigh a vicious look: she shouldn't have said anything.

"It's all right," Penny said. "I'm not a faculty stooge or some informer or something. We all have our curiosities about this place."

"Show him," Kaileigh said, encouraging Penny.

"I need his agreement first." Penny faced Kaileigh with full intensity. "Do you promise not to tell anyone what I'm about to show you? If you should tell, I will find out something about you and expose you. I'm quite capable of that, and I promise that whatever it is, it will get you in trouble. And if there isn't anything there, then I'll invent it and you'll still get in trouble."

"I told him about your father," Kaileigh admitted.

"Like that," Penny Cardwell said. "Exactly like that."

"I promise," Steel said.

Steel was sized up one final time, and then Penny hit some keys, and the screens changed from Sudoku to video. Each monitor was divided into four windows. It took Steel a long few seconds to see that each window showed a part of the campus. Some were in color. Most were black and white.

"I hacked the admin computer late last year, just before summer break. It took me all year. It started out . . . All I was after were some library books. Rentals. You know: you have to put your name on a list? I wanted to move my name up so I could get the new Artemis Fowl before anyone else. It turned out I had to hack the school system to break into the library. Besides grades and financials, I found this."

"Security cameras," Steel said.

"Funny that they don't tell us they're watching everything we do," Penny said.

"How many locations?" Steel asked, his curiosity piqued.

"Enough. All three floors of the four dorms—no cameras inside actual dorm rooms or bathrooms. But all of the school buildings, including classrooms, the gym—but not the locker rooms—a lot of cameras covering the grounds." He pointed out many of the areas on screen as he listed them.

"The chapel?" Steel asked.

"Most of the outside. *Nothing* inside."

"Which I found interesting," Kaileigh added.

"The administration building. The common room and dining hall. The gym, inside and out . . . I think I said that already."

"I asked him to show me the other night when you said those guys went missing in the Lower Three bathroom."

"They were *recorded?*" Steel gasped.

"The cameras record through a blade server to a disk farm," Pennington Cardwell said. "I haven't been able to find where the farm's at, but I can lift the information from it. All of the images—every single camera—are left on a disk for a week—seven days exactly—then compressed and archived to the memory farm. They probably use tape backup, or optical disk. Without the backups, the only thing I've got is from the previous week. That may be a storage limitation. It's entirely possible that they don't keep anything for longer than a week, though I doubt it. You gotta believe they keep the stuff a lot longer. That way if they spot something—someone smoking, or a boy and girl messing around—they can go back and try to establish a history."

"And you were right," Kaileigh said to Steel.

"Was I?"

"You're mocking me," she said. "It's not that I didn't believe you."

"It isn't?" he said.

"About the bathroom. About the door opening an odd number of times," she said.

"When she first told me you'd counted the times the bathroom door opened and closed . . ." Cardwell said. "But then I counted them on tape. I gotta say, it like totally blew me away that you were right."

Steel shot a look at Kailiegh. She'd obviously told Cardwell about his incredible memory. He didn't want that going around school. Wynncliff Academy was his chance to start fresh, to avoid the freak label.

Cardwell III cued up the video in question, directing Steel to watch the center computer, where instead of four panes, now the view from a single camera filled the screen.

"Lower Three, just after curfew last Sunday night," Penny said. He hit the space bar and the video played. It wasn't the clearest image. Black and white, dimly lit and fuzzy.

Steel watched two large boys come down the hall and enter the washroom.

"Now look at the time code," Penny said. He set the video into a faster play mode. A clock timer in the upper corner advanced through ten o'clock and beyond. Steel saw himself enter the washroom. He recalled hearing the squeaking hinge and then finding no one inside the washroom. Then at 11:23 p.m. three large boys exited the washroom. The faces were not clear enough to recognize.

"I was in there," Steel muttered to himself. "And they were not."

"Show him the other one," Kaileigh said.

It took Penny a few minutes to set up another video. During this time, Kaileigh and Steel said nothing. They exchanged a few looks. Steel's curiosity would not let go.

"Okay," Penny said. "There are four cameras mounted up on the chapel, giving a bird's-eye view of the front lawn, the dining hall, and other stuff. This is the one looking toward the street."

The staticky, dark image, lit only by some distant streetlights, included the chapel's side entrance to the choir room. Steel watched as two blobs—he and Kaileigh, he realized—sneaked up on the door and went inside.

"Just let it play," Kaileigh said, catching Penny before he advanced the video.

They waited about a minute. Four large lumps came out of the same door and disappeared around the corner and out of sight. Steel clearly remembered peering out from beneath the pipe organ and seeing the face of a boy he now knew to be Victor DesConte.

"Is that the last we see of them?" Steel asked.

"No," Penny said.

He advanced the video. The time clock read 11:25 p.m. If Steel was right, that gave enough time for DesConte to have gotten to the admin building, met with Randolph, and returned—though it didn't begin to *explain* it.

"It's about the same time of night as they left the washroom last Sunday night."

"So this is something they do regularly?" Steel said. "What do you supposed they're planning?"

"No clue," Penny said.

"We need to get into those tunnels," said Steel.

"And that would help us, how?" Kaileigh inquired.

"We talked about this! What if these guys are planning something awful?" he asked. "You know, something really bad, like what you read about in the newspapers? A school shooting. What if we can stop that?"

"Couldn't we just tell someone?" Kaileigh asked.

"We can't tell the headmaster about my hacking the system," Penny said. "You gotta find another way."

"We need to get into those tunnels."

"It feels wrong to me," she said. "I was *invited* to go here. I don't want to get kicked out. This is way better than home."

"Are you saying you're not going to do it?" Steel said.

"No, of course I'll do it," she said. "I just don't want to get caught missing curfew." Her face tightened with the thought.

"Yeah . . . but if Penny can watch the cameras and help us move around campus without being seen, how would we get caught?" Steel said.

"Knowing us, we'll find a way," Kaileigh said.

14.

SHREDDED WHEAT

The dining hall teemed with bleary-eyed students dressed in disheveled uniforms staggering through a cafeteria line while half asleep. Coffee and tea flowed freely, as did the Coca-Cola and Red Bull. The school expected students to use caffeine in moderation but did nothing to police the situation, leaving some students cranked before the first class bell, their eyes stuck open as if held that way by toothpicks, their lips twitching, their feet dancing beneath their desks.

Steel was presented with his choice of hot or cold: an assortment of cereals and yogurts, or today's offering of biscuits and gravy: a sallow breaded material on top of "mystery meat" and slathered beneath a ghostly gray gravy. He headed for the Frosted

Shredded Wheat, snagged a watered-down orange juice, and poured himself a breakfast tea.

He exited the kitchen into the dining hall, an enormous room with pale maple-paneled walls from which hung this month's gallery of student art— ghastly attempts to paint Campbell's soup cans. There were forty round tables, each surrounded by ten uncomfortable wooden ladder-back chairs built sturdily enough to survive decades of abuse. At each table sat one faculty member and nine students. Lunch and dinner had mandated seating; breakfast was a free-for-all.

Steel spotted Kaileigh sitting at a table of all girls. He found a chair at a table with his roommate, Verne. He sat down, said nothing to anyone, and began eating. Third Form students risked all sorts of derision and razzing if they spoke first at the break-fast table. The conversation only included you when your name was mentioned.

His attention landed on the headmaster's table, where he spotted Victor DesConte, two other boys Victor's size, three snobby-looking Fifth Form girls, and three students he didn't recognize. Steel had long since learned to read lips—a skill he kept to himself. Not even his parents knew how good he was at it. But for him, reading lips was only a matter of memory—how words were formed by the mouth, tongue, and lips.

He tried to eavesdrop on the conversation at the headmaster's table, only to realize they weren't speaking English. In fact, the more he watched, the more he came to understand they weren't all speaking the same foreign language. Instead, they seemed to be speaking three or four languages at once, but back and forth as if each understood clearly what the other was saying. Wynncliff was widely recognized as the prep-school equivalent of Middlebury College—a language-intensive school (six foreign languages were offered), but he'd never expected to see something like this.

Benny the Bulb was overseeing Steel's table. He chastised a student for hogging the milk and told him to refill the pitcher. He caught Steel staring across the hall at the headmaster's table.

"Foreign languages, Mr. Trapp," Benny the Bulb said. "Breakfast at the headmaster's table forbids English. He's something of an expert, is our headmaster. He speaks German, Chinese, Japanese, French, Italian, and Spanish. Fluently, I might add. He can lapse into any at any time. It's quite a challenge to keep up with him. Only a few students are up to the task."

Steel found it amazing that the brutish Victor DesConte was fluent in anything other than bullying.

"Have you considered pursuing a foreign language, Mr. Trapp?" the Bulb asked.

"I'm taking Mandarin," Steel said. He had his father to thank for that.

"Advanced mathematics? Computer science?"

These were Mr. Morgan's courses. Steel knew better than to speak ill of either.

"Maybe when I get to Sixth Form," Steel said, thinking this the politically correct answer. But he was shot a hot look from one of the upperclassmen at Morgan's side.

Wrong answer. Obviously, you didn't wait until senior year to take a Morgan class.

Morgan's thin lips twisted into a gnarly smile. "While true that I instruct primarily Sixth Form students, Mr. Trapp, it would hardly be a precedent for an underclassman such as yourself to express at least a passing interest in the subject matter. And should such an interest be voiced, said student might also discover that said master offers tutorial instruction in said courses, the tutoring often resulting in early acceptance to advanced placement study. Computer science is at the very heart of all business, commerce, communication, health care, finance, and even the arts, Mr. Trapp." This part sounded rehearsed to Steel. "Getting an early start can be beneficial to a student's acquisition of certain upper-classmen's privileges. I can see on your face that this is news to you. Oh yes, Mr. Trapp: academic advancement has its rewards at Wynncliff Academy. We treat AP placement as incentives. If you want to discuss this further, I'm in my office every evening after football practice."

Benny the Bulb had been the JV football coach for something like twenty-four years. He'd had a los-ing record only one of those years, when a medical complication had sidelined him. It was said that he applied the advanced mathematical concept of statis-tical probability to his play-calling, and that it gave him an enormous advantage over the competition.

"Yes, sir," Steel said.

"I've heard about that memory of yours," he said. "Wouldn't mind putting it through the paces."

Steel felt himself blush, astounded that he might be the subject of gossip among the faculty.

"We've all heard," said one of the upperclassmen to Morgan's right. She was a handsome girl with vibrant green eyes and a contagious smile. Steel felt a little jolt of electricity at being the object of her attention. Most upperclassmen wouldn't give a Third Former the time of day. And here was an upperclassman *girl* staring at him like she was dying for him to say something back to her.

"It's not like I have a choice about it," he said modestly. "It's just one of those things."

"Nell Campbell," she said, introducing herself.

"Any relation to Seymore "Soupy" Campbell, class of seventy-two, Yale graduate in astrophysics?" Steel said, showing off. He'd read about him in the alumni directory.

Nell's eyes widened and her mouth dropped open. Her teeth were as white as his mother's best table china. Mr. Morgan cocked his head, clearly impressed as well.

"So it's true," Nell said, as if she'd discovered some national secret. "How'd you do that?"

"Is he your father?" Steel asked. He knew he was: he could see the similarity from the picture that had also been in the book. He was about to display this knowledge when a beefy guy with a freckled face came up behind Nell Campbell and laid his hands on her shoulders. The behemoth looked right at Steel and let him know to shut up. The hands on the shoulders indicated some kind of possession. Steel felt certain of it.

Nell Campbell did not look pleased to be interrupted, and Steel suddenly felt in the middle of things.

He was only halfway through the shredded wheat, but he asked the Bulb to be excused, and was up and away from the table before he did something stupid.

The whole girl thing was new territory to him. He didn't know all the rules.

He ran smack into Kaileigh. She looked a little miffed as she said, "Who's your new friend?" She was staring directly at Nell Campbell.

All he'd wanted was a bowl of cereal. Suddenly everything seemed too complicated.

"I'm out of here," Steel said. It was the only thing he could think to say.

15.
A WORD HE DIDN'T KNOW

Today, Mrs. D. had come to the Corinthians to tutor the boys in math and reading. This was their least favorite thing to do. But the right to a bed and three meals a day came with this string attached. More important to the boys, she rewarded the two best students each week with tokens to a nearby video game arcade, or gift certificates to California Pizza Kitchen. For this reason, and this reason alone, competition was fierce. Some actually studied throughout the week in anticipation of the quiz that came at the end of tutoring.

Now, with the quiz over and with Little Peter and Saul the week's winners, the boys were eager to have Mrs. D. gone so they could get back to life at the boathouse.

"Boys!" Mrs. D. announced. She never raised her voice. The mere act of addressing them as a group won silence and their undivided attention.

"Taddler and Johnny. You nearly fouled up the Haymarket job. You took risks you shouldn't have taken. You put yourselves in intractable positions that could have jeopardized everyone in this room." She paused, and as she did, it seemed that no one but she was breathing. "But the fact is, you succeeded, and succeeded without being caught. You displayed bravery, cunning, and the ability to work under pressure, and for that you are to be commended."

From her purse she produced two small cell phones. "We can no longer risk using the walkie-talkies. These are push-to-talk cell phones, far more secure than the walkie-talkies. They operate on pre-paid accounts, so there is no way to trace them to the owner, if found. Taddler and Johnny," she announced to the others, "will be team leaders on this upcoming job." She handed each a cell phone; the boys admired them greatly.

"You are now entering the planning phase of a job at the Armstrad Hotel."

There was a collective gasp in the room. The Armstrad was known as the fanciest, most expensive, most lavish hotel in all of Boston. It had been in operation for more than a hundred and fifty years. It was also known as the hotel with the best security in town. For this reason—as explained many times by Mrs. D. herself—the boys had never attempted a job at the Armstrad. Just the mention of its name made some of them fear the assignment before they even heard it.

Taddler swelled with pride as he received the cell phone. But there was something else going on inside him as well: curiosity. This wasn't the Mrs. D. the boys had come to love and fear. She never passed out such rewards—some money here and there, yes, but never anything that could be pawned; poverty, it seemed, was one of the ways she kept the boys beholden to her. Even her tone of voice was different. The hard edge was gone. She was almost *motherly* to them. Taddler didn't know what to make of it, but he suspected it was intentional. She was sending them a signal that this job was different. Very different.

"Now listen up," she said, as if the boys were not already hanging on her every word. "I have secured an incredible opportunity for two of you. Only two." She looked right at Taddler, then Johnny. "The two boys who please me most on the Armstrad job will be given a real chance at something big."

She surveyed the group, one young face at a time. "You boys mean the world to me. And yet you must understand I would never hesitate to expel you for bad behavior. I've done so many times. But now I'm offering you a way to *get out of here*. Do not take this lightly. I will select my two choices at the end of the Armstrad project. I expect you all to keep that in mind as you go forward with your assignments. We will start with general surveillance. This will be coordinated by Taddler. Johnny will plan the entrance and exit strategy. As you are all aware, the Armstrad represents a formidable challenge. Made more so by the fact that now, following the Haymarket incident, hotel security across the city has intensified even more, and there is a high alert for boys your age. You must be vigilant, extra careful in your surveillance. Whatever you do, be extremely cautious about how you return to the Corinthians, in case you're being followed. Johnny, I expect you to make a different route for each boy, one that provides opportunity to check for tails. We can't be too careful, gentlemen. Your futures are literally at stake."

Brian Taddler heard mention of his future and hardly knew what to do. It caught in his throat like a fish bone. If he'd ever considered his future—and he couldn't remember having done so—it had only been to fear it: prison, a gang, drugs, the street. What Mrs. D. was talking about was none of that, but something different altogether. He rolled the word around in mouth like a piece of candy. *The future.* It tasted sweet.

16.
THE TRYOUT

It began as what should have been a simple ga-ga tryout. Steel had progressed under Hinchman's coaching. He'd studied both solo play and team strategy, where the five players on either side attempted to avoid striking each other with the ball while also defending each other from the opponents' attacks. As a game of elimination, one by one, a team member was eventually struck with the ball and forced to leave the game. The idea was to strike first and strike fast, quickly turning the numbers to your team's advantage. If you could get up five–three or four–two, the odds put the win in your favor. For this reason, teams worked on passing and defensive drills that required lightning-quick reflexes and split-second timing. With proper movement within the octagon, and passing between players, a team could surround an opponent and strike on the back of the legs, a difficult, if not impossible area to defend. Conversely, with good communication between teammates, such attempted strikes could be avoided with jumps or deflections.

Steel's incredible powers of memory had worked to his favor. Hinchman never had to repeat a concept twice. If he outlined a play on a whiteboard, Steel had it memorized instantly, requiring only repetition in the pit to perfect it. But over the weeks of early morning practice, another benefit of his reliable memory revealed itself. He came to realize that each ball possessed individual characteristics. Some were smoother than others; some were slightly more or less inflated; each ball bounced differently. Steel could visually capture each bounce, each reflected angle like a camera taking high-speed shots. If he and Hinchman spent a few minutes passing and shooting at each other, Steel's photographic brain recorded and learned the nuances of each ball. He taught himself to measure the force with which the ball was struck, so that the next time Hinchman's hand started five inches, or a foot from the ball, Steel knew how fast it would travel and at what angle it would leave the ground. He then calculated the trajectory, and he found it easy to predict both its path and its rate of travel. All of this happened in but an instant, and yet he found it an effortless task—he knew *exactly* where the ball would go practically before it was hit.

He had never adapted his gift to a sport; he'd always considered himself more brainiac than jock, so his early success with ga-ga inspired him to try all the harder, to practice agility moves on his own, to learn striking techniques—slapping, spinning, and clubbing the ball—and to listen carefully to everything Hinchman taught him. It was not uncommon to hear the slap of an open palm striking a ball across the playing fields in the free time between the end of organized sports and the dinner bell, and to look out to see a solitary figure—Trapp—working against the brick wall of the gymnasium.

The tryout, with twenty students competing for the seven spots on Sparta, began just after lunch, in a forty-minute time period before the start of afternoon classes. As a club sport, ga-ga could not cut into organized athletics, so Hinchman and the other club coaches found, and took advantage of, whatever free time could be had. The boys didn't bother removing their ties; they simply peeled off their school blazers and entered the pit. The girls wore stretch-fabric bike shorts beneath the khaki skirts they were required to wear to classes. The twenty students were divided into four teams, and play began. Ten players became nine, eight, seven . . . and the play intensified. Five . . . three . . . and finally a team won. The other ten players entered the pit, and another round began. At the end of play, the teams were recombined by Hinchman, who was furiously taking down and studying notes on his aluminum clipboard.

It should have been simple enough. The twenty students would be reduced to fifteen after the first cut; to ten following the second tryout; and down to eight, by the end of the third.

It might have been simple enough if it hadn't been for Steel. Nineteen of the tryouts were Fifth and Sixth Formers, many returning team players. All except for Steel. Just the idea that a Third Form student would tryout for a club team rankled many of the upperclassmen who had tried, and failed, to make a club team in the years prior.

So on this particular warm September afternoon, with students having little to do until the 1 p.m. bell, group by group, they began to fill the octagonal wooden bleachers that had surrounded the ga-ga pit for the past forty years. Matches often filled up the stands as students came out to support their club teams. Tournaments at the end of each semester were standing room only. But seldom, if ever, had more than a handful of the curious or bored gathered to watch a tryout.

The phenomenal abilities of the young Third Form student escaped no one. It seemed that the spud was magnetically repelled from him. Moreover, he was an unselfish player, willing to pass rather than to take the strike. He seemed to see the pit, the angles, the movement of players, in ways others did not. He stood out from the moment play began.

Steel had been coached by Hinchman to not worry too much about this first round of tryouts. The competition would be tough, but there were always four or five students out of their depth. Hinchman felt that, with all the hard work Steel had put into it, he was fairly certain to make the first cut. After that, it was anyone's game. But Hinchman had only been vaguely aware of a boy out playing shots against the gymnasium wall late afternoons. Had failed to connect that this boy might possibly have been Steel.

Steel's superiority and confidence revealed itself immediately. In the first round alone, he had three assists and two strikes, had been the last player standing for his group, meaning he played a role in the elimination of every player in the opposing group. Hinchman had to recheck his notes several times to believe this. Such dominance had not been seen in the pits for over twenty years. It had to be some kind of fluke.

By the time the second round began, Hinchman secretly tested Steel further by saddling him with three of the worst performers from the first round. Word spread quickly through the small school—the action was at the ga-ga pit. The stands filled.

Hinchman had never seen anything like it: faculty and students alike crammed onto the bleachers, pointing out players and talking among themselves— *at a tryout.*

Steel paid little attention to his own accomplishments. His focus was on each player, the bounce of the ball, the method of striking, the footwork. Watching the first round both as a spectator and player, he had recorded the patterns of each player. Just as Hinchman had told him, a player performed in predictable ways. This player rose to her toes before a strike, but onto her heels in anticipation of a pass. One of the boys held his breath and pursed his lips before an attempted strike; another lifted his elbow higher before the attack. Each move, each face, each pattern was recorded into the neocortex of his brain, where it was permanently filed. Hinchman could recombine the groups all he wanted: Steel knew exactly what competition he faced before the first whistle ever blew.

The second round proved more difficult than the first. He would pass the ball, only to have his teammate miss it. Two on his team were incredibly slow to pick up a shot off the wall, and were quickly eliminated. Only minutes into the game, it was five players to Steel's three, and Steel understood from Hinchman's coaching the tremendous disadvantage this put him in. A few shots later it was four to two: he and a girl were facing four others. One of the opposition grew overconfident and struck the spud too hard. The ball bounced over the wall, and the player left the game. Three to two. Steel's teammate was surrounded in a brilliant show of team play, and before Steel could offer a counter move to free her, she was struck and it was down to just him. Three to his one.

He knew what was coming—the triangle. They had performed it on the girl, and now they would come after him with the same technique.

The whistle blew.

Passing the ball, the other team worked to isolate Steel between them, to move him to the center of the pit. If he stayed too close to the wall, they could use quick passing and a deflection to hit him. But a properly executed triangle meant defeat. He and Hinchman had reviewed the problem formation a dozen times on the whiteboard. The one sure way—the only real way—to beat it was to intercept an early pass and make an immediate strike. Once a triangle formed and the passing sped up, the captured player was all but out. Eventually the legs would be exposed and hit.

Steel had memorized most of the idiosyncrasies of his opponents. It was now a matter of pushing away the pressure, of seeing his predicament as opportunity instead of challenge. Here was his chance to put into practice everything he and Hinchman had discussed.

Two of the three he faced were seniors, veteran players with championship competitions under their belts. They worked fluidly as teammates, so comfortable with the other person's play as to use head and eye signals instead of words to set their plays. But Steel had seen most of this in the first round and had it committed to memory.

When the tall one—the captain—cocked his head to the left, Steel knew the triangle was coming. Before he ever saw the second senior move to occupy the position, Steel measured the movement of the captain's hand from the ball, and he jumped into the passing lane, a step ahead of the boy for whom the pass was intended. Steel stole the pass, spun, and slapped the spud into a low skid. The senior jumped to avoid the strike, but what he didn't realize was that Steel already knew that jump of his; Steel's strike was not intended to hit him directly, but to rebound off the wall behind him and hit him in the calves as he came down.

The crowd erupted into a cheer. Many of the spectators came to their feet. The senior left the pit, snarling at Steel on his way out.

Hinchman held the ball, ready to resume play.

Steel felt good about his chances: two to one. The remaining senior, a girl, was a problem . . . She was a very good player. The junior, a boy, presented Steel with possibilities. He had a slow left hand and was clumsy when forced to spin to the left.

The spud hovered in Hinchman's hand, ready to fall.

Steel spotted a familiar face in the stands. It was Nell Campbell, on her feet, eyes bright, her cheeks flushed with excitement. Her full attention, every bit of her energy, was focused on him. She was cheering, bouncing up and down, her hair lifting like a curtain over her head.

The whistle blew. The ball fell.

Steel turned too late.

He felt the cold slap of the spud sting his left leg. He'd been hit. He was out.

The crowd let out a collective sigh. Steel, confused and caught, glanced once to Hinchman—his coach was disappointed. Then to Nell Campbell. All the excitement had left her face. She turned, disinterested in him now, collected her books and left the bleachers. A good number of other students left as well.

Steel stepped over the wall of the pit, his first real taste of failure like a poison in his system. He wanted to hide. He wanted to run away. He wasn't used to being beaten, and it hurt him all the more.

He found a seat with the other *losers*. Having lasted as he had, he was certain to make the cut and play in the second round. But he'd let himself down, allowed himself to be distracted. Worse, he'd let Hinchman down.

The following tryouts had yet to be scheduled. He understood he had more to learn than just technique. He had beaten himself, and that hurt most of all.

Worse, he could relive the cheers, the stands exploding as he broke the triangle. He'd never experienced anything like that—the thrill of massive adoration.

He wanted it again. He wanted more.

17.
AN EYE TOWARD
THE ALTAR

"There will be more ga-ga tryouts after classes today, but before athletics begin." Kaileigh had snuck up behind him as Steel was on his way back to his dorm, intending to lick his wounds.

"You saw?" he asked.

"Yes. And you were incredible."

"I got knocked out."

"So what? For a while there . . . Anyway, the point is there will be more tryouts."

"I won't go again until tomorrow or Wednesday. The next round."

"I'm not talking about *you*, as amazing as that may be to you. I'm talking about all the team try-outs and the attention they receive."

She was right. He was focused entirely on his loss. It had consumed him.

"So? What about it?" he said.

"So half the school will be watching. Meaning that would be an excellent time to—"

"Check out the chapel." He stopped and turned. Kaileigh's face revealed her reluctance. "But I thought you didn't want to risk getting into trouble," he said.

"That was until you brought up the idea of something horrible happening, of those boys pulling off a Columbine. If I did anything that . . . If I ever looked back and thought I could have stopped something like that from happening. Well . . . no one needs another school shooting."

"It's about time," he said. "So you'll go with me? I can't do it without a guard."

"Penny can help out. He can monitor the cameras and let us know if anyone's coming."

"Last I checked, neither of us had a cell phone."

"No, but the maintenance guys use walkie-talkies, and Penny knows where they're kept."

"We can 'borrow' a few?"

"It can be arranged," she said.

"After class?"

"Between our last class and the start of sports,"

she suggested. "No one will use the chapel until choir practice, and that's not until after dinner."

"Done your homework, have you?"

She blushed and lowered her head, averting her eyes.

"What?" he asked.

"Nothing," she answered. Steel knew better than to pursue this awkward moment.

"We'll meet under the silver ash around back."

Steel and Kaileigh entered the chapel through the choir room as they had done before. Steel carried the two-way radio Kaileigh had brought for him, the volume turned down low, but loud enough to hear.

They opened the door that led into the chancel, the pipe organ to their right. Immediately, no matter how quietly they attempted to walk, their footfalls echoed off the stone and up to the high ceiling with its massive wooden crossbeams.

Steel walked about the chancel, looking for a spot to hide a tiny camera.

"Shouldn't we try to move Sir David?" she asked. "Remember the spilled coffee? I bet two of us could move it."

"Using the camera was Penny's idea, not mine," Steel answered. "And it's smart. If we see something going on, then we'll know what to do. And this way we don't have to be here all night waiting around."

"But are we sure the camera will work? What if it's too dark?"

"You're the one who thinks Penny is so cool."

"Do not."

"It's a wireless camera from the library. He *borrowed* it." Steel slipped it out of his pocket and showed it to her. It was nothing but a bead of clear plastic on a box about the size of a pack of cigarettes. It had a single switch and a short black wire as an antenna. He needed to find somewhere to install it that had a view of most of the chapel, yet a place not easily noticed.

"The balcony," Steel said.

A hundred years earlier, a small choir had sung down into the nave from the balcony. It held three rows of stair-stepped wooden benches with a center aisle between them. It was only used now when the nave filled to overflowing—Christmas and Easter services.

Steel and Kaileigh climbed a set of rickety wooden stairs. The stairwell smelled musty and old the higher they climbed.

"You sure about this?" she asked in a whisper.

"It's the best spot," Steel said.

They entered the balcony, Kaileigh following Steel closely. Neither said a thing. The view was awe inspiring: the white marble Sir David kneeling with his massive sword; the rows of dark wood pews facing each other across the gray marble floor; the raised pulpit that slightly hid the pipe organ; the distant altar with a white linen cloth draped over it; the tall silver cross that rose from the altar majestically; and all of it bathed in a multicolored kaleidoscopic glow that emanated from the towering stained-glass windows in the transept and along the walls.

Steel kneeled to get a look between the balustrades that supported the front rail. From here the camera would have a view of most of the chapel. Penny had provided him a ball of a claylike white adhesive, and Steel used it to stick the camera to the underside of the rail. He felt certain no one would see it. The lower rail was decorated with large dental molding; the box blended in well.

Kaileigh followed his efforts and nodded at him, still not speaking.

There was a reverence to the place, a holiness that seemed to demand their silence. But Steel had to speak. He switched the camera on.

He clicked the transmission button and said, "P,

do you see anything?" They couldn't be absolutely certain their conversation wouldn't be overheard, so they'd decided to keep things as cryptic as possible.

"Got it. Angle it a little lower."

Steel worked with the small metal box. "Now?"

"Better. Try a little to the left—your left."

Steel rocked the box on a slight angle.

"Perfect. Wait a second . . ." Penny's voice rang with concern. "You got company. Front door."

Steel double-checked the camera, confirming that it had been adhered good and tight.

Kaileigh slipped beneath the bench. Steel had every intention of finding a place to hide as well, but he'd taken too long with the camera. A bang and groan thundered into the chapel as one of the heavy doors opened.

Boom, it shut again.

Steel twisted the volume button, shutting off the radio. He remained absolutely still. He dared not even breathe.

Footsteps.

And then, directly below him, a white-haired head appeared. An adult. A man.

The man walked up the center of the marble floor, kneeled, held his hands to his lips, and then stood, finding a seat in the front row of the pews. He folded his hands and lowered his head.

Steel slowly exhaled. He looked down, his eyes meeting Kaileigh's. She looked slightly terrified, lying on her side beneath the low bench. He felt an urge to reach out and touch her face and calm her. He resisted it.

They waited. And waited.

Kaileigh tapped her watch, indicating the time: sports started in five minutes. They would both be marked absent. Not only would that have disciplinary consequences, but sometimes a coach would send a student off looking for the missing person. They didn't need a search party coming after them. Worse: Penny would abandon his electronic surveillance soon. They would need his spying services in order to get out of the chapel without being seen.

The next time he looked at Kaileigh she touched her lips, kissing the end of her finger, and pointed to him, reminding him to kiss her if they were caught.

His nerves got the better of him. Steel barked a short, nervous laugh. It wasn't much, but in the hollow quietude of the chapel it may as well have been a bomb going off.

Through the balustrades, Steel saw the man look up, and identified him for the first time.

It was Mr. Randolph, the physics teacher.

"Hello?" Randolph called out in his thick British voice. "Is someone there?"

Steel slumped to the floor and remained stone still.

"I said, is there someone there? Show yourself, please."

A moment later, footsteps creaked up the old stairs as Randolph climbed to the balcony.

He reached the top of the stairs and looked out into the empty rows of bare benches.

From where he stood, the balcony appeared to be empty, the bench perfectly hiding the two students who were currently wrapped in a tight embrace. They lay beneath the farthest of the benches, their lips touching in a long, awkward kiss—the first such intimate kiss for either of them.

Randolph leaned right and left, but saw nothing. He turned and headed back down, mumbling to himself. A moment later, the chapel door thumped shut.

Kaileigh and Steel broke off their kiss—a kiss that seemed to have gone on far longer than necessary. Neither said anything. Steel wiped his mouth on his arm; Kaileigh pulled at her hair and straightened her clothes.

They hurried down the stairs and into the choir room, where they waited.

They checked with Penny—he was still there, on the other end of the radio—and waited for the "all clear." An uncomfortable thirty seconds passed.

They separated without another word, heading off to their respective sports.

Steel caught one last look at Kaileigh in profile, when she was only yards away.

She was blushing, and he thought he caught something of a slight turn to her lips.

Kaileigh was smiling.

18.
A PERFECT COVER

Saturday dinner was the first time every week that boys could eat in the dining hall without wearing a necktie, and girls could leave the plaid or khaki skirt in the closet. It started a half hour earlier, at 6:30, because the Saturday movie started at 8:00, and in part because of the large appetites resulting from afternoon athletics and off-campus competitions with other New England boarding schools. The Saturday dinner was also cafeteria style, unlike the more formal weekday dinners, where students acted as waiters. Sadly, the weekend dinners were rarely edible: mystery meat in gray gravy, soggy vegetables, frozen pizzas reheated to the texture of modeling clay. Variety was not the spice of life.

Steel found a seat at a table with other Third

Form students rather than face the derision of upper-classmen. Most of the students, if not all the names, were familiar to him by now. He spotted his room-mate, Verne, at a nearby table with other African Americans; a number of Asian students were also sitting together. It struck him as odd that when left on their own, students showed no desire to cross the lines that separated them; but he didn't challenge it. He was as guilty as the next guy of not wanting to draw attention to himself. Such attention at this school meant harassment . . . days, sometimes weeks of it.

He ate his meal quickly. There was zero conversation at his table. It seemed like some kind of law that during Saturday and Sunday dinners, only the upperclassmen spoke.

As he neared completion of a dish of warm sliced peaches (they'd started out at room temperature, or maybe were cool to begin with, but were served in a thick white bowl that had just come out of the sterilizing dishwasher at approximately the temperature of the surface of the sun), he happened to look across the dining hall to see Pennington Cardwell III looking at him, *staring* in fact, his right eye twitching in a way that implied the boy was trying to wink.

Steel looked behind him. Nothing but a large bay

window looking out onto the back of the library. He felt heat in his face. Penny—a boy!—was winking *at him*. Steel made a face, attempting to communicate his confusion; he didn't want to be winked at. Penny cocked his head toward the common room—the student lounge at the front of the building that acted as a holding area prior to the dining room doors opening, and where students drank coffee and played cards before and after meals. Steel nodded. He was done anyway, so he stood up, bussed his tray and plates, and headed out to await the nerdy Fourth Form computer hacker.

On his way, he looked around for Kaileigh. He didn't see her. He thought they'd agreed to sit together at the movie—the most recent Harry Potter, a film that had only been in theaters for two months. There was genuine excitement about the film; Steel had seen it twice before he came to school and was looking forward to a third viewing. Whether Kaileigh would actually sit with him was the real question. Such agreements tended to vaporize at the last moment. The fact that he'd missed her at dinner wasn't a good indicator.

Steel sat on a couch to wait. Penny's face carried a weird expression as he approached, then sat way too close. The couch was huge, yet Penny was practically in Steel's lap. Steel inched away.

"What?" Steel said, anxious to have this over with before it had begun.

"The chap-cam," Penny said. It took Steel a beat to understand he meant the chapel camera. Tech heads like Penny loved abbreviations and acronyms; it drove Steel nuts. "We got a hit."

"What?"

"Four guys. Came right out of the wall by the choir room. I gotta show you."

There she was! Steel spotted Kaileigh over Penny's shoulder. She pointed toward the front doors, and Steel interpreted this as a renewal of their agreement to sit together. For a moment, Penny wasn't there at all.

". . . it right now."

"What?" Steel said to Penny.

"We ought to go see it right now."

"You going to the movie?"

"Before the movie. They come *right out of the wall.* You coming or not?"

"Ah . . . yeah, okay. But I gotta make the movie."

"Are you telling me you're the one remaining human on the civilized planet who has not seen that movie?"

"No. I've seen it. But only twice."

"Oh! Well, point taken. You *do* have to see it. I promise it'll be quick. You'll get to the movie in plenty of time."

"The whole school's going to be there."

"No kidding."

"So I've got to be there early."

"So why are we sitting here talking?" Penny stood.

Steel glanced back, hoping to catch Kaileigh, but she was gone. She'd taken off with a bunch of girls, and Steel could already see the choice he was going to have to make: if he wanted to sit with her, he'd have to also sit with her friends.

Penny led him back to the science building. They didn't have to worry about being seen: nobody, but nobody, was going to study tonight.

Penny produced a crowded key chain from deep within his left pocket.

"You didn't see this," he said. He then proceeded to look in both directions down the hall before admitting them. How could a student come into possession of a master key? Steel wondered. What kind of connections did Penny have?

"Jeez," Steel said, as Penny used the same key to lock the door from the inside.

"There's nowhere I can't go, no room I can't get

into, though I never said that." Penny tried way too hard to be the secret agent of Wynncliff. Steel wished he would give it a rest.

"Yeah. Well, how 'bout the video?"

"Over here."

A few minutes later, Penny had the screen displaying the image of the darkened chapel. The chapel tilted to the right, and part of the lower pews were missing; Steel hadn't realized he'd set up the camera so crooked.

"This is last night, just after second curfew." He pointed to the date and time stamp that ran in the corner of the screen. 11:19 p.m. That was about the same time, weeks before, that Steel had heard the fifteen squeaks, had discovered an empty washroom.

The image quality wasn't much. Without enough light, black pixels fluttered across the darkest parts of the picture. Sir David's white marble was pretty clear, as was the marble floor and the distant altar. There was a geometry to the pews, but they looked more like black pens in a drawer than wooden benches; the organ was nothing but a black blob in the upper left of the screen, while the choir pews looked like the tines of a dirty comb.

"It's not like you can see anything," Steel said.

"Wait!" Penny said, his chewed-up fingernail pointing to the time stamp. "Four . . . three . . . two . . ."

Sure enough, out of the gray on the right side of the screen appeared a pinprick of light. Then the pinprick disappeared and four boys came out of the wall in single file. The last stopped and turned around—maybe closing whatever door they'd come through. A moment later, all four crossed the chancel, past the pipe organ, and vanished into the choir room—just as four boys had done the night Steel and Kaileigh had hidden beneath the organ keyboard.

Steel watched it three times in a row.

"What's with that white dot?" he said.

"Not sure," Penny said. "At first I thought it might be a bad pixel on the screen, but it's not. It stays lit exactly five seconds."

"A flashlight? Or one of those laser pointers?"

"Could be a penlight, I suppose. Not an actual flashlight, or it would have given off more light, and we'd have seen it."

"It's weird."

"It is," Penny said.

"It worked," Steel said, of their hiding the camera.

"Yes, it did."

"I've got to get in there," Steel said, "and find that door."

"Yeah, I kinda thought you might feel that way." Penny sat down at the equipment. "No better time than tonight during the movie."

That, Steel now understood, was why Penny had been so eager to talk to him immediately after dinner.

"Tonight is not great," Steel said. He could picture Kaileigh holding a seat for him. An empty seat.

"Tonight is perfect," Penny said, indicating the gear. "I can keep watch. Nobody's going to be anywhere near the chapel. You can get in, find it, and get out. Miss maybe fifteen minutes of the movie. It's a perfect cover."

There he went again: Secret Agent Man.

Steel tried to find an argument against Penny's reasoning. He wanted to say something about Kaileigh not being here, not doing this with him. But he knew that would sound lame.

"You go in right at eight o'clock. Right as credits roll. It'll take you a couple of minutes, max. Then we'll know. We'll actually know how they're doing this."

Temptation was something Steel had not yet learned to overcome.

* * *

He stood at the back of the auditorium, surveying the crowd, wondering if it had ever been this packed. It wasn't just students, either. There were a dozen or more faculty members, their heads towering over most of the audience, with their spouses and kids. The room was loud with chatter. He scanned rows, looking for Kaileigh, and as he did, he captured the conversation as well. Such crowds were chaotic and difficult for him. He avoided them whenever possible, his unrelenting memory pushed to the limit. If he stayed here too long he would suffer an unforgiving headache: *too much to process.*

Finally, he spotted Kaileigh. He hurried down the aisle on the right and reached her row. They made eye contact just as the lights went dark, and Kaileigh patted the seat next to her. In the strobe light effect of the projector, Steel tapped his watch, trying to mime that he'd be a few minutes late. Then, as students behind him jeered for him to "sit or split," he took off up the aisle.

He entered the chapel through the main doors, walked a few paces, and kneeled, as he had seen Mr. Randolph do. It was pretty dark inside, and he debated turning on the lights (in part because Penny would see him better), but knew it would light all the stained-glass windows, and he didn't want to announce himself.

He folded his hands as if in prayer and then peered out with shifting eyes, trying to see if he was alone. He took a minute down on one knee and, seeing no one, rose. He approached a pew and repeated the inspection process, this time sneaking a look up into the balcony as well.

No one. As far as he could tell, he was all alone.

He walked quietly up to Sir David and went behind him, as if interested in the Bible. He flipped pages, still checking around him. He wore an earpiece that connected to a radio that Penny had provided him.

"I'm telling you, there's been no action in there since you left," Penny said into his ear.

Steel waved at the camera.

"Go for it before we lose so much light I can't see you."

Steel's heart was racing. He wasn't sure he wanted to find the door, wasn't sure he wanted to know what these upperclassmen were up to. It had been one thing doing this with Kaileigh, but with her out of the equation, it felt more sinister, more wrong. More risky. As much as he'd scoffed at the excuse of the kiss to get them off the hook, without it, things felt much more dangerous.

"Are you going to do this or not?" Penny asked.

Steel took the earpiece out of his ear. He did this dramatically so that Penny could see him do it on screen. Then he reconsidered, realizing Penny was his only link to the outside. He put the earpiece back in.

"Okay," Penny said. "I get it. You're there. I'm here. Big difference. Take your time, but not too much. Okay? You gotta do this right now." Penny paused, static crackling in Steel's ear. "As in, someone's coming. Front door. Headed right for it. You gotta hide!"

Steel turned and hurried deeper into the chapel.

19.
CLICK

With Penny panicking in his ear, Steel headed toward the altar, hoping he could make it to the choir room door alongside the organ. But as the hinges of the main doors cried out, echoing off the hallowed walls, Steel leaped to his right and crawled up into the choir pews. He was on the wrong side, the opposite side of the chancel from the organ—and the door to freedom. If he tried to cross the chancel there was no question he'd be spotted. He backed up on hands and knees, deciding to hide. But with his attention ahead of him, not behind, he miscalculated and bumped into the paneled wall. And as he did, he heard a click.

He glanced over his shoulder to see that one of the dark wood panels had popped open on a spring lock.

As the chapel's heavy door clapped shut, warning him that he was about to be discovered, he pulled the mysterious panel toward him and saw inside to lines of shining metal flashing from within. It all made sense: the organ pipes occupied a large chamber facing the organ, and this door led inside to the pipes. This door had been how the upperclassmen mysteriously appeared or disappeared. This door not only accessed the pipes for maintenance and cleaning—*it led somewhere*. The discovery made him want to cheer, but instead he hurried inside and quietly pulled the door closed behind him.

There were rows and rows of silver colored pipes staggered in an ascending array and growing longer and wider with each level. Halfway up they changed to a darker color: wood, or a different metal, some as thick as his arms, and, behind them, more rows of pipes as wide as his legs. Beginning at eye height, and facing the organ, the wood panels had been replaced by screening that allowed the sound to escape. He'd never noticed the screening from inside the chapel, but the result was that he could see into the chapel; he was certain that standing in the dark pipe chamber, he would not be seen. This explained how the upperclassmen could arrive, scope out the situation, and wait for the right moment to cross the chancel and escape through the church.

Immediately in front of him, a wooden ladder leaned into the darkness. There was a narrow passageway between the wall and the first row of pipes. The pipe room stretched twenty to thirty feet overhead, and was ten to fifteen feet deep.

He heard footsteps coming toward the chancel, past Sir David and into the choir. He peered out through the screen: it was a grown-up. A man. He sat down at the organ.

Steel glanced behind him as clicks and pops filled his ear, followed by a whooshing sound: the organ mechanics had been switched on.

The man lit a small light above sheet music that blocked Steel's view of him. Steel made the connection, then, between the man at the organ and the huge pipes behind him.

At once, it was like a bomb going off as all the pipes came alive with sound. A deafening blast of Bach exploded all around him.

He covered his ears and made his way along the narrow passageway. It turned at the end and descended through a series of steps alongside the rows of wind boxes that powered the pipes. It led to a small dark room that clattered and hissed behind the equipment that drove the pipes.

He pulled the radio from his pocket and touched a button, causing a small green screen to light up dimly. It provided just enough light for him to see that he'd guessed right: he was in a small room cluttered with dusty equipment. He stuffed the radio back into his pocket, not wanting to risk revealing himself, though he'd descended at least eight feet. No light would escape into the chapel from here.

The pipe organ was booming, leaving Steel deaf. He covered his ears again, hoping that whoever it was would stop playing. The movie would run for two hours. What if he wound up trapped here . . . this man used the school movie time for his practice?

He searched his memory for a possible exit. The passageway had widened briefly. In a hurry, he hadn't paid it any attention, but he returned there now.

He discovered a wooden panel. He pushed against it. In the cacophony of the organ music he did not hear it click, but he felt it vibrate through his fingers, and the panel popped open. He aimed the radio's green light inside.

He faced an extremely narrow stone stairway leading precipitously straight down. The steps had been hand chiseled out of the stone, and were very old. He recognized this for what it was the moment he saw it: the route the boys had taken. And he knew where it led: somehow this connected to the lavatory in Lower Three. This explained how the four boys reached the chapel unseen each night.

With the organ music screaming in his ears, Steel stepped into the stairwell and pulled the trick door shut behind him. It locked into place. He tested it once: it popped back open. Again, he pulled it shut. He could return this way if necessary—that was good to know.

Penny was trying to talk to him, but with the metal of the pipes and density of the stone stairway leading lower, the radio went to static. Steel pulled the earphone out but kept the radio in hand, its tiny screen illuminating the way in an eerie, haunting, green light. Down, down, down. It smelled of mold and metal and left a bitter taste in his throat. He grew cooler with every step. The nape of his neck tingled. It seemed that just beneath the chapel, he was heading into hell, and he wondered at the irony of that.

This was, after all, what he'd wanted so desperately to find. But now that he'd found it, he had to wonder what had driven him to look for it in the first place. He thought of Kaileigh sitting in the movie with the empty chair beside her, and wished she were here with him. He considered turning around, but the farther he got from that organ music, the better; it was loud enough to turn his brain to tapioca.

The stairway curved right. Suddenly the air grew warmer and dryer. Holding the radio out as a lantern, Steel stepped onto a level concrete floor.

There was a light switch to his right.

Did he dare?

He switched it on and gasped.

He stood in a narrow five-foot-high tunnel with lights every thirty feet. From the ceiling hung dozens of pipes from iron supports. A hundred wires of all thicknesses and colors ran like sagging bunting along the near wall. He recognized some: the grays were phone lines, the blues, Ethernet. The tunnel stretched out impossibly long before him—a hundred yards or more.

Toward the administration building.

The dorms.

It suddenly made sense to him: the campus didn't have a single power or phone pole. All the utilities ran underground, including water, gas, and sewer.

He'd entered a network of underground utility tunnels.

He glanced behind him, up the narrow stone

staircase he'd descended from, where the music continued to blare. Then he looked ahead. Would there be another light switch—some way to turn them off at the other end? Where did the tunnel lead?

He had no choice but to find out.

He ducked his head, stuffed the radio away, and made off down the longest tunnel he'd ever seen.

20.
UNDERGROUND

Nearly a hundred yards into the tunnel, Steel encountered a metal ladder mounted to the concrete wall. He looked up and saw a hatch door. He was tempted to climb the ladder, tempted to try to open the hatch, but he'd taken precisely forty-three paces—he'd been counting—and if his sense of direction and mental math were correct, it all combined to place him somewhere under the common room.

Just past the ladder, the tunnel reached an intersection. The continuation of the tunnel he now occupied led in the general direction of the administration building; the tunnel to the right probably aimed more toward the school library.

At the base of the ladder he saw a triple light

switch. He tried each switch and ended up toggling the lights in the three sections of tunnel. He turned off the lights behind him and left on those that lit the way to the administration building and the school auditorium.

He began to feel the vibrations from the Harry Potter sound track as he continued. He reached yet another ladder and climbed it out of curiosity. It led to a hole in a floor with a low metal handrail. Pipes and wires ran from the tunnel into the space. He pulled himself up and shined the radio's green light. It was a utility room, most likely in the basement of the administration building, quite large and containing tanks and vented metal boxes, electric panels and telephone punchboards. Seeing the wires reminded him of Penny, and he stuffed the earpiece back in.

"Penny?" he whispered, pushing TALK.

"Sweet Jesus! I thought you'd died! Whoever that teacher is, he's still playing the organ. You can't go back out. Hey . . . why am I not hearing the music?"

"Because I'm in the basement of the admin building. There are tunnels connecting all the buildings on campus. It's how the boys from my dorm made it over here after hours without being seen. It's wickedly cool. I've come all the way from the chapel to here underground."

Static.

"Tunnels?" Penny said, incredulous.

"I'll bet the video cables run down here. Everything else does. Ethernet, phone, all kinds of pipes."

"I gotta see this."

"Not now. I'm going upstairs, to the movie. Meet me afterward."

"No way. It's got to be now. The whole school's at the movie. I've got the track camera. I could plant it down there in the tunnels."

Although he had no idea what a track camera was, Steel liked the idea. A hidden camera could prove that the upperclassmen were sneaking out and using the tunnels.

"Okay. Bring the camera. And bring a flashlight. But we've got to be quick. I've got to make it to at least half the movie."

For the five minutes it took Penny to reach the door on the basement level of the theater, Steel took a look around at all the equipment, committing it to memory. It was not only a central distribution point for hot water—the size of the boilers suggested it supplied the dorms and/or perhaps the steam heat to the school buildings—but it also housed two large gray panel boxes into which dozens of phone wires disappeared—one white, one gray—and another black box on the wall with blue Ethernet wires coming out in fat bundles held together with white plastic ties. If the administration building was the brains of the campus, this room was the heart.

Two light knocks on the door signaled Steel to open it, and Penny was inside. It was hard for Steel to believe Penny was a grade above him, given how short he was. The boy set down a tote bag and dug around inside.

"This camera is used at track meets. A laser is bounced off a reflector," he said, removing the first of several parts involved, "and when the beam is broken, it stops the official clock and signals the camera"—he held out a photo—"allowing for the proverbial photo finish. For us . . . if I set up the laser in one of these tunnels, the camera will capture their faces, and you'll have proof."

"But even with the lights on, it's not exactly blinding down here."

Steel moved to the hole in the wall, turned around and backed through it into the dark, the toes of his shoes finding the top rung of the ladder. A moment later he popped on the lights, and Penny, his head through the opening, gasped at the sight.

"Oh, man . . ."

"Yeah, I know," Steel said.

"This is freakin' incredible."

"The way it looks, the tunnels connect all the buildings. This one Ts down there at the dining hall, with a tunnel that runs between the chapel and the library. We don't know which of these leads to the dorms, so the best place for the camera is after the T."

"But it's gotta be this tunnel," Penny said, complaining. He pointed up the tunnel, which did, in fact, point toward the dorms.

"I still think the chapel tunnel is where to put the camera. What if there are guys entering from the common room?"

"Good point," Penny said.

Steel saw on Penny's face what was really going on: he was afraid. His realm of existence was the lab; the idea of "field work" terrified him. Steel's father had told him how the FBI and CIA divided their ranks between two equally important groups: the analysts and the operatives. He figured Penny for more of an analyst. It made him miss Kaileigh all the more. Like Steel, she possessed the qualities of both.

"You want me to do this alone?" Steel asked.

"Yeah, kind of." Penny had brought a penlight

along with him. He handed it to Steel.

"Okay. I'll take the tunnel. But you've got to show me how to set it up, and you've got to stand guard. If anyone comes into the tunnels, they'll expect them to be dark. They'll turn on the lights, and I'll see that—hopefully before they see me. But if they *don't* turn on the lights, if they come down the tunnel with flashlights, or in the dark or something, I won't see them coming. So you're going to hide over there in the corner. You'll have a view of the tunnel. If someone comes through this room or down the tunnel, then you've got to go down the ladder and flash the lights. Flash them just once so you won't be seen, and then go back up the ladder and straight out the door, quiet as a mouse. Without that warning from you, I'm toast."

"But no one's going to come. Right?"

"Of course no one's going to come. Everyone's watching the movie."

"Which is the perfect time to use the tunnels," Penny said. "You're not saying it, but that's what you're thinking."

"It crossed my mind. We're down here, after all, aren't we?"

"Why don't I like the sound of that?"

Steel switched on the flashlight. "Get into your

corner, and don't mess this up, Penny. You got that?"

Penny nodded sheepishly.

Heading off down the tunnel, Steel did not have a good feeling about this.

21.
INTO THE PIPES

Steel soon reached the T. He turned left toward the chapel. A few yards beyond the ladder rungs that led up to the common room he set about installing the camera and the reflector that triggered it. Fixing the reflector to something solid, and adjusting its surface to bounce the invisible laser light back perfectly, took far longer than Penny had suggested. Steel was approaching a full sweat when the lights flashed on and off in the connecting hallway.

"What was that?" a low voice said, speaking in a harsh, nervous tone.

"Something's up with the electricity down here," a second voice answered. "Keep moving."

Steel had just, that very moment, managed to get the reflector into place, and so took an extra few seconds to stick it firmly where it belonged rather than start the whole process over again. With the camera now placed and ready, Steel judged that he no longer had enough time to make it to the common room ladder.

He could turn and run toward the chapel, but it was a long hallway—he would likely be both heard and seen. Reversing direction was out of the question as well: he would run into them. He spun once in a full circle, feeling as if the walls were moving in on him.

And then he looked up.

The four boys, all of them big, turned left, following the network of tunnels toward the chapel. The overhead lights flashing on and off had made them uneasy, and they moved quickly, their way lit by the pale beam of a flashlight held by the boy in the lead. He had a thick body and surprisingly big hands. His watchband was shiny metal. All four wore leather boat shoes, blue jeans, and school blazers.

They walked with their heads bent to avoid striking the tangle of pipes and wires suspended both from the tunnel ceiling and along the walls. They were almost certainly upperclassmen.

Had any one of them looked up a few yards past

the iron-rung ladder to the common room, they would have seen a boy lying prone, tucked between the pipes and the ceiling, his face mushed down by two pipes, his mouth spread open, making his nose look something like a beak. His mouth being forced open in this way, he'd begun to drool; his tongue licked constantly at his lips, trying to catch a big glob of spit from falling. At last, the task proved impossible. A blob of clear saliva, roughly the size of a nickel, fell from the boy's lip like a bomb, catching the last of the four boys below, squarely in the hair.

The boy made it several paces past the location where Steel was suspended before the spit slipped from his hair, sliding down onto the back of his neck. He slapped at it and then groaned, disgusted as he pulled his hand away.

"Gross! The pipes are leaking." He flashed a look over his left shoulder and up toward the pipes. In the shifting shadows that resulted from the dim flashlight in the lead, the trailing boy failed to distinguish the soles of two shoes bent and wedged amid the pipes.

"Wait up," he said, scrambling nervously to catch his buddies.

* * *

Steel exhaled for the first time in what felt like minutes. He didn't dare move—not until the upper-classmen were long gone. He would lie atop the hot pipes as long as necessary, because getting down was not going to be easy or quiet.

He had the confirmation he'd come for. He hoped the camera had caught what he'd just seen. There was no way the headmaster wouldn't believe him now. He felt sure one of the boys was Victor DesConte—he was up to something, roaming the school tunnels at all hours, avoiding being seen, using the chapel to—

Why? Steel wondered. He had no idea what it was he was accusing the older boys of, beyond sneaking around—a crime for which he was now guilty.

When it sounded safe, he lowered his head down through the pipes and saw that he was alone in an empty tunnel. He swung a leg down and dropped. Rather than head in the direction of safety—either up the ladder into the common room, or down the adjoining tunnel toward the administration building—he started creeping toward the chapel, his back against the cool concrete wall. He told him-self that if he heard anything he'd climb back up onto the top of the pipes, though an inner voice wondered if he'd have time for that. In all likelihood he'd be caught, a possibility that slowed him down.

He reached the rebar ladder leading up into the chapel, and hesitated. Up ahead he could make out a square hole in the roof of the tunnel. He checked it out: a rock wall shaft, like he was standing at the bottom of an old well, leading fifteen feet straight up. And now it made sense: this was the marble base of Sir David! At some point, years before, there must have been a secret access into the tunnels or a crypt by moving Sir David. The more modern concrete tunnels had been built around it, the statue cemented into place.

He returned and climbed the rebar ladder slowly, his ears pricked for the slightest of sounds.

Voices. Muffled and at a distance, but clearly conversational. Several people were talking.

He stepped through to the tightly packed space housing the towering organ pipes and walked carefully toward the fabric screening. He peered into the chancel.

The four upperclassmen stood alongside the organ. DesConte was speaking, addressing whoever was sitting behind the organ, the player's face still blocked by sheet music. Steel, eager to identify the player, moved slightly to his right, leading the way in the dark by carefully sliding his feet ahead. By doing so, he accidentally triggered a valve box that delivered forced air into one of the tall pipes. The resulting note, the lowest E-flat, erupted like a foghorn, shaking the floor beneath him.

He got his wish: Mr. Randolph's head shot out from behind the sheet music.

"That wasn't my doing," Randolph said.

The four boys all looked over toward the pipe room.

Steel froze.

But with the pipe room dark, and the screen acting as a one-way window, he could see them, but they could not see him.

"Well? Have a look!" Randolph said.

Steel turned. He knew the way out of the small room, remembering the route. But he could also calculate DesConte's speed. The upperclassman was going to come through the door to the pipe room at the same moment Steel would make the turn toward the ladder leading down into the tunnel. He was certain to be spotted.

Instead of running away, he stepped deeper into the dark room and felt his way around a row of towering pipes. The pipes ascended in rows mounted to small wooden platforms. Between each row of pipes was a narrow gap, but wide enough to allow a man to reach inside to make repairs. Wide enough for Steel to crawl inside. He pulled himself into the space, turned sideways, and, carefully avoiding the valve boxes, lay down. It was pitch dark in the space; a person would have to shine a flashlight to see him.

He heard DesConte burst through the hidden door, and caught a faint glimpse of the boy's head as he made straight for the tunnels. The other three were fast on his heels. They rumbled down the ladder and flicked on the lights. Strange shadows, like tall black candles, filled the room. It looked alternately like a shark's mouth and prison bars. With the boys off searching the tunnel, the only way to explain the sound of feet approaching was that Randolph had entered the pipe room himself. Then, through the narrow slits between pipes, Steel saw Randolph's profile silhouetted against the screen. The man bent over. The E-flat sounded again, sounded loudly, Steel's ear nearly pressing against the giant pipe. Steel thought his teeth might rattle out of his head. Randolph stood and patrolled down the line of pipes, heading for the end of the row. Was he going to check between the rows? Had he figured out where Steel was hiding? Steel had felt so confident that it would be nearly impossible to see him where he was, but suddenly he had no desire to test his theory.

He flattened himself further—stretched his arms over his head to make himself long and narrow. And he watched as Randolph did exactly as Steel had feared: came around the first row of pipes and glanced down through the space that separated one pipe from the next. For a brief second or two, Randolph and Steel were looking directly at each other. Randolph manually tripped a valve, and a low pipe sounded.

"Was that you?" It was DesConte speaking, having returned from the tunnel.

"Yes," Randolph said, turning away from the end of the row. He had not given his eyes time to adjust. "Testing the box. Seems fine."

"Meaning?"

"Someone was in here."

"You think?"

"I know," Randolph said. "Someone followed you."

"Not possible."

"At this school? *Anything* is possible. Okay . . . we're going to cancel tonight. Get back down those tunnels and return to the movie before it ends. Who knows who that might have been?"

"Maybe your foot hit a pedal," DesConte proposed. "I mean, it could have happened."

"They are my feet, Mr. DesConte. I think I know where they were and what they were doing, and what is and is not possible."

Steel heard the other three join DesConte. None spoke. Only DesConte.

"Yes, sir."

"Into the tunnels. Keep an eye out for anyone hiding, though I would bet we've lost whoever it was. Exit at the common room. Head to the auditorium for the end of the movie. I want you seen by other kids when the movie lets out. You understand?"

"Yes, sir."

"And next time . . . Well, we'd all better be more careful. I do not enjoy the thought of someone following you. You'd better come in twos from now on. We can't afford all four of you being caught at once. We've put too much into this operation."

Operation, Steel noted. He'd been right! Something was up with DesConte and the other three.

"We're on it."

"Go," Randolph said.

The boys took off down the ladder and through the tunnel. A moment later the pale light from the tunnel entrance switched off. But Randolph had not moved. His silhouette squatted. Another loud blast of a ship's horn—Randolph had triggered the valve on the farthest pipe. Steel watched as one by one the small metal arms of the valve mechanisms that were attached to the wooden bellows boxes moved toward him. Each time, a different low note, bone-jarring in volume and intensity, filled him. Randolph moved down the line—a line that came right to Steel. If he didn't move at least a few inches, his body and limbs would block a pipe's mechanics and prevent the note from sounding. It was as if Randolph had sensed him lying back there, and now couldn't leave without testing his suspicions.

As the metal valve arms moved box to box, Randolph tripping each in succession, Steel lifted into a sideways push-up, supported only by the fingers of his left hand and the toe of his right foot. The valve below his elbow moved cleanly—the low note groaned. Then a valve beneath his armpit. The next was to be directly beneath his rib cage. He arched as high as he could to give the valve clearance, bending himself awkwardly and painfully. The metal arm jumped with the release of forced air. Yet another note roared—deafening him. Next were his hips, then his knees. Valve by valve, Steel contorted his body to accommodate the movement of the mechanism.

Randolph worked his way down the entire row, hesitating on the last and final note. There he paused, as if debating saying something into the darkness. A warning? An announcement?

But at last he stood and left the pipe room. As he switched off the organ, the system sighed—a release of pent-up air like an inanimate gasp.

Steel relaxed and lay back down. He waited several minutes, waited until silence had filled the chapel, waited for his own pulse to subside.

An operation.

He could hardly wait to tell Kaileigh.

22.
A VOICE FROM THE DARK

Steel left Tuesday night study hall at 9:30 p.m., puzzled and confused. Not by homework—he never had any trouble with homework—but by Kaileigh. Since the events of Saturday night, he'd tried several times to get her off by herself. He had so much to tell her. At first he'd thought she was not picking up on his signals, but then it became clear there was nothing wrong with the signals; there was something wrong with Kaileigh. She wasn't having anything to do with him. She sat on the opposite side of the classroom; looked the other way if he actually managed to catch her eye, itself a rarity.

In his typically numb-brain way, it had taken him nearly three days to trace her avoidance of him back to *Harry Potter*. He'd left the seat next to her empty, which was apparently an unforgivable offense. All the coolest discoveries in the world apparently couldn't excuse him from causing her humiliation and embarrassment. Worse, he couldn't even get close enough to her to apologize.

There was so much to tell, to think about, that he found his school studies—typically a breeze—something of a chore. Not a challenge, not hardly, but reading was time consuming; homework had to be completed, no matter how easy. Adding to his frustration, study hall lasted two hours, and even the most difficult night of assignments rarely took him more than an hour to complete, leaving him with way too much time on his hands, confined to a shared desk in what by day was the art room. He usually took advantage of the surplus time by getting ahead on his reading, but since his adventure in the pipe room he'd had trouble focusing. Having perfect recollection wasn't always such a good thing.

He'd tried to signal Kaileigh several times during study hall. He couldn't see how she might have missed him, but she hadn't returned so much as a nose flare in his direction, so he gave up any thought of walking back to the dorms with her. The study hall monitor released them. Steel hung back, avoiding the first wave of kids who charged the door, secretly hoping he might connect with Kaileigh. But looking around, he realized he'd missed her somehow. Again. He headed off with the other stragglers and soon found himself alone, leaving the main building out through the post office door. He passed through the covered passageway and took the stairs down to the field level, the backside of the dormitories.

"Psst!"

He jumped with the sound. It had come from the shadows of the base of the stairs to his left. He couldn't see anyone.

"Psst!"

DesConte? he wondered. *Kaileigh?* He backed nervously away from the steps.

"Steven!"

A girl's voice. But Kaileigh never addressed him by his proper name. Was she so mad at him that she wouldn't even use his nickname? If so, he had real problems. This was new territory.

A door opened to the passageway up the stairs, spreading light and making noise. He had to make a decision. Whoever it was obviously didn't feel like showing herself.

Steel gathered his courage and moved toward the

dark—toward the voice. Deep in the corner, where the brick of the stairs met the brick of the building, he discerned a figure standing. A blob of blackness in the gray.

"Closer," she said.

Definitely not Kaileigh. Too tall, for one thing. He stepped deeper into the dark, his eyes quickly adjusting to the low light. And now he saw who it was.

"Nell? Nell Campbell?"

"Shhh!" She reached out and grabbed him—though exactly how she managed to reach across such a considerable distance puzzled him.

"What's going on?" he croaked out.

She held on to him. He could smell a flowery scent, could feel blood pulsing frantically at his ears. His eyes stung. Her grip was strong as she pulled him right next to her—he could feel the warmth of her body, though they didn't exactly touch—and she spun him around so that his back was to the bricks, and her form—a woman's form—loomed between him and the light spilling across the fields beyond. For the briefest of moments he thought she meant to kiss him. His head swooned. He had no idea what to do, what was expected of him, and yet . . . he kind of wanted it to happen. This was a new discovery as well.

"I can't be seen talking to you," she said. Her breath smelled sweet, like lemonade or ginger ale.

"Ah . . . okay."

"And I . . . well . . . I *care* about you."

He found the lump in his throat too thick to push air past. He couldn't speak.

"Care about your staying in school."

"What?" That didn't sound good.

"You're studying Chinese."

"Mandarin," he said. "So what?"

"With Zeke Goddard."

"Yeah?" How did she know any of this? He remembered her from the ga-ga bleachers, the way she'd cheered for him. Now she'd cornered him and was standing so close he could hear her breathing, could see the silhouette of her rib cage expanding and collapsing, like she'd been running. Or was nervous. *Or anxious*, he realized.

"I'm the student aide to Mrs. Jian."

Had he known that? he wondered. It wasn't as if he could *forget* anything, so he assumed he had not known it in the first place, but something told him that a girl like Nell Campbell could make him forget things—a novel and intriguing thought. He tried to open his mind to that concept.

"So?" he said, thinking how stupid a thing it was

to say. He might have said any number of things, but that was what came out of his mouth.

"Zeke Goddard cheats."

"What?"

"He cheats. On his homework. On tests. He's a cheater."

"Zeke? But I just met him. He seems like a—"

"That's the point. Why do you think I'm talking to you like this?" She glanced over her shoulder as if afraid someone might see them.

"Well . . . honestly, I was wondering about that."

"Mrs. Jian tricked Zeke. She suspected he'd been cheating, but couldn't prove it, so she devised a trap, and he took the bait. The point is, if you're studying with him for the quiz, which I think you are—" At this point, Steel nodded. "And you have the kind of memory everyone says you have—"

"Who's talking about me?"

"Certain people. I can't talk about that now. I shouldn't be talking to you at all."

This comment of hers puzzled him all the more. What people? Why couldn't she tell him? Who *was* she?

"The point is, you have to unlearn whatever Zeke has told you. You're studying for the quiz, right?"

"Sort of," he said. "I don't . . . Studying . . ." He

couldn't figure out how to say it without sounding arrogant.

"If you're caught cheating along with Zeke—the thing is—then they won't—then they can't—and you're perfect for this. I know I'm not making any sense. I'm not, am I?" She bent over to come down the few inches to his height. He supposed she was trying to look him in the eyes, although in the dark that wasn't going to happen. "This is so frustrating."

Again he felt his throat constrict. "For me too," he gasped. "Who are you talking about? You said 'They.' Who do you mean?"

"You'll find out," she said.

"How?"

"Not if you cheat. If you cheat . . . who knows? They might expel you."

"I'm not cheating!"

"But it'll look that way. To them. It'll be a black mark against you."

"Who?"

"I want . . . I like you, you see? The way you think. The way your mind works. You're perfect for this."

"For what?"

"I can't say. It's not for me to say. It's up to them. When you're ready. I imagine that's sooner than you think. But you must not get yourself in trouble. Not this kind of trouble. It could all be over before it begins, and that's just not right. You've got to forget everything Zeke has told you, although I suppose for you that's impossible, so maybe you actually have to first remember everything Zeke has helped you with, and then figure out some way to block it, or replace it, or something. I could tutor you, I suppose. That's it! Ask Mrs. Jian if you can work with a tutor. That would be me. Then I can help you. Please. Okay? Just ask her for help. Why didn't I think of this before?"

His head swam as his perfect recall allowed him to review everything she'd just said. He couldn't form the right question.

"You are freaking me out," he said.

"Steel?" It was a voice beyond Nell Campbell. A girl's voice. Kaileigh's voice.

He ducked his head around and past Nell.

Kaileigh looked as if she'd seen a ghost.

Then he understood the paralyzed expression she wore: Nell Campbell was still holding Steel by the arms, and he could only imagine how it must look to Kaileigh—the two of them hiding in the shadows, Nell standing about one inch from him. Leaning over him.

"Kai!" he said, calling out.

But she turned away, her curtain of hair swinging and hiding her face. A face he didn't have to see to know how to read.

Nell placed her hand over his mouth and shushed him. The contact—her hand on his lips—startled Steel, and yet it wasn't unpleasant.

"Are you kissing my hand?" she said, pulling it away.

"No! I . . . ah . . ."

"Eew," she said, stepping back. "Who was that?"

"A friend."

"Augustine. Kaileigh Augustine."

"Yes."

"She can't say anything about this—about our talking. If Mrs. Jian finds out I warned you . . . If it looks like I was trying to stop you from cheating—"

"But I'm not cheating!"

"It'll ruin everything. They'll never ask you."

"Who? Never ask what?"

"I didn't say that . . . Didn't mean to say that. You hear me?"

"I hear you."

"Go find your friend. Hurry. Tell her—I don't know what to tell her—but tell her something. Make this right."

"Who's going to invite me to what?"

"Are you listening to anything I said?"

"I remember *everything* you said." He nearly added: *This is me we're talking about.*

"Oh, yeah," she said, sounding deeply concerned.

"It's all right. I'll figure out something. And I'll ask for help in Mandarin. I'll do everything you told me to do."

"You can trust me," she said.

He hadn't even considered he might not be able to trust her. The idea threw him. He couldn't trust DesConte. Or Randolph.

"I want to trust you," he said, almost begging. "But how am I supposed to? You tell me all this stuff that doesn't make any sense, and then . . . I don't know. What? Just go on faith?"

"Yes, that's it: faith—and patience," she said. "You have to have patience, too. But ultimately it's worth it. I promise you, it's worth it."

"By the way . . ." She stepped forward and hugged him. "Congratulations on making the team."

"What are you talking about?" Steel croaked out, his voice catching as he felt her press against him.

"The Spartans," she said. "They posted it after dinner. You're a reserve!"

He felt a rush of heat, conflicted as to what caused

it. *He'd made the team! As a reserve, but still!* How had he missed that? He had gone through two more tryouts and was waiting to find out if he'd made it. He felt like screaming.

Nell turned and hurried away.

He stood there, his head spinning. Nell Campbell had just hugged him. *The* Nell Campbell.

Maybe he was dreaming. He hit his fist against the brick. It hurt something fierce. No, not dreaming.

So what was going on?

23.
NUMBER SEVENTEEN

"Tell her I had a . . . spiritual moment in the chapel. Please." Steel faced a Sixth Form girl who served as floor monitor for Kaileigh's dorm. The girl had a severe face, a long chin, and attitude. She represented the only way for Steel to get a message through to Kaileigh. For this reason, he was determined to win her help.

"You heard me. I spoke to her," the girl reminded. "She said she didn't want to talk to you, didn't want to see you. Remember? That's pretty clear to me. I'm not a relationship counselor. Better luck next time."

"Just once more, please? 'A spiritual moment in the chapel.' That exact wording."

"Pass."

Steel's memories jumped like photographs at high speed. *Visions*, his mother called them. But they weren't visions; they were what had happened. *Exactly* what had happened. He could no more dismiss them as worthless and random than he could change them. But he was able to ignore those he found unimportant, and to hold on to, or focus and study those he deemed worthy. He searched for . . .

"Let me see the back of your head, please," he said.

She looked at him indignantly. "As if."

"Just turn around, please. I'm not going to do anything. For one thing, there's a desk between us."

Perhaps her curiosity won out, or maybe she just wanted to be rid of him, but she did it.

"Monday's school assembly," he said, the memory now locked. "You sat in the . . . eighth row, four seats into the center section from the right aisle. . . ."

Her brow furrowed. He didn't know if she doubted him or was simply impressed by his powers of recollection. He didn't want her thinking he was some kind of stalker. He spoke without a break, to keep her from interrupting.

"There was this guy one row behind you— couldn't stop looking at you. His friend caught him staring at you and punched him in the arm.

You never turned around or anything."

"Who?" She was blushing. "Who was it?"

"I'm new here. Brown hair. A jock. Pretty tall."

"Did he have zits? Zits on his forehead?"

Steel shrugged. "I mostly saw him from the back."

"You're making it up."

"Am not."

"You saw all that?"

"I see all sorts of things."

"I don't believe you."

"He plays soccer. Varsity soccer. Midfielder."

"Mike Darling? No way!"

"Number seventeen. His jersey."

She gasped. "You . . . are . . . bizarre." She looked around haphazardly. "This is some kind of prank, right? Some kind of hazing ritual or something? Who put you up to this? Did Danny Lightyear put you up to this?"

"Please. I've got curfew coming up. You've got to call her back for me."

"Mike Darling? Seriously?"

"I don't know his name. But he couldn't stop looking at you."

She picked up the phone. "If this is a prank, if you're pulling something on me, you're going to regret it. I'm talking *big time*!"

"A spiritual—"

"Yeah, yeah! I've got it."

A few minutes later, Kaileigh's face appeared in the safety glass of the door, the last barrier between her and him.

Steel made no effort to encourage her through to meet him, but every fiber of his body wanted it. Finally she swung open the door and walked out. Her eyes were red—had she been crying? Just the thought of that confused him.

"Will you come outside for a minute?"

Kaileigh pouted and shrugged, made a face like she didn't care what she did.

He held the door for her. She moved with the speed of a slug.

Alone with her in the chill of the night air, he sensed that the rules between them had changed. He hadn't known there were any rules to begin with, but that was the way it felt, and his first reaction was to want to figure out what the rules were and where they'd come from. But first they had business to discuss.

He spoke faintly, in a whisper, a voice designed to draw her close to him, and it worked.

"That wasn't what it looked like."

"It's none of my business. It's not like . . . I don't know."

"You got it all wrong."

"It was Nell Campbell. Wasn't it?"

"Yeah," he said sheepishly.

"As in Fifth Form hottie?"

"It was about Mandarin class. She's the student aide to Mrs. Jian."

"Mandarin class. So you're telling me she pulled you into a dark corner under the post office stairs to talk about Mandarin class?" She crossed her arms tightly in front of her. "I don't know why I'm even here. Talking to you. At this school. I think I made a big mistake."

"Listen, it was *nothing*. She wanted to warn me that Zeke cheats and that I could get in serious trouble."

"So she's protecting you. She cares about you. Good for you."

"Kai . . . she said something about how if I blow it I won't get invited. Not by her, but other people. Wouldn't tell me what she was talking about. Made it all this big secret. Said I couldn't tell anyone, and I'm telling you."

"Goody for me."

"Earth to Kaileigh!" He was angry at her for not understanding. He could present the facts, could recite them as precisely as they'd happened, but if she chose to misinterpret them, then what could he do?

She must have sensed his frustration. "Okay. So are we good here?"

"No, no, no!" He started telling her about Penny, but jumped over that and moved straight to following DesConte and the three others into the chapel, about seeing Randolph, and how Randolph had almost caught him. "'We're going to cancel tonight.' That's what he said."

"Are you sure?" she asked. But then, remembering to whom she was speaking, said, "Never mind. I didn't mean that." The spell over her seemed to have broken. "But . . . what's the big deal?"

If a teacher like Randolph wants to meet with four of his students, why all the secrecy? Any teacher could invite any number of students over to his place, or to the chapel, or whatever, *any* time he wanted."

"How do you know they're his students?"

"That's not the point!" Realizing he'd raised his voice, he collected himself and returned to a whisper. "Something is going on, and Randolph doesn't want to risk being discovered. He's taking all kinds of precautions."

"It's none of our business," she declared. "You were worried those boys were trying to pull off something dangerous. If a teacher's involved, then that's obviously not what's happening."

"But *something's* happening," he said.

She looked at him impatiently.

"And I'm going to find out what it is."

She shook her head. It reminded him of the way his mother would too quickly dismiss one of his ideas.

"I have to find out. *We* have to find out."

"Wrong. *You* found out everything *we* needed to know. There's a teacher involved. End of story."

"No story ever ends," he said. "Someone just decides to stop telling it."

"Well, I'm done," she said. "With the tunnels. With DesConte. Mr. Randolph. With—" She stopped abruptly, then lowered her head.

"Me?" he said. He realized his fists were clenched nervously at his side, and he forced himself to relax.

"I didn't say that."

"You almost did."

"No I didn't. That's your interpretation. You know what I think? I think we both should focus on our studies, and you on your ga-ga, and we should forget about all the other stuff going on."

"Then you admit there's stuff going on?" He'd caught her, and she knew it.

A smile twisted across her lips.

"I got you."

"Did not," she said. She was still smiling.

"I . . . got . . . you." He shook his index finger at her, and her smile widened.

They half waved good-byes at each other and headed off through the rattle of fallen leaves. He'd wanted to win her over completely—to convince her to join him. He had to find out what DesConte was up to, if for no other reason than it was DesConte, and he didn't like the guy.

But he wasn't going to push it. Not tonight.

Quit while you're ahead.

He was learning.

24.
SWORDS

Living at the Corinthians was not without its rules, and there was one Mrs. D. was particularly firm about: the boys were expected to return directly from school each day. Mrs. D. would not tolerate their loitering on city street corners, something she believed was the "root of all evil" and a major factor in boys their age having brushes with the law. More to the point, even a single encounter with police could mean expulsion from the Corinthians. None of the boys wanted that.

Taddler stuck to the rules as much as possible, as much as any boy could stick to any set of rules, which meant at least some of the time, but nothing close to *all* of the time. The straight-back-from-school rule was a little fuzzy when an operation was underway. As co-leaders of Project Armstrad, he and Johnny were allowed some leeway.

That was why Taddler was currently riding a city bus down Commonwealth Avenue. For these fifteen minutes he was just another kid in the city, not someone cast out of a state institution. Not a kid all alone. Not hungry and feeling sorry for himself. He was just a regular kid. He enjoyed the ride and the resulting ten-minute walk from the bus stop toward the hotel. The streets were alive with traffic—big beautiful cars spit-polished shiny and clean. He promised himself that someday he would own three, maybe four, such cars; that he'd have a garage big enough to fit all of them, and a house that made the garage look tiny. Everyone in the house would have their own room, and each room its own bathroom, and there would be a kitchen with a refrigerator stuffed full of food—glorious food like mac and cheese and hamburgers and vanilla milk shakes— and a drawer in the kitchen packed with bags of potato chips, another brimming with candy. This was the dream of nearly every boy at the Corinthians, and one they took turns elaborating on. What else might such a house contain? A giant plasma TV? A computer with video games? A foos- ball table?

His plan was simple. He would walk fully around the Armstrad, as he'd already done more than ten times, each lap on a different day of the week, always with a pad and pencil close by so that he could duck into a coffee shop and write down anything special he'd seen. (He also happened to like the shortcake cookies at the Coffee House.) With Project Armstrad so important to Mrs. D., and the promise of leaving Corinthians in the offing, Taddler intended to do this right. Johnny was supposed to be doing much the same as Taddler, but he tended to procrastinate. His assignment was to watch the front door for how the bellmen handled the arrival of children, to identify the house detectives, to find out which kitchen workers took cigarette breaks and when, and if possible, to identify the kind of radios used by the staff. This last bit was the most important. Mrs. D. could then buy them two of the same make and model, allowing them to listen in on everything said between the staff. This would give them a leg up when it came time to execute Project Armstrad, and might even keep them from being caught.

He reached his stop and got off the bus. Just then Taddler spotted Johnny on the opposite sidewalk, also walking in the direction of the hotel. He was pleased to see him because it meant that Johnny was actually holding up his side of the assignment. He considered calling across the street, but the point of any operation was to remain independent, to not be seen with other members of the team, to limit the carnage if one or more boys should ever be caught.

Taddler watched from across the street as Johnny slowed and headed up the steps toward a tiny storefront. A giant playing card hung in the window of the store, bearing the image of an airbrushed half-naked Medieval woman with a tangle of blond curls. She wore a leather blindfold and held two swords, one in either hand. *Swords* it read at the bottom. This turned out to be name of the store as well. *Tarot Readings*, it read in blue neon in the same window.

Johnny went inside without hesitation, suggesting to Taddler that he'd been there before.

Taddler's assignment was surveillance, so he stopped and stood with his shoulder against a building's warm brick and studied the storefront while pedestrians walked past.

Johnny's visiting a fortune-teller wasn't part of the assignment. Contact outside the boathouse was forbidden, everybody knew that. One slip of the tongue might lead authorities to the discovery of the Corinthians, sending its inhabitants back onto the streets as runaways, or into juvenile detention facilities—jail. Johnny was violating Mrs. D.'s no-contact rule, putting everyone at risk.

Taddler waited for a break in traffic and darted across the street. He didn't climb the stairs immediately, but instead hung around in front of the entrance to The Rocking Horse, a store with a purple door that, judging by the window display, sold children's books and plush stuffed animals. He climbed the steps to The Rocking Horse's front door and tried to get a look inside Swords. The angle was wrong. . . . All he could see was the small shop's far wall. But the wall held a dozen or more mirrors with frames of every kind—gilded, carved, painted, decorated—and in several of these mirrors Taddler could make out Johnny in profile, sitting at a table and talking to a beautiful woman who, he realized after a moment, was the same woman on the card in the window—the only difference being that she was fully clothed.

Taddler spied on his friend in rapt fascination, for it appeared the two were deep in conversation. What if Johnny was asking the fortune-teller to predict how the Armstrad operation would go? That would threaten everything! Presently, Johnny reached into his back pocket and produced a piece of paper that the woman unfolded and studied carefully. From time to time she looked up from the letter to Johnny, and then back to the letter. She nodded, refolded the page, and slipped it away so quickly and cleverly that Taddler couldn't see what she'd done with it. The ease with which she made the paper disappear sent a shiver up Taddler's spine—she was a clever one, this beauty, and perhaps she had Johnny under some kind of spell. Maybe Johnny wasn't to blame at all.

Two things happened then: the purple door to The Rocking Horse swung open, bumping Taddler and pinning him between the open door and a wrought-iron railing as a mother and daughter left the store without so much as seeing him; and, unseen in Taddler's confusion, Johnny stood up from the tarot table. By the time Taddler next looked into the wall of mirrors, Johnny was gone. A moment later the door to Swords opened and out came Johnny.

Taddler spun around, caught the door to the bookstore as it was closing, and slipped around it, using it as a screen. He ducked inside the store.

"May I help you?" The proprietor was a woman older than time, with a face like a crumpled paper bag. Taddler nearly yelped with surprise.

"Just looking," he said, edging to the store

window in time to catch sight of Johnny. The boy turned to the right, *away* from the Armstrad Hotel. He seemed to carry a lightness to his step. It was almost as if he were . . . happy.

Something was definitely up.

None of the boys living at the Corinthians were ever anything close to happy.

25.
BRANCHING OUT

Steel thought of it as a two-pronged mission.

"So first we'll get the camera back from the chapel," he said. It was just past dinner, the forty minutes of downtime before study hall. He, Kaileigh, and Penny shared a concrete bench in the rarely occupied patio outside the school library.

"If we don't, I'm toast," Penny said. He'd explained his situation about five times. Steel didn't want to hear it again. Penny's obsession with hacking the school's computer system and constantly monitoring faculty and administration e-mails, student report cards, and departmental reports had led him to discover that maintenance planned to replace backup batteries in every security camera and smoke detector in the school. There was no question they would discover that one of the cameras was missing: the one that the three had moved into the chapel. Unless it was returned this very evening, an investigation would be launched, and just the thought of that terrified Penny.

"It will be easier to get it back than it was to put it there," Kaileigh said. "Don't worry, Penny."

Her genuine concern for Pennington Cardwell III annoyed Steel, in part because she was treating the two boys so differently: she seemed barely aware of Steel's existence while doting on Penny.

"Once you have your precious camera back," Steel said, "we'll need a leg up. Specifically, *I* will need a leg up," he clarified. "The plan is that Kaileigh will already be up in the tree. So don't go anywhere."

"You're doing this with him?" Penny asked Kaileigh in a whining voice.

"He needs a scout," she said. "I have one of the best pigeon calls you've ever heard, if I do say so. I took care of an injured pigeon for most of the summer a few years ago, and we learned to communicate."

"You talk to birds?" Penny sounded suspicious.

"Only pigeons," she corrected. "And I didn't say I can talk to them, I just said I can sound like one." Kaileigh was proud when it came to her pigeon speak.

You learn something new every day, Steel thought.

"But I thought you two . . ." Penny said.

"We were what?" she asked.

"You know," Penny said.

"I *know* what?"

"That the two of you weren't exactly . . . speaking."

"Us? No. That is *so* yesterday."

"Remember: immediately after study hall," Steel told Penny. "Kai and I will leave our books in cubbies and head straight over to the chapel while we're still allowed to walk around campus. We've got to get the camera out and be up in the ash before curfew."

"I'll wait for you at the sundial," Penny said.

"And why should I do this?" Verne asked, his face buried in a volume of Chaucer.

"Because I'll help you with that book."

"You've read it already?"

"Yesterday."

"You finished it yesterday?" Verne said, astonished. "But it was only assigned yesterday." He was on page ten. "Besides, this jerk doesn't even write in English!"

"I had some free time. It's Middle English. That's part of the point of the assignment."

"You'll write my paper for me?"

"No, but I can help you understand what's going on in the book."

"Crocodile Done Deal!" Verne said.

"We could both get in trouble," Steel cautioned.

"I'll get in a lot more trouble if I fail English," Verne said. "Besides, White Socks doesn't do anything but swing open the door on that first check and look at the bunks. It'll be fine."

Their dorm master had gotten his nickname years before. Steel didn't know if it had to do with the baseball team or the fact that the man only seemed to own one color of socks. "He does a roll call."

"I'll tell him you're out cold, that ga-ga practice got to you and you're zonked. You think he's going to come in and pull back the covers? You walk on water as far as the faculty goes."

"Not true."

"Is too, and you know it. The first Third Former ever to play for the Spartans? Are you kidding me? "You know how many teachers are impressed by that?" He laid the book down on his chest. You know how many kids hate you for that?"

Steel hadn't considered this, and hoped Verne was wrong. Kids hating him? That had been what he'd come to Wynncliff to get away from. Was it something he would never shake, something he was bound to endure forever? He'd been working hard to hide his memory skills from his fellow students. Speaking up less in class, keeping his quiz scores hidden from prying eyes. He'd been given the chance at a fresh start—his parents must have known how badly he'd wanted that—and now Verne was telling him he'd already failed.

"You okay?" Verne said.

"Yeah." He considered his options. He needed Verne's help. "If you wouldn't mind, maybe you could set up my bed for me right after study hall. You can use both our laundry bags for your body, and Mr. Henry for my head."

Mr. Henry was a modeling bust that Steel had smuggled out of the art room. The head was incredibly lifelike and wore a wig roughly the same color as Steel's hair.

"Yeah, okay," Steel said.

"You just better not get caught coming back into the dorm," Verne said. "Can't help you there."

"I've got that covered," Steel said. In fact he hadn't explored on this end of campus, but the tunnels were his and Kaileigh's only chance to go unseen on their way back.

"Second check is at eleven sharp. Don't screw that up."

The eleven o'clock bed check often involved White Socks confirming a boy's presence in his bunk. In truth, the ten o'clock curfew wasn't that big a deal; it was the final curfew that the dorm masters paid strict attention to.

"I'll be back by ten thirty."

"You'd better be." Verne picked up the book and returned to reading. "Stupid thing might as well be in Latin. I'm counting on your help."

Steel, Kaileigh, and Penny met at the sundial shortly after study hall, the campus teeming with Third and Fourth Form students eager for a few minutes outside before being confined to their dormitories for the night. They headed into the chapel and, after a few minutes of ensuring that they were alone, hurried upstairs and retrieved the security camera. Why Penny couldn't have done this on his own, Steel didn't know, except that Penny was a bookish, pale boy who didn't seem to have an ounce of nerve or adventure in him.

With the camera in hand, they left the chapel and

approached the giant ash tree at the back, which formed a sixty-foot-wide umbrella of foliage that bridged an area between the chapel and Mr. Randolph's three-story Victorian. The tree was over six feet in diameter and nearly two hundred years old, its silver bark having peeled off in places, giving it a sick, patchwork appearance. The lowest branch was well out of reach. With Penny serving as lookout, Steel gave Kaileigh a boost, lacing his fingers together and providing a step for her. Even this was not enough. He had to lift her foot high in order for her to hook her arms around the wide branch. On the third try she managed to hook a knee over the branch and pull herself up.

Steel was next. Penny gave him a boost, and Steel bounded effortlessly into the tree, trying to show Kaileigh that boys were good at some things, even if girls thought them useless.

"Good luck," Penny said.

"And to you," Kaileigh returned, for Penny now faced the chore of returning the security camera to where it belonged, inside the library, and all before curfew.

"Is your roommate covering for you?" Steel asked Kaileigh as they ascended through the branches.

"She'd better. I gave her a leather-bound journal

that my father bought me as a kind of diary. It wasn't cheap."

"I told Verne I'd help him with Chaucer."

"Seriously? Will you help me too?"

"Sure," he said, happy at the thought. This surprised him. He'd never really thought much about spending time with friends. Maybe that was why he hadn't had all that many back home. Maybe starting over at Wynncliff was about more than hiding his incredible powers of memorization from others.

Up they climbed, higher and higher, the lights from the chapel windows fading to the thick of the leaves. There was music playing from Randolph's house—a solo violin piece that was too good to be anything but a recording.

Halfway up the tree, about thirty feet, Steel paused in the crook of a branch. As in the lower branches, Steel found clusters of initials carved into the bark, some dating back over eighty years. It was as if the tree were a living yearbook, recalling all the students that had climbed it, all the students that had come and gone, many dead by now. The discovery both excited and chilled him, for lately the thought of death had been present in his mind.

"Perfect!" Kaileigh said in a whisper, seeing that from where they were, they had a good view through the branches of both the chapel to their left, Randolph's house to their right, and the route between the two.

"Now we wait," Steel said.

"And we hope."

"They'll come."

"You think they will."

"He called it an operation," Steel reminded, "and they aren't surgeons."

Kaileigh suppressed a giggle, covering her mouth with her hand. For a moment Steel recalled what a strange and indefinable feeling it had been to have Nell Campbell's hand across his own mouth.

The minutes dragged by and the campus emptied. The darkness settled around them, and for a moment Steel wondered about what they were doing, the risk they were taking compared to any possible gain. Kaileigh had tried to reason with him, had tried to tell him, but he hadn't listened. Not until now, when it was too late. He checked the glowing hands of his wristwatch: first curfew had come and gone fifteen minutes ago. They hadn't seen any teachers out searching, so they figured their roommates had covered for them so far. But how much longer could the ruse hold?

At twenty-five minutes past the hour, four

people—upperclassmen—appeared from around the chapel. They moved silently and quickly, and just the way they hunched and hurried suggested something secretive, almost sinister. They cut a straight line between the chapel and Randolph's house, where, to Steel's utter amazement, they made their way to a side door that accessed the screened-in porch and let themselves in without knocking.

This convinced Steel that he was on to something. He swelled with a sense of purpose and nodded to Kaileigh through the branches. He pantomimed, pointing first to himself and then to the ground. She nodded. Once he dropped out of the tree, without a boost he couldn't climb back into it. They were separating now. He'd promised he would come back to help her out of the tree, but both of them knew it wasn't necessarily a promise he could keep.

"I know you'll try," she said.

"I will. I promise. No matter what, I don't want you getting in trouble."

"That's sweet."

"No . . ." he said, not wanting to be sweet. "It's the truth."

"I know. Forget it. Okay? I'll be fine."

"No heroics."

"Shut up," she said.

Steel smiled in the dark.

Steel dropped from the lowest branch and hit the soft ground silently. He stayed in shadows thrown from lights in the chapel and made his way to Randolph's. The house, painted white with black trim, was surrounded by handsomely maintained gardens of rhododendron, forsythia, and honeysuckle. Steel ducked through the planting to get his eyes to a window. He hesitated, taking a moment to look up into the tree and see if could spot Kaileigh. He felt desperate to see her, to make contact, to gain encouragement, for his heart was pounding in his chest, his hands were cold, and his mouth was dry. He pushed out all thought of what might happen to him if caught, focusing on the task at hand.

He sneaked a look inside from the corner of the windowsill: an empty parlor lit by light from a hallway. He kept moving, next eyeing a butler's pantry, also dark.

He was forced to leave the security of the bushes, hurrying around the screened-in porch and reentering the planting on the other side. He lifted to his tiptoes, raising his eyes above the sill, and then dropped like a sack of stones.

Not Mrs. Randolph, since Kaileigh had told him the woman had died. An older lady, she removed doughnuts from a box and arranged them on a large plate. Maybe she was a teacher Steel hadn't met yet, or a kitchen worker, or school housekeeper. She had four glasses of orange juice and a cup of coffee on a tray.

Steel pushed his back against the house, his heart beating wildly.

"*Who-who . . . Who-who . . .*" Kaileigh's warning call sounded impossibly real. It flushed him with heat. He slumped lower, blood pulsing at his temples, and tried to slow his breathing so as not to be heard. He waited for what seemed like an impossibly long time.

Someone was either approaching him and the house, or Kaileigh had managed to see someone inside the house. Either way, she'd warned him off.

Then he spotted it: a shadow out across the grass. And he understood that the woman with the tray was standing in the window directly over his head. Had he made noise to attract her attention? Was she looking for him, for someone creeping around in the bushes? Steel didn't know what to do. If he moved, if he made any attempt to run, she'd see him. If he didn't, and she somehow knew there was someone out there, then he was a sitting duck.

The shadow moved.

"*Coo-coo*," came the call from the tree. *All clear.*

He understood then that he wasn't going to find Randolph and the boys on this side of the house. He was going to have to continue around the house, away from the protective eyes of Kaileigh.

He made his move. Low and quiet, he dodged a set of back steps, continuing past a storm cellar entrance, and hugged the next corner of the house, arriving to a long line of equally sized windows.

The flower beds along this side of the house had not been raked recently, so the fallen leaves crackled underfoot as Steel crept toward the first window. He saw inside to a music room and study, also dark. He hated to take even a single step, the crunching of the leaves seeming so loud to sensitive ears.

He slipped ahead to the next window and discovered the dining room. DesConte sat in a chair at the dining table, his back to the window. The three other boys flanked him. Randolph sat facing the far wall, where a portable screen had been erected. A projector, connected to a laptop computer, showed slides of what looked like a foreign country. A building in the pictures was large and surrounded by a tall wall. There was a guard booth. It looked to Steel like an embassy or some kind of official building.

The next slide revealed a neighborhood, but not like any Steel had ever seen. Each boy had a pad of paper and a pen and was taking notes on every new slide.

A class? Was Randolph . . . tutoring the boys? History? Something for extra credit?

Steel felt like a moron. All this for . . .

But if just tutoring, then why had the boys snuck around, arriving here through the tunnels? That made no sense. Why tutor after hours when the boys belonged in their dorm rooms? Why try to hide that the boys were here in the first place? It couldn't be tutoring—*not exactly*—and yet . . .

"*Who-who. Who-who.*" The warning cry carried faintly around the house. Kaileigh's second warning.

The old woman?

Something jumped at him. It sprang from the sill of the very window he'd been peering through. A cat! It had been right there, right next to him, sitting so quietly, so dead still, that he hadn't seen it. It pounced and landed on him, sticking its claws into his arm.

"Oww!" Steel shouted.

Everyone in the dining room spun toward the window. Steel ducked.

He heard Randolph shout, "GO!" Chairs banged to the floor. Footfalls pounded against and squeaked the plank flooring.

DesConte and the three others were coming after him.

"*Who-who! Who-who!*" The pigeon sounded far more agitated.

Steel took off toward the chapel. If he could only make it into the tunnels . . .

Kaileigh would see him running and could join him in the choir room. There was still a chance of getting away.

As he cleared the front corner of the house, he caught a blur through a window: two of the boys racing toward the front door.

The other two were no doubt headed to the back.

The screen door flew open just as Steel skidded to a stop.

He was facing Verne and a friend of Verne's, an African American student named Earl Coleman.

What the heck was Verne doing here?

"Go!" Verne whispered. "We got you covered. Go!"

Steel scrambled away just as the boys came off the porch. He dove and hid in some bushes.

"What-a-we-got-here?" It was DesConte.

"Just out for a stroll," Verne said. His eyes flashed in the dark.

The other two boys from the dining room reached them. Verne and Earl stepped forward, blocking the way to Steel's hiding place.

Steel saw Kaileigh drop from the lowest branch and run around to the far side of the chapel. DesConte glanced in that direction, but missed getting a good look a her.

Steel sneaked away toward a stone wall.

"You want a piece of me?" Steel heard DesConte ask Verne and Earl.

Three minutes later, Steel and Kaileigh met at the chapel's main doors. They ran inside, and Steel led her through the hidden door into the pipe room. They were in the tunnel now, keeping their heads low and moving as fast as their feet would carry them.

He led the way, turning right at the common room, heading past the metal rungs that led to the auditorium, and into new territory. The tunnel angled slightly left. Steel switched on and off sets of lights. Suddenly the tunnel extended a hundred yards or more in front of them: the dorms.

He found a ladder that roughly matched the distance to Kaileigh's dorm. He led her up the ladder and found himself facing a panel of lumber construction. He worked with the panel and then noticed a peephole. He put his eye to it.

"It's the boys' bathroom," he said. "Lower Two. A shower stall."

Now he understood where, in his own dorm's washroom, he'd lost track of the boys he'd gone after weeks before.

"The *boys'* room?"

"I don't think you have any choice."

He found that by pulling the panel toward him, it clicked and released. And he swung it open.

The washroom was empty.

"You know where you are?" he asked.

"Yes. My dorm's directly overhead." She looked terrified.

"Can you do this?"

She nodded.

"Okay. Better hurry."

She stepped through the hidden panel and pushed it shut.

"What the heck?" he asked Verne when his room-mate returned to their room fifteen minutes later.

"Is that 'Thank you'?"

"Yes. It's that and: What the heck? Where did you come from?"

"I followed you. Not me, actually. It was Earl who did that."

"Followed me?"

"Went looking for you. You asked me to cover for you, you got me all curious."

"And White Socks?"

"No sweat. He bought it."

The boys undressed quickly, changing into pajamas. Steel tossed the laundry bags into the closet and moved the dummy head there as well. Second curfew was in three minutes. They could hear White Socks making his way from room to room.

"But—"

"You've got some explaining to do," Verne said. "DesConte was ready to split your head open, I think."

"You're going to get into trouble," Steel said. "You think he saw me?"

"He saw you, but I don't think he knew who it was."

"Why would you do that?"

"I got your back."

"But why?"

"We're roomies. 'Sides which, you're now going to tell me everything that's going on."

"You think?"

"I know. I saved your butt. Me and Earl."

"It's complicated, and I don't know it all."

"I'm listening."

"I can't tell you," Steel said, "what I don't know."

"We're roomies," Verne repeated. "So you'll tell me what you do know."

White Socks opened the door. "Keep it down in here. Shut your . . . Trapp." He'd amused himself. He pulled the door closed, and they heard him move to the next room.

"That's original," Steel said.

Verne chuckled.

Roomies, Steel thought.

26.
THE SPUD AND
THE OCTAGON

The bleachers that surrounded the ga-ga pit on three sides were overflowing with students and faculty. Even more people were standing or sitting crossed-legged on the grass. The ever-present Connecticut wind was lessened by the pit's position in the lee of the gymnasium, and the early afternoon sun remained high enough in the sky to cast strong but barely slanting shadows so that the pit seemed lit by spotlights.

As a reserve Spartan, Steel sat in the front row of one of the aluminum bleachers, with a few empty spaces between him and Hinchman. To his right sat Cloris Twiler, a horse-faced girl with wide shoulders and amazingly quick reaction times, the other

Spartan reserve. Cloris expressed anxiety by worming her hands like a ball of snakes in her lap.

"Can you stop that, please?" Steel said to her.

"No," she answered, without taking her eyes off the ga-ga pit.

The first of seven games had been no match at all. The Argos players—the Argives—led by DesConte, had proved themselves far more agile and fleet-footed. Their use of the boards—the octagonal walls of the pit—was precise and devastating for the Spartans. When in the hands of the Argives, the spud traveled as if it had a mind of its own, seeking out all Spartans and striking them below the knee with authority. The game was over nearly before it began, with the Spartans' five members quickly whittled down to just one, Brenda Simple, who didn't last long, being outnumbered as she was.

Hinchman psyched up the team for the second game, placing the Spartans into a defensive formation known as *gammon*—a play on the word *backgammon*, for the teammates lined up in an I-formation, but back to back. The gammon defense worked; the Spartans stayed in the game longer and got the upper hand, five players to three. Some adroit passing and the Argives' striker, DesConte, was eliminated. A few strategic passes and the Spartans had won.

In a surprising move, the Argos coach retired a player and called upon a reserve, the results devastating: the Argives handily won the next two games, quickly getting up four players to two and then "running the pit"—eliminating the remaining players. In the process, Ronald Martinez, the Spartans' foremost striker, was hit with a wild ball to the stomach and went over the pit wall backward, twisting his knee. The crowd hushed as Martinez went down, and groaned as he came up limping.

Hinchman turned to his bench: Cloris and Steel. There were no rules preventing him from loading his team with three girls, all of whom were formidable players, but his tightly set eyes lingered on Steel.

"Trapp," he said.

Steel swallowed with difficulty, his eyes lighting upon two faces in the crowd: Nell Campbell and Kaileigh. He'd been so focused on the ga-ga pit in the early going, he hadn't paid any attention whatsoever to the crowd. But now he felt both the joy and terror of being picked to play. They were behind three games to one, meaning a single defeat would cost Sparta the match.

Hinchman pulled him by the shoulders, leaned down, and spoke into his ear. "You've been watching the game," he said. "I'm counting on that.

Anticipate their every move. Exploit their weaknesses. You can do this."

Steel nodded. Hinchman turned him toward the pit. He was greeted by his teammates with fist-pounds as he climbed over the wall.

There was DesConte grinning at him the way a wolf grins at a wounded lamb. The two teams, five players each, lined up on opposite sides of the pit. Hinchman elected a "2-3"—two players in front, three behind. The Argives stayed with the "1-3-1" they'd been using—a player out front, in this case a girl, three players behind her, with DesConte in the middle, and a remaining player behind the row of three, the other girl. DesConte, the team's strongest player and best striker, was protected within a diamond of teammates. If the team structure could be maintained, it meant that there was a high percentage of probability that he would remain in play the longest, be the last Argive standing. This gave their team the best chance of winning.

The 2-3 chosen by Hinchman was a more aggressive lineup, as it put two strikers, Steel and Toby Taggart, up front against the Argives' one. Their best overall player, their team captain, a boy named Reddie Long, was in the middle of their two girls, in the back row.

The referee tossed the ball into the middle of the pit and the play began.

Steel, while never taking his eyes off the spud, focused less on the play and more on what Hinchman had told him: *Anticipate, exploit.* Without giving it direct thought, he shook off his nerves and immediately knew exactly what each player was going to do *before* he or she did it. This included his own teammates. His ability to anticipate—*to know*—slowed the game down for him. He blocked out the crowd noise, even the voice of his coach, and watched as the ball began to move as if heavy and tired. He could calculate its direction and destination long before the spud arrived at a given point.

Reddie slapped the spud against the octagon's midcourt section, striving for a rebound that would reach DesConte. But Steel quickly saw the spud's movement in terms of vectors, like a pool player knowing how the cue ball will come off the bumper. He took Reddie's strike not as a challenge to DesConte, but as a pass to himself, darting past the front girl and assaulting the Argos formation. As DesConte braced to defend the strike, Steel intercepted and redirected the spud off the back wall. The spud leaped with a backspin and caught the rear defender in the back of the leg. She was out.

The crowd cheered.

DesConte collided with Steel, laying a shoulder into him and nearly knocking him down.

The serve to restart play required the spud to touch two walls. The Argives, overeager to balance the teams with a strike of their own, touched the ball before it hit the second wall, and the ball was served by the Spartans instead.

Players darted in and around one another, vying for positions of advantage, but being well coached, returned to formation. The Argives, down one player, adopted a 1-2-1, a straight diamond with DesConte on the left side, in the middle pair.

Play continued. The constant shifting of formations clearly caught the Argives off guard. A second and third Argive were out. The Spartans retained all five of their players while the Argives were reduced to DesConte and the girl playing forward.

It was as if DesConte changed gears—as if he'd been waiting for the pit to clear out some. He hit three Spartans in a row. In less than a minute he'd single-handedly evened the teams.

Steel and Brenda Simple spread out. Whenever the pit got this empty, the game nearly became every man for himself. But Hinchman had coached them to resist playing alone, especially in reduced numbers, and Steel knew if he didn't work with Brenda, he'd be sitting on the bench for the next game, and Cloris would be the one playing.

DesConte played like a madman, seemingly everywhere at once. He moved with lightning-quick reactions, catching Steel from behind off a perfectly calculated rebound that Steel should have seen coming. He was out.

The crowd sighed.

But Brenda caught DesConte celebrating, and the Argive captain was retired, to more complaints from the crowd.

The Spartans remained in the match: 3–2.

Hinchman kept Steel in the next game. He personally eliminated three of the Argive starters, to enormous cheers from the crowd, and the Spartans won the game easily. The match was tied: 3–3.

As play to the final and deciding game began, Steel realized the advantage he gained from repeated play, from facing the same five players in every game. By this, his third game, it wasn't just a matter of anticipation, his ability to predict play, to see a few milliseconds ahead of each strike, every block and rebound. It felt more like he'd already watched the game on a DVR and knew exactly what was coming. He moved around the pit through openings other players didn't see. He avoided DesConte's shoulder blocks, darting through gaps and redirecting the spud without even giving it much thought—he seemed to just *know* where the spud was going to go. He took out three players, matching man for man the expert play of DesConte. It was down to two against two: him and Toby Taggart against DesConte and a thin, flashy boy with quick reactions.

The thin kid took out Taggart by redirecting a strike aimed at Steel. It was not only a terrific play, but one that Steel had not seen coming. He caught a glint in the thin boy's eyes: Argos knew what Steel was up to. Their coach had put in a player that Steel hadn't seen yet. He'd saved some new plays to surprise him.

With Taggart out, it was two on one. Steel got lucky and caught the thin guy on the heel. He hadn't been trying to hit him, but the referee spotted the glancing blow, and the boy was out.

Steel faced DesConte.

The crowd was on its feet.

He saw the heads of spectators bouncing up and down like they were dancing to wild music. He saw DesConte, crouched, shoulders thrown forward, about to serve. The spud struck two walls, and Steel redirected it. DesConte jumped up, and the spud passed beneath him without touching him.

The crowd roared.

DesConte sent a vicious strike straight at Steel. Steel dove to the side and avoided it, but was off balance as DesConte raced across the pit and sent the rebound at Steel again.

Steel jumped, caught the ball, and sent it off a wall at DesConte. But with an easy block, DesConte avoided contact with his legs. He bounced it off a wall, passing it to himself and launched the ball backward between his own legs.

Steel had never seen that move.

It caught him in the shins.

The crowd exploded: the match was over. The Argives rushed the pit and surrounded DesConte.

Steel stood there, frozen, unable to move.

But then DesConte broke from the celebration, approached Steel, and offered his hand to shake.

Steel took the boy's hand, and the crowd responded with a roar.

"That was amazing play for a first match, kid," DesConte said.

The Argives grabbed DesConte and continued their celebration. Steel climbed out of the pit and Hinchman wrapped an arm around him.

"I'm sorry," Steel apologized.

"Don't be ridiculous," Hinchman said. "You've got nothing to be sorry for. This is only the beginning of the season. And yet this match will be talked about for a long time to come—and for only one reason. Because it was the first time people saw you play."

"But I lost the game."

"The team lost. It's true. But it's not a one-man team. Go take a shower. You did very well."

Steel looked around the crowd for the first time in a long while. He spotted Kaileigh, who was looking right at him. Her face brightened with the eye contact: admiration . . . concern that he was upset by the loss.

He forced a smile onto his unwilling face and won a smile back from her. A friend tugged on her arm at the same time the Spartans headed toward the gym, and the moment was gone.

Steel took his time undressing, letting the upperclassmen on both teams use the showers first. Everyone but him seemed to have already forgotten the match, whereas Steel couldn't help but remember every detail, every shot, reliving the plays that had gone wrong. Especially the leaping, backward-through-the-legs shot that DesConte had won the game on. He'd won dramatically, triumphantly. There was the usual locker-room banter going back and forth, jokes and teasing, and Steel wanted none of it.

He was the last to leave the locker room. His hair was still wet, and he hadn't fully tightened his necktie, wearing it knotted but loose beneath an open shirt collar. If he spotted a teacher he could cinch it up quickly enough.

He was four steps down the hall when someone grabbed him from behind. The person was strong and lifted him right off his feet. A strong hand clamped down over his mouth. Before he could even think to kick, a second person had him by the legs, and he was being rushed down the hall and into the empty wrestling room.

The boy holding his legs wore a bandana tied over his face as a mask, which prevented Steel from seeing his face. The same was true for the guy who had him by the shoulders. Steel was dropped onto a cushioned mat in the wrestling room, and he heard the door being closed and bolted.

He faced the two boys. Their matching blazers and ties made them look a lot alike, but there were differences. Steel noted their shirts, belts, and shoes.

"What the—?"

"Shut up," said the taller and stockier of the two

in a voice that wasn't his own. He disguised it by making it into more of a growl. Not DesConte, as Steel had originally wondered: the shoes didn't match. This was a student he'd never met face-to-face before. He'd have remembered him otherwise.

The two upperclassmen just stood there, staring down at him. As if they were . . . waiting for something. Or someone. Steel knew better than to try to run for it, or, for that matter, to even speak. He raised up onto his elbows, dread seeping into him. Were they going to hurt him? Punish him for being the only Third Former to make a ga-ga club team? Hit him with a blow dart? Maybe some kind of hazing ritual. He'd just completed his first match as a club player—perhaps there was a rite he was meant to pass through. On the other hand, perhaps they were going to beat the snot out of him for nearly winning.

The door banged open. Two other boys entered, carrying another victim headfirst. Their faces were covered too. Time seemed to slow as they spun their captive around. As the person's face came into view, Steel nearly screamed.

Kaileigh!

She whipped the red hair out of her flushed face, glanced at Steel, then to the boys, and straightened her skirt.

"If you touch me again, you'll all go to jail," she said. She appeared ready to continue her complaint, but the leader held up his hand.

"Trapp . . . your shoes. Would you care to explain the mud on them?"

Steel looked down at his shoes. He hadn't even seen the mud until that moment. He knew he could easily explain it, so he simply "rewound" his memory, like a DVD going backward at high speed. He searched for that moment when he'd stepped onto the JV football field or some part of the front lawn . . . put his mind's eye in an entirely different scene: he was in Randolph's garden; he was hiding beneath a window.

He swallowed dryly.

"Ms. Augustine," the growling boy said, "can you explain the sap on your left hand?"

Kaileigh looked at her hand as if it belonged to someone else.

Then, in unison, Kaileigh and Steel looked at each other. They were two criminals caught by the police.

"Mr. Trapp, whatever you saw—and I think we both know what I'm talking about—you are urged to forget, to dismiss. As hard as that may be for someone with your memorization skills, it's wickedly important to your remaining at Wynncliff. If you like it here, and I think you both do, you'll go back to your studies and forget whatever it is you think you were doing putting your noses into other people's business."

"Who are you?" Steel said.

"That is not the response I was hoping for," the boy said. But then Steel wondered if he had it right. Was this, in fact, a boy? Or was it an adult, a teacher, perhaps, dressed in a school uniform? The thought of that gave him a chill. What was going on? Nell Campbell's warning came back to him.

"Ms. Augustine," the boy/man continued, "your situation is far more precarious. . . ." And that was another thing, Steel thought: the growling boy didn't talk like a boy at all. "You have a keen and intelligent mind. You have demonstrated language skills that are far superior to those of your peers. But don't think that buys you a position here at Wynncliff. The school is bigger than any one student."

Steel again wondered if the stocky boy behind the leader wasn't DesConte. There was something so familiar about him.

"If you continue to snoop around, you'll both be expelled."

"Because you're hiding something," Steel blurted out.

Even though the boy was wearing a hockey mask, Steel could tell the person was grimacing.

"I will answer that in this way: Wynncliff is not your normal school. I think you are *both* aware of that by now. It is special. Unique. You are here because you are also special and unique. Not everyone at the school is so special. You might say there are two schools in one. But that's all I can say for now. You'll have to . . . trust me . . . that it's in your best interest to wait just a little bit longer."

"How long? Wait for what?"

"I respect and admire such curiosity. Yours is a special situation. Never before have two students been in the situation you've been in."

"We didn't mean to make any trouble," Kaileigh said. "Steel thought . . . we both thought . . . we were worried someone was planning something awful . . . like the kind of thing you hear about on the news. That's all it was! We didn't want to be hating ourselves the rest of our lives because we let something like that happen. We had no idea about some secret society or something. No idea whatsoever."

"Well, now you know," said the voice behind the bandana. "If you tell anyone what you think you saw, it will be denied and you will be expelled. If you break curfew or do any more exploring, same thing: you're out."

"How long before we know what's going on?" Steel repeated.

"Soon," he said.

"How soon?"

"It doesn't matter!" Kaileigh said.

"I'm not sure you're going to make it, Trapp. You'd be well advised to listen to Ms. Augustine. What we have in mind for you—where this is all leading—it requires a great deal of patience. And at your age, patience is one skill that can't be taught. It has to be learned."

At your age, the person had said. It wasn't a student behind that bandana: Steel had been right.

27.
ALL FREAKS

"Nice game," Verne said from the comfort of his bunk. He pulled the iPod earbuds from his ears. "What's bugging you?"

"Nothing."

"Yeah, right."

"Okay, there is something, but I can't talk about it. You've got to respect that."

"Whatever. The coach come down on you or something?"

"Something like that."

"I can't help if I don't know."

"Let me ask you something," Steel said. "Before coming here, did you take some tests, or do something unusual or incredible, or anything like that?"

"I took tests. We all took those tests, right? Why?"

"Just curious," Steel said.

"I won the Hunt."

"You hunt?"

"The newspaper thing. It's this weekend deal. There are these clues . . . It starts with a clue in the newspaper and—I don't know—it's like a treasure hunt, only really big, like for the whole city, for the whole day—and I entered it. I wasn't supposed to. You had to be eighteen or something—and it's supposed to be a team event—but I entered by myself and I won, and it was like this big deal."

"And then the school contacted your parents," Steel said.

"How'd you know that?"

"Is that what happened?"

"Yeah, this woman showed up. Mrs. DeWulf—I remember because I was thinking 'da wolf.'" He cracked himself up, and Steel suffered through his recovery. "And she talked to my mom for a long time. Then I took the tests and stuff—"

"*After* the newspaper hunt, not before?"

"That's what I just said, didn't I? Why?"

"So I take it your winning . . . that was in the papers—"

"And on the news. Yeah. Youngest person ever to win the Hunt, and they made a big deal about how

253

I'd done it all by myself. Listen, I mean, I know they asked me here because of the Hunt, but what's the big deal?"

"What about your friends? How'd they get asked here?" Steel sat up on the top of his desk, facing the bunks. He saw a story unfolding, but he kept it to himself. He felt like he could answer the questions himself, but he allowed his roommate to speak.

"Well, Twiney . . . You know those stores, ExcelSport?"

"Yeah?"

"They have these rock-climbing walls *inside* the store."

"Yeah?"

"So Twiney . . . he like *borrowed* a pair of gloves that he wasn't exactly going to pay for—"

"He stole them."

"Not exactly. He never made it out the door. His dad caught him, and Twiney's dad is not exactly the most forgiving person, and he basically was going to smack Twiney back into the Stone Age for lifting those gloves. Except there was the rock wall, and so Twiney . . . he like jumped on that wall and went up it like Spider Man. No ropes, no nothing. Straight to the top in about zero seconds."

"Let me guess: it made the news."

"No. Not exactly. Sort of. There *was* this TV thing going on, this live deal, you know, the end of some road race or something where the winner got to shop in the store for five minutes without paying. And there was Twiney in the background, climbing that wall and all."

"So it was on TV."

"Yeah, definitely. Ten o'clock news. But not exactly on purpose or anything." He set his iPod on a box that acted as a table, and he rolled onto his side. "What's up with that, anyway?"

"Just curious," Steel said, the words suddenly catching in his throat. He supposed just asking questions like this was in violation of what he'd been told to do.

"Yeah, well . . . you know what they say about that and the cat," Verne said.

"Do me a favor: don't tell anyone I asked you any of this."

"Because?"

"I'm kinda like on probation."

"I'm the one pulling weekend study hall because of the thing at Randolph's. I didn't think they even got a look at you."

"Neither did I," Steel said. And bending over to clean his shoes, he left it at that.

"We're all freaks," Steel told Kaileigh.

Entering the common room before dinner had been maybe the best two minutes of his life. About a million kids, including Nell Campbell, had congratulated him on his ga-ga game, even though he'd lost. For a few minutes he'd felt like Lance Armstrong or Tiger Woods or somebody. Interestingly enough, DesConte and the other Argives, while receiving some attention, did not get near the reception Steel had.

But now dinner—a Saturday special of rubbery meat in a gray gravy—was behind them, and he'd led Kaileigh out to the giant sundial that was situated on the front lawn, about thirty yards from the chapel. It was marble, with a series of marble steps surrounding its base, and it reached about twenty feet high. They sat on the second step, looking back toward the main building.

"What do you mean?"

"Not freaks, but with special skills. And probably not all of us, I suppose. There are too many students, but at least some of us. Me with my memory. And Verne solved this treasure hunt all by himself. There are obviously kids with physical skills, too—the guys I saw shooting the blowguns. A friend of

Verne's can free-climb." A thought occurred to him. "Or maybe the physical skills are something you eventually need to know." He paused. "You're good with languages, right?"

Kaileigh didn't often look embarrassed, but she did now.

"What?" Steel asked her.

"I won something too. Like Verne. It was . . ." But she couldn't say it.

"What? Come on, Kai!"

"This impersonation thing. This stupid talent contest. It's just this thing I can do."

"Impersonation?"

She looked at him, closed her eyes, and said, "What? Come on, Kai!" sounding *exactly* like Steel. It was as if a tape recorder had played his voice back to him.

"Whoa!" he gasped.

"I know . . ." She blushed.

"Can you do that for anyone?"

"Anyone," she said. She rattled off a few lines from President Obama, Miley Cyrus, and Orlando Bloom, each pitch perfect.

"Well," he said, looking at her strangely, "that confirms it."

"Confirms what?"

"That we've been chosen by Wynncliff for our . . . *unusual* talents."

"We're supposed to let it go. Remember? This is what the guy was talking about."

"He scared you?"

"Duh! What do you think?"

"I think he was supposed to, but I don't think they'll expel us."

"And this is based on?" She sounded angry with him. Or maybe she was frustrated.

"They need us."

"As if!"

"That's why Nell warned me, and why this guy warned us both."

"Note the word, 'warn.'"

"We're part of something, and we don't even know what it is."

"The trouble with you is you think too much."

"Reddie Long was one of them."

"What?"

"Reddie Long. My own teammate on the Spartans. His belt and shoes. I spotted him tonight in the common room. His belt and shoes—same as one of the guys in the hockey masks."

"I didn't hear that."

"There's something going on."

"You think?" Pure sarcasm on her part.

"They recruit kids with special talents."

"You need therapy."

"But for what?"

"Let it go. They told us to let it go."

"If they were going to expel us, they would have already."

"Based on some mud on your shoes? I don't think so. They couldn't do that, but they've warned us that one more thing like that and we're gone. And I, for one, am listening."

She stood.

"You're going?"

"You're going to get me kicked out of here, and I don't want to get kicked out. For me, home is a governess and parents who are out of the country all the time. It is like majorly boring. I happen to like this place."

"You're ditching me?"

"I can't do this, Steel. I'm willing to wait for whatever. I can't risk it."

"Who said I was going to do anything?"

"You have that look."

"I was going to have Penny do it," he said. "If Penny can hack the grades, then he can hack admissions. We can see what, if any, special skills the new kids have."

"For what? What will that accomplish besides getting you thrown out?"

"Nell told me that someone was going to invite me to do something. The guy today. Same thing. Even my *dad* hinted that I'd be told something around Thanksgiving. 'Information is the most important weapon,' he said. Who knows if they're going to tell us the truth? If we can figure this out ahead of time, then we're better informed. Better prepared."

"Not me," she said.

"Kai!" he pleaded.

"Don't get thrown out, Steel. I would miss you."

"You're seriously not going to do this? It was you who introduced me to Penny!" *I would miss you*; her words swam around in his head.

"Until you quit this stuff, I can't even talk to you."

"What?"

"I can't talk to you. I don't even *know* you anymore."

She turned her back on him and walked away. Steel felt as if he'd been betrayed—his father was the reason she'd been invited to the school in the first place. And now she was deserting him.

"Kai!"

But she just kept on walking.

28.
A DAY TO BE
REMEMBERED

Taddler had attended a couple of small meetings before with Mrs. D., but he'd never been the focus of her full attention. He thought he now understood what a small plant felt like in the noonday sun, the strength of that persistent heat, the way it begged you to be bigger and stronger than how you really felt.

She had this grown-up quality about her—the way her hair was so carefully taken care of, her clothes expensive and without a wrinkle, the strength behind her eyes, the way she controlled her voice. That, he realized, was the one word that came to mind with Mrs. D.: *control*. Maybe that described grown-ups in general; maybe that was what separated kids and adults. But when it came to Mrs. D., it was everything.

She had led him and Johnny up to the second floor of the boathouse, out onto a balcony that over-looked the Charles River, where college crews were rowing—fours and eights, men and women—the perfectly synchronized oars looking like a bug's legs dipping into and disturbing the shining water.

"Tell me," she said in a calm, soothing voice.

He cowered under the glare of her eyes. He wanted most of all to please her, to never let her down, to never do anything to upset her. She was at the very center of his universe, which made him think of the sun again. The boathouse—this run-down, ramshackle building—now felt like home, and yet he thrilled at the idea of graduating out of here.

"It's fancy," Taddler said. Johnny nodded. "Never fewer than three bellmen at the main entrance. No way we're going to get past them." Johnny shook his head. Taddler wished he wouldn't keep doing that, but said nothing. "There's a side entrance into a bunch of shops, and there's an elevator on that level, but it only goes up one flight. From there you have to cross the lobby to get to the main elevators. I suppose if we stayed pretty close to a family we could pull it off, but if they gave us any kind of look or asked a question, we might be in trouble."

"I'm well aware of the hotel's physical layout," she said, her enunciation perfect, her gaze unrelenting. "But your observations about your ability to make it inside safely are exactly the kind of insight I was hoping for. Johnny?"

He looked a little panicked. Taddler wondered if he should bring up the fortune-teller, and that Johnny hadn't been spending his time conducting surveillance, but wasting it with a tarot card reader.

"It's like Taddler said." Johnny was having a hard time meeting Mrs. D.'s eyes. "Kind of looks impossible to get in there."

"Is that what you're saying, Mr. Taddler?" She sounded as if she were accusing him of a crime.

"No, ma'am. I just said the front entrance and the lobby elevators present problems."

"And do you have a way around these problems? Either of you?" She aimed that last part at Johnny, who knitted his brow, confused.

"I have an idea," Taddler volunteered.

"Speak."

"Smoking."

"Excuse me?" she said.

"The workers are always standing around outside smoking. The kitchen guys, housecleaners. Even security, or at least guys in suits, every now and then."

"Yes? Explain yourself?" Her voice could be so soothing and reassuring.

"We've tried that before!" Johnny barked out.

"I'm not talking about some kitchen door off an alley," Taddler said.

"But?" Johnny scrunched his face. Their attempts to sneak into hotels had often included such doors—areas where workers loitered while taking breaks. Taddler seemed to be contradicting himself.

"It's some kind of balcony. On the second or third floor. Off the mezzanine, I'll bet. A place where all the conventioneers can sneak out for a smoke. I've seen 'em up there—people smoking. And not workers, either! A door like that's got to be left unlocked—open—right? Or else they'd constantly be locking themselves out."

Mrs. D.'s eyes glowed. She seemed positively fascinated with him. "Oh, this is marvelous work, Taddler. Exceptional. And at what hours have you seen people? And have you ever *not* seen people? Is it ever empty, this balcony?"

"It comes and goes, that is, the people do. And there's this fire escape going up to it. What I'd like to do . . . What I'd like permission to do . . . is to try a run at it—climb the ladder and sneak up there and like just check it out. If I get inside, then we know that's the way in."

"Then I suggest you try it."

"I'll need some cigarettes," Taddler said. Mrs. D. had strict rules regarding cigarettes, and if she took this as a ruse for him trying to win smokes off her, he'd be in big trouble.

She cocked her head, again giving him that hawkish look.

He did not flinch.

"Very well. That can be arranged."

Johnny looked stunned and envious.

Taddler's chest swelled with pride. Not only a mission, but cigarettes to go with it. It was a day to be remembered.

29.
WHITE SOCKS AND BLACK TUNNELS

A week passed, the longest week of Steel's life. Not only was the warning from the wrestling room on his mind, but, more important, Kaileigh was still not speaking to him. He attended classes. He practiced with the Spartan ga-ga team. He called home twice and talked to his mother. But nothing had prepared him for the ache in his chest that came with Kaileigh's cold shoulder.

If he approached her in the common room, she clustered with girlfriends and ignored him. If he saw her walking to class, she turned on the afterburners and practically ran to stay ahead of him. During class, she wouldn't so much as look at him.

Finally, on Thursday evening, pent up with frustration, he walked out of the dorm, threw his head back, and screamed up into the gray sky. "Ahhhhh!" That felt surprisingly better. But as he turned back toward the dorm, he faced the full, round, gloating face of Victor DesConte.

"Trapp."

"Victor."

"At ten minutes past ten you're going to tell your roommate that you don't feel so hot."

"Am I?"

"And you're going to head to the bathroom in our dorm."

Steel felt his heart doing somersaults in his chest. *The fifteen squeaks.* He suddenly wondered what his time at the school would have been like had he never heard them.

"Okay," he said, though reluctantly.

"You need to wear dark clothes to bed. A dark T-shirt. Maybe you leave a pair of jeans on a hook in the bathroom, a pair of running shoes, like you forgot them after a shower."

"I could do that. But why would I?"

"Because I said so."

"Past ten, I'm after curfew."

"White Socks has already made his first round by then. You'll be back by eleven." DesConte looked at him with a weird, penetrating expression. He seemed on the verge of saying something like *I know it was you we were chasing that night,* but he held it back.

"And don't try bringing a phone or recorder or anything, because you're going to be searched."

Steel experienced a quick spike of terror. *What the . . . ?* "Whatever," he said, trying to sound unimpressed.

If the days had passed slowly, the next several hours—through study hall, back to the dorm, a shower (leaving his clothes in the washroom) and into bed—were positively glacial. If anyone had asked, he might have said a day or two had gone by in that short period. Finally he turned off the room light, and a few minutes later White Socks appeared in the door and checked on Steel and his roommate.

"Trapp?"

"Here, sir."

"Dundee."

"Present."

The door shut. Since Verne's probation-earning encounter outside Randolph's house, a simple visual check was no longer sufficient.

Steel sat up, checking the glowing clock: 10:04. He heard White Socks going door to door down the hall.

"My stomach's not so great. I feel like I'm going to puke," Steel said.

"That's because they feed us roadkill," Verne said. "Calling what they put on our plates meat is an insult to all cows and pigs."

"Don't talk about food."

"Don't hurl here, dude. This is a no-hurl zone. A no-fart zone. A shower-before-you-enter zone. Just because I have to room with you doesn't mean I have to breathe you."

Typically, when his 10 p.m. rounds were completed, White Socks left via the dorm's far door and returned to his apartment. On rare occasions he would turn around and patrol the dorm a second time. Steel waited to see which it was to be tonight. After a prolonged silence in the hallway, he faked a groan and came off the bunk as if tender.

"I gotta get out of here."

"I'm telling you: don't blow that roadkill in here."

Steel, clutching his stomach, sneaked a look into the hall and then made for the washroom. As he pushed through the door, there was DesConte, his index finger held to his chapped lips, indicating silence.

"Reddie?" Steel hissed at the boy standing to DesConte's right.

His fellow Spartan also held his finger to his lips. He moved to block the door as DesConte told Steel to pull his pants on. Steel did so, and was then pushed into a shower stall. Suddenly he feared that this was nothing but more hazing by upperclassmen, that DesConte had suckered him. But the Argive reached up to the showerhead until there was a distinct click, then DesConte twisted it to the right and pushed it toward the tile wall. It looked like he'd broken the thing. But as the showerhead jammed against the wall, a deeper click resonated through the tile. DesConte pushed Steel out of the way, grabbed hold of the tile soap holder built into the wall, and pushed. The entire wall of the shower swung open like a door, revealing darkness beyond.

"You ever tell anyone about this, you're a dead man," DesConte whispered. He stepped into the void and signaled Steel to follow. A moment later, Reddie Long came through, and DesConte pushed the wall shut.

"Whoa," Steel said in the consuming darkness.

"Yeah . . . just wait," said DesConte. He switched on some lights. They were above the tunnels.

Steel tried to seem impressed, as if he were seeing this for the first time. He wasn't sure how convincing a performance it was. DesConte led the way down the rebar ladder rungs and into the tunnel, and the three of them were off. DesConte kept looking back at Steel to measure how impressed he was. Steel did his best to continue to look surprised.

The tunnel passed the administration building. They turned left at the next junction, and DesConte led them up into the chapel's organ pipe room, where he stopped to use a peephole to ensure that the chapel was empty. Then they slipped into the choir pews, past the organ, and into the choir room. Out this door and in shadow, to beneath the ash. Here, DesConte turned toward Steel, and his glaring eyes told him that he knew it had been Steel out here spying on them. Steel wondered if DesConte had been one of the boys in the wrestling room, but didn't think so. Reddie had been there, however, and Steel didn't love that Reddie was looming behind him the whole way.

To his relief, DesConte moved on. They stayed in shadows and reached the screened-in porch of Randolph's home. Without knocking, DesConte let them inside. He did this comfortably and without hesitation, and it told Steel a great deal: they were expected, and DesConte had likely been coming here, this same way, for a long time.

He was led into a sitting room containing a small

fireplace, two couches, and some chairs. He spotted the back of a girl's head and tensed as Kaileigh glared over her shoulder at him. There were now six students in the room: he and Kaileigh, DesConte, Reddie Long, and two girls from the Sixth Form, whom he recognized by their faces though didn't know by name.

Randolph entered the room. He wore gray pants and a starched white shirt unbuttoned at the neck. Close up, he looked older and tired. Steel's grandmother had looked the same way after his granddad had died, and he attributed the look to Randolph's having recently lost his wife.

Randolph motioned for Steel to sit next to Kaileigh, which he did. The teacher thanked the four students for their help, and they left the room, but not the house, Randolph asking them to stay in order to return his guests to their respective dorms.

"Do you know why you're here?" Randolph said.

"We didn't mean any disrespect, sir," Kaileigh said, "to the rules or to the school. And we promise it won't happen again."

"I think he's asking why we're at Wynncliff," Steel said, not taking his eyes off Randolph, who nodded slightly.

"Yes, Mr. Trapp. Why is that?"

"Kaileigh for her ability to pick up languages and mimic people—her impersonations. Me . . . well . . . I'm okay at remembering things."

Randolph smirked.

"Because of Steel's father?" Kaileigh asked.

"Well, we can't discount legacy, can we?" Randolph said. "So, yes. That's partly correct. But do you know why Wynncliff?"

Steel said, "No, sir. We don't know what's going on."

"He means that there are times it feels different here at Wynncliff," Kaileigh said, piping up. She flashed a disapproving look at Steel. "Not that anything is actually going on. We're very sorry for nosing around, and it won't happen again." She wanted out of there.

"But your 'nosing around,' as you call it, is important to me. To us. To Wynncliff."

"Are you going to expel us?" Steel said, blurting out what was on both their minds.

Randolph grinned. "Expel, Mr. Trapp? Far from it. I'm going to . . . *promote* you. I'm going to explain things, to answer the very questions you've no doubt been asking yourselves. But first I have to lay the ground rules. Anything—everything—I tell you I will deny ever having said. If you repeat any of what

I'm about to tell you to a single other person, including your parents or your entrusted Mr. Pennington Cardwell, you will most definitely be expelled, you will find it impossible to be accepted at any other private educational institution, and there will be severe financial repercussions for your parents. The simplest of matters—applying for a driver's license, for instance—you will discover becomes almost insurmountable. It will follow you for years to come. I cannot begin to express how much you will regret the day. Am I clear?"

Steel nodded his head. *He knows about Penny.*

Kaileigh said, "What if I'd rather not hear it?"

"Too late," Randolph said, finding room to smile at her. He paused. "So do we understand one another?"

Kaileigh nodded. But she looked terrified.

"Very well. Wynncliff is not your normal private school, as you've no doubt surmised. There are reasons for its physical isolation, for our not playing any home games in competitive sports. We like to keep as low a profile as possible."

Steel felt goose bumps rush up both arms.

"It is an institution," he continued, "that prides itself on enrolling some of the most intelligent and uniquely gifted students in the country. In the *country*," he repeated. "There is a school within the school, hence the need for utmost secrecy. Only a handful of students, such as yourselves, are in a position to be enrolled in this inner school. Ten students? Fifty? Even I don't know the number. That is privileged information known only to Mr. Hastings and a handful of board members. A few faculty members, such as myself, are responsible for our own small team of students. We keep to ourselves and we make *no attempts* to invade the privacy of others. Do we understand one another?"

Both Steel and Kaileigh nodded. Then Kaileigh changed her mind and shook her head.

"What kind of school?" she asked.

"This country is fighting a war. I'm not talking about *that* war. I'm talking about a war of intelligence that has been going on since its inception, a war that has multiple fronts and one that expanded greatly during the Cold War. Knowledge is everything. Information is knowledge. And this nation collects as much information as it possibly can, sometimes using technology, sometimes what we call human assets.

"Over the years—decades, really—it became apparent that we, as a nation, were lacking a means of intrusion, what we call a conduit, into certain aspects of foreign affairs. Particularly foreign embassies, where prospective employees are vetted—that is, background checked—so thoroughly as to often prevent any intelligence gathering. Quite by accident, a young person changed all that while visiting with a family in the mid-1960s. He was an overnight guest of a school chum at a foreign embassy—which one doesn't matter—and overheard something that proved vital to our national interests. As luck would have it, he reported what he heard to his father. He and his friend attended an international school, and over the next several months, he gleaned a good deal of intelligence for us. He never broke any laws. He merely kept his ears open. And we learned something of vital importance: people will say things around children that they wouldn't around adults. It's as simple as that.

"Wynncliff Academy became the only school in the country—as far as we know—to begin training such students. Only certain students interested us for the program—"

"Those good with language, or with special memory skills," Kaileigh said.

"Or a kid who could run fast, or climb well," Steel said.

"There were many skill sets that interested us. In

some cases, in students over eighteen, that is graduating seniors, students who were no longer minors,
the assignments took on more covert activities, and
physical attributes became important. That's possible. Yes.

"Some students are recruited to Wynncliff for the
wonderful private education the school offers.
Others . . . like yourselves . . . are recruited for your
individual skill sets that might prove useful to this
other program. It's a voluntary program. No one is
going to force you to join. You face discipline only if
you discuss what I'm telling you. Not for refusing to
join. Do we understand one another?"

They both nodded.

"Normally, we, the school faculty, wait several
months or even an entire school year before recruit-
ing our special students. But a situation has arisen
that has forced my hand. That, coupled with your
curiosity." He looked like he'd bitten into a lemon.
"For these reasons, you are becoming involved much
sooner than usual. Your situation is being accelerated.
I'm required to recruit you ahead of time. As it
happens, the timing is critical. There's an assignment that needs your particular skills, and your
ages, immediately. So I must ask you to carefully
consider everything I've just told you, and to

contemplate admission to our program. Questions?"

"Only about a thousand," Steel said.

"I can field one at a time."

Steel and Kaileigh exchanged looks: bewilderment, excitement.

"I realize," Randolph said, "that all this can be overwhelming. I'm more than happy to send you back to your dorms to think about it. But I will ask that you not only not speak of it with your friends or parents, but that you not speak of it to each other. We cannot afford this to reach any ears outside the Program—and for your reference, that is how we refer to it. You may only discuss the Program inside my home for the time being. Do we under—"

"Yes," said Steel.

"Let me leave you for a moment." Randolph left the room, shutting the door behind him.

"So, this can't be for real, right?" Kaileigh said. "I mean it's got to be some kind of major hazing ritual to involve a teacher and all—and I certainly fell for it—I mean I actually believed the guy—but there's no way something like this is actually going on and they're asking us to be part of it. I mean, right?" Her eyes begged Steel to agree with her.

Steel said nothing. He felt sorry for her because he knew that on some level she'd been blocking out all their discoveries, that she would far prefer to deny anything was going on than to face the consequences of her own involvement in it. Whereas he suddenly felt that a burden had been lifted. It was as if all his suspicions had been confirmed and he felt powerfully good as a result. He exhaled like someone who'd been holding his breath in a contest.

"Steel?"

"I wonder what happens if we turn him down," he said. "It can't be good."

"But it's a joke, right? An elaborate hoax. Right?"

He ignored her. "And I'm not sure what it means that he's told us ahead of the others. My father warned me. I'm *so* stupid because I paid no attention at the time. But he warned me. He said I had to hang in there *until Thanksgiving*, that everything would be clearer after the break. I thought it was just typical Mom-and-Dad stuff: 'Patience is a virtue' and 'Good things come to those who wait.' But now I think it was my bad, that he was trying to tell me to chill until after the break. He probably knew I would be invited into the Program at some point, and he knew me well enough to know that I'd see things that would bug me."

"He sent me here to be in the Program?"

"Think about it," Steel said. "Think what we did

in Washington, D.C. last year. With basically no training and having no idea what we were doing, we pulled that off. Obviously, people were going to hear about that. And obviously, the right people did. On top of that, you can do languages and sound like other people. That's got to be of value. And obviously, stuff like that is what got us invited to go to school here."

"What do we do?"

"We decide to join or not," Steel said. "By ourselves, because neither of us can ever look back and think that the other person dragged them into this."

"You actually think it's *real*?" Her voice cracked. "Face it: Victor and Reddie are going to come through that door laughing their butts off."

Steel answered by simply meeting eyes with her.

"Oh, come on . . ." she gasped. "You can't be serious."

"Totally."

"He made it sound like we'd be . . . *spying*."

"Not exactly. I think it's more like they would put us into some place where a lot of embassy kids go, and if you happen to hear something important, you report it."

"That's called spying."

"He made it sound like the older kids like

DesConte and Reddie Long do the heavy lifting, not kids our age," Steel said.

"It still sounds like spying to me."

"In a way, I suppose. But I think there are a lot of definitions of spying. And I think the point is: who's going to hurt a kid? A foreign country is not going to hurt a kid, and it would be way too embarrassing to accuse a kid, to admit that some thirteen- or fourteen-year-old was able to spy on you. It's basically genius, if you ask me. If the kid doesn't break any laws, then what's anyone going to do about it, and I can see how grown-ups wouldn't take the same precautions with kids as they would with other grown-ups."

"It's totally random."

A knock on the door silenced them both. Randolph entered, but not the other kids. Steel thought they must be in the house somewhere, but he saw no sign of them.

"Have you had a chance to discuss it?" Randolph said.

Neither Kaileigh nor Steel answered.

"The assignment I have you in mind for is over the long Halloween weekend. We will have to move very quickly. Training. Study. Both of you would be operational."

"Do we get our parents' permissions, or what?" Kaileigh asked.

"No, Ms. Augustine. You are in our charge. Your parents signed a contract upon acceptance of admission. Do you think we could do this for as long as we have without protecting ourselves? Don't worry about your parents, Ms. Augustine. We are not putting you into any harm. We are just enlarging your skill set, preparing you for the possibility of service to your country when you become an adult. The CIA, NSA, FBI, Homeland Security, and a dozen other agencies all recruit Wynncliff graduates. You will find yourself invited to attend the nation's premier colleges. I doubt you'll get much complaint from your parents."

"Are you trying to tell me that my parents are spies?" she blurted out.

All color had left her face.

"I am certainly saying no such thing," Randolph said, though his face implied otherwise.

Steel thought back to Kaileigh's saying her father was an art dealer, constantly traveling. What better cover for a spy? She'd processed this as well and seemed ready to cry.

"I'm in," Steel told Randolph.

Kaileigh snapped her head in Steel's direction,

her jaw set forward in angry disbelief.

Steel's attention remained on Randolph. "What do you mean 'operational'?"

"Your Third Form year is typically devoted to training," Randolph said. "You don't usually go operational until Fifth Form abroad, though there are always exceptions. You two are the exception." He winced a smile.

Kaileigh continued staring at Steel as if she expected him to reverse his decision.

"How do we get out of the Program if we don't like it?" she asked.

"An excellent question," Randolph said. "The answer to which is a little tricky. A process exists. A procedure. For now, that's all you need to know."

"Do you get to stay at the school?"

"Very, very few are recruited into the Program, Ms. Augustine. Those that decline enrollment—and there have been precious few, I might add—often end up transferring to other schools. Fine schools. There is some minor debriefing involved. Parents are part of it, of course. Certain documents are signed and processed."

"Nondisclosure agreements," Steel said. He'd once heard his father talking about a legal document that prevented a person from saying anything about a specific topic.

"Something akin to that," Randolph conceded, "yes." He grimaced, put off by the current line of discussion.

"You're saying that if I refuse, I'll be expelled," Kaileigh said.

"Transferred," Randolph said. "And with the highest of recommendations and often a full scholarship. To some of the best, most prominent schools. I assure you, we've never received a complaint. Ms. Augustine, should you, with your parents' guidance, opt out, believe me, you will be very pleased with where you end up. I . . . we . . . don't want you feeling any pressure. As I said, typically we wait until second session. Our current situation requires drastic measures. There you have it. You must not feel obligated in any way. The Program is an extra burden on students. There's additional study involved. Training. More of your time is required. The decision is not to be taken lightly."

Kaileigh mulled it over.

"I would like to know, Mr. Trapp"—Randolph turned, addressing only Steel—"how it was you discovered us in the first place? It was you in the pipe room, was it not? Blind luck? Did you stumble upon the tunnels somehow, or what exactly was it?"

Steel nearly answered him directly. But at the last second, he held his tongue. "I think," he said, "it might be better discussed at another time."

Randolph furrowed his brow. "I see."

"But no, not blind luck."

"Then we have a problem in the conduct of our operations."

"Not one that others would uncover," Kaileigh said. "It's that brain of his."

Steel bristled.

"It's of major significance to me," Randolph said.

"I'm in," Kaileigh said, interrupting them. "I'm willing to do this as long as I have a way out if I don't like it."

"Of course," Randolph said, though Steel detected for the first time that, if not lying, he was at least stretching the truth. "Excellent. Excellent!"

Randolph must have given some signal, though Steel did not see it. Reddie Long entered the room carrying two thick documents, one bearing Steel's legal name, the other with Kaileigh's.

"You may read through these agreements now, at your leisure. Once you've signed them, we can discuss your first . . . assignment."

Steel turned directly to the final page of the

document, pulled out a pen, and signed it without reading a word.

Kaileigh looked at him as if he'd committed high treason.

"What?" he said. "I'm in. In is in. A contract is not going to change that, and honestly, I don't want to know what it says. It'll just freak me out."

Kaileigh began reading the first page. She glanced up at Randolph, over at Steel, and then turned to the last page. She signed.

"You are now, by signing these documents, sworn to secrecy. It is a secrecy not to be taken lightly. Federal charges can and will result if any of what you learn or are told, going forward, were ever to leak. Do we understand one another?"

Both kids nodded.

Reddie Long collected the documents like there was a fire in the room. A moment later he was gone.

"Welcome to the Program," Randolph said.

30.
GRINNING IN
THE DARK

For the next few weeks, Steel and Kaileigh found themselves living double lives. To their new friends and teammates, they were Third Form students with busy schedules. To Mr. Randolph, DesConte, Reddie Long, and a limited number of other students, they were the latest recruits into the Program.

There was a great deal to learn, and the instruction often came after the second curfew check at 11 p.m. They would take the tunnels to the chapel and then sneak across to Randolph's house and sometimes stay as late as 1 a.m.

Confronted by Verne about the late-night sojourns, Steel could tell him only that he was being hazed by upperclassmen and that any report to the faculty would get him into big trouble. Verne accepted the explanation—rumors were rampant among Third Form students about the existence of secret societies and clubs, and all were eager to be invited into one or more of the groups. Only now did those rumors begin to make sense to Steel: stories had been invented to counter the truth of the Program; the administrators had figured out a way to create so much speculation about what was going on at Wynncliff that if the truth ever surfaced, it would be discounted along with the dozen other stories circulating around. "It's a school for student spies." Oh, sure.

As the Halloween weekend approached—Friday afternoon through Sunday—Steel grew increasingly nervous about the exact nature of the assignment. On the Thursday night before the break, he and Kaileigh were due at Randolph's for a final briefing. By prior agreement, they left their dorms early and entered the tunnels. Steel led Kaileigh in a new direction: toward the library instead of the chapel.

"Where are we going?" she questioned.

"Someplace we can talk," he said.

They traveled another fifty yards in the tunnel before Steel stopped at a ladder.

"The science lab," he said.

They climbed the ladder and settled into a utility

room, much like the one in the basement of the administration building. He switched off the lights so no one would know the direction they'd come from.

"What do you think about the Program?" he asked.

"I've wanted to talk to you so bad," she said. "It's almost like—"

"They're keeping us apart to make sure we don't talk too much."

"Yes!"

"Do you have any clue what we're supposed to be doing in Boston?" he asked.

"No. You?"

"Not really. Randolph has me memorizing all sorts of scientific stuff. Tons of it. He quizzes me on it. And they've created this kind of fake identity thing—my *role*, as they call it—which makes me think it's going to be weird. I'm supposed to be poor and I've been in a lot of trouble."

"Same here! Exact same thing! They've got me talking like trailer trash and working on Spanish, Farsi, and Russian."

"Farsi and Russian?" He tried to think that through. "Oh! And he had me memorize hotel floor plans, city maps, and stuff like that. You think we're going to steal something?"

"I didn't think we ever actually break the law, right? We just listen and stuff like that. So that doesn't make sense. How do those two things fit together?"

"Got me." He wished he could see her face in the dark. "What about Penny?"

"He knows something is up."

"You think?" he asked.

"Yeah. He's got to. We've barely talked to him since, you know, that night. And who knows what he sees on those cameras of his? He could know more than we do. I thought about telling Randolph about him."

"But you didn't," Steel said, seriously concerned.

"I'm not busting Penny," she said. "He helped us out a ton. And I like him, and they'd probably expel him for what he's done. And besides, I think he'll be recruited at some point. He must have been invited here because of how techie he is."

"I suppose," Steel said.

"You don't think he'll get us into trouble, do you?"

"I think we should both agree on a story to tell him. Our being hazed by a secret society works the best. I think we just tell him that and apologize for the last couple of weeks."

"I suppose."

"Are you scared?" he asked.

"About tonight? A little, I guess. Or worked up is maybe more like it. It just all seems so—"

"Weird?"

"Yeah."

"I know," he said. "But it's gotta be important. Otherwise they wouldn't have rushed us."

"He made it sound like they needed us. Like the older kids couldn't do it."

"We'll find out, I suppose." Steel reached out and took her hand. She squeezed his strongly. "We're cool, right?"

"I'm glad that whatever it is, I'm doing it with you," she said.

"Yeah, me too," he said.

"A good team."

"Yeah." He waited a second, his heart beating so strongly he wondered if she could hear it. "So here we go."

Randolph paced his study as if rehearsing what to say, Kaileigh and Steel facing him in uncomfortable chairs. He had a projector on the table and a screen set up in the corner. He stole a look at them several times, causing Steel to wonder if he'd reconsidered allowing them to participate.

"How do you feel?" he finally asked, turning to face them.

"Fine," Kaileigh said.

"Ready," Steel answered.

"That's the spirit, Mr. Trapp," Randolph said.

He rattled off something in a foreign language at Kaileigh, and she answered in the same tongue, sounding far more foreign than Randolph.

"Brilliant," he said. "Excellent, Ms. Augustine."

"Whatever it is, you can tell us," Steel said.

Randolph found it in himself to smile openly. "You think?"

Steel nodded.

"I think so too," Randolph said. "Very well. Mr. Trapp, I'm assuming you will remember everything I'm about to tell you. Ms. Augustine, you may not take notes. I'll ask you to put the pen down. Thank you. Mr. Trapp can remind you if necessary. Do I have your attention?" This last bit was directed at Steel, who nodded.

He faced Steel and spoke slowly.

"The operation will be this weekend during our Halloween break, as I told you before. We . . . our government . . . is not the only one that understands the usefulness of younger partners—operatives such as yourself. . . ."

Steel loved being called that.

"We have gained intel—*intelligence*—that there are secrets being passed between the Iranians and Russians. The nature of these secrets is unknown, but we never leave such things to chance. As it happens, the exchange is to be made between two minors such as yourselves—the daughter of the Iranian deputy ambassador, and the son of a Russian consulate general." He tripped a remote control, and the photographs of a boy and a girl appeared on the screen. "Memorize these faces, Mr. Trapp." A moment later he changed slides. "This is the Armstrad Hotel, downtown Boston, and the temporary residence of the Iranian ambassador. The embassy is currently undergoing renovations, thereby making the ambassador's hotel suite foreign territory and therefore off-limits to our law enforcement or military. We believe the exchange will take place inside the hotel suite, out of reach of U.S. law. Are you with me, Mr. Trapp?"

Steel nodded, saying, "It's like the hotel suite is part of Iran, as long as they're in there."

"Precisely."

"So we can't do anything to stop what goes on."

"Exactly."

"Including them giving each other stuff."

"And by using minors," Randolph continued,

"they further tie our hands. The ambassador's family members are, like the ambassador himself, immune from prosecution. Even if we caught them, we couldn't do anything."

"That's why you've had me learn some Farsi and Russian," Kaileigh said. "But how does it work?"

"Very good, Ms. Augustine! Yes, indeed. The children are being used as cutouts—that is, they very likely have no idea what it is they are exchanging. We assume they will meet at a Halloween party, a fundraiser scheduled in the hotel on Friday night by a law firm. It offers them good cover. They will proceed to the suite and make the exchange. From there on the information is protected by immunity and they are untouchable."

"Then . . . what can you do?" Steel asked.

"It's what *you* can do," Randolph answered. "The two of you."

"We're going to take their places," Kaileigh said. "The phrases I've been working on . . . I'm speaking to someone . . . who? A guard maybe. Someone who can let me in to—"

"The suite!" Steel said. "I've memorized the hotel plans."

"You see?" Randolph said. "You two are the perfect choices."

"But if I'm to imitate the girl, I'll need—"

"To meet her," Randolph said. "To hear her speak, to see her move. That's correct. That will happen at the party. From there, the two of you will change costumes—we have reliable intel that the Russians have ordered an Aladdin costume for the boy, and the Iranians a Jasmine for the girl. All of that has been worked out. The complication comes from what we call a 'wild card.' That is, specifically, the possible involvement of a third party. There's a group of delinquents working the Boston hotels—stealing from guests. We know that this group has targeted the fund-raiser I spoke of. They'll be in attendance Friday night as well. If we're to prevent them from interfering, which will be the responsibility of Mr. DesConte and Mr. Long, we need to identify them *ahead* of time. This is the first leg of your assignment. Early Friday evening you will attempt to identify the woman in charge and follow her to get a look, if possible, at her team. If that isn't possible then you'll follow her operatives to the Armstrad and identify them there. The point being, we must know who her operatives are if we're to stop them. If they were to steal the information—which we believe will be contained on a thumb drive—we could have an international incident."

"You mean *we* are stealing some thumb drive?" Kaileigh said, objection in her voice. "I thought you said we didn't do that kind of thing, that the older kids did that kind of thing, and only when necessary."

"It's okay," Steel said, eager for the assignment.

"Once the party has begun, your assignment, Ms. Augustine, will be to assist Mr. Trapp in getting into the suite. Mr. Trapp's assignment is to examine and memorize the contents of the thumb drive, identify the purpose of its contents, and to advise me of such. If there is to be any intervention, it will, indeed, be left to other operatives."

"Victor and Reddie," Steel said under his breath.

"You needn't concern yourselves with anything beyond your immediate assignments. You are well aware of the rules. We've discussed them in detail."

"Yes, sir," they said, nearly in unison.

"If we had other operatives available, believe me, they would—"

"It's because of our size, and her language, and my memory," Steel said, interrupting. "These other kids . . . we can pass for them."

"Let's hope so," Randolph said, "or the operation is doomed before it begins."

31.
BREAK

As school let out on Friday at noon, the campus became frenzied with students heading in every direction. Four chartered buses were waiting in the semicircle out front, as were several dozen cars driven by parents, and more than one town car. The trees were, for the most part, barren of leaves, the lawn covered in golds and browns and the red of maples, the wind stirring as students hurried past, lugging bags and backpacks.

Steel and Kaileigh boarded the bus marked for Boston along with thirty other students. As instructed, they did not sit together. Soon, Steel felt as if he were on the bus alone. He spent most of the ninety-minute ride staring out the window. He counted barns. He tried to see in the windows of people's houses, and he looked down through car windshields, trying to imagine where each driver was going and what he or she was up to. But mostly he reviewed his instructions and the enormous volume of scientific data he had committed to memory. To him the evening assignment was simple enough, the burden of the job on Kaileigh. It was the job this afternoon that troubled him: finding, identifying, and following some woman. One thing was certain: nothing would be the same after this weekend.

The city loomed big in his mind, perhaps because of his weeks on a windblown campus far from anywhere, perhaps because of the assignment that was etched into his formidable memory, and his sense of being so small in a place so vast. He took a moment to glance back at Kaileigh, who, like him, was staring out the window. He caught sight of Penny staring at him from three rows back. The sight of Penny surprised him, though he tried not to show it. Penny lived in Boston—he and Kaileigh should have thought of that, should have prepared to have to deal with him.

The bus charged on, giving Steel views of outlying neighborhoods with their laundry lines, old cars, and muffler shops. Billboards streamed past, offering white-toothed smiles, sale items, and political candidates. With each mile, Steel felt his gut twist a little tighter, his skin prickle with perspiration.

Finally they were in the city proper, driving the city streets, and the walls closed in around him, the buildings blocking sunlight, the sidewalks suddenly alive with people. At the stoplights he saw the poor and the rich, the old and the young, the healthy and the not-so healthy, the cops, the shoppers, the smokers, the joggers, the bike riders, the happy, the sad, and a street musician playing a harmonica with a scruffy dog on a leash tied to his ankle. He saw himself trying to fit into the mix, trying to blend in, trying to look right. He studied and memorized things of importance: the way a street bum hunched his back like he was carrying an enormous weight, the way the less fortunate seemed to walk slower, the way hunger could show in a person's face, and how bitterness and despair could be worn like a coat, or disguise a face like a veil.

He'd been warned by Randolph that taking on an alias was not simply a matter of "changing clothes." He'd practiced things like speaking less properly— difficult at first but easier as he went along; eating without table manners—more fun than he could have imagined; frequently complaining and blaming others—something he found repugnant.

Since a very early age, he'd learned to control his uncanny memory, to hold it back, to stop the flood of thought that often threatened him. He lived with a database of images in his head that would have crashed a supercomputer. "Steel?"

He jumped.

Kaileigh had sneaked into the seat next to him.

"What do we do about you-know-who?" she said, screening her hand and pointing to the back, where Penny sat.

"I've been thinking about that," Steel said. "When in doubt, try the truth."

"*What?!*"

"My mother says that all the time."

"But we're sworn to—"

"Our secret society," Steel said, cutting her off, "is hazing us this weekend. We have to dress up and do weird things, and if we pass, then we're in."

"Ah . . ." she said, nodding. "That works for me."

"And no one can know about it, or we're out, so he's got to promise to leave us alone. 'Cause you know, the way he spies on everyone, I don't trust him."

"Who's going to tell him?" she whispered.

"Both of us. Right now."

"Okay. We're almost there. I agree."

The explanation to Penny went smoothly enough. Kaileigh stepped on Steel's attempt and took over and made Penny see how cool it was, and Penny nodded a lot and looked back and forth between the two of them.

"Well, I brought all my stuff along," Penny said, holding up a bulging backpack. "GPS. Radio-tracking. Listening devices. Video. I never go anywhere without this stuff, so if you need a hand . . . ?"

"Actually, I think that would disqualify us," Steel said.

"We shouldn't even be talking to you," Kaileigh said, glancing around. "We weren't supposed to talk to anyone on the ride."

"My lips are sealed." Penny pretended to zip his mouth shut.

"See you Sunday night, back on the bus," Steel said.

"Roger, that," Penny said. "I can't wait to hear what's up."

Steel and Kaileigh split up and returned to their seats. He thought that had gone quite well.

The bus pulled into the terminal. Everyone stood at once, fighting to get off first. Steel hung back, knowing his and Kaileigh's first stop was the public restrooms, where they would change their identities.

They wouldn't want any classmates hanging around when they came out looking like homeless kids. He was in no hurry.

A few minutes later, Steel was in a stall of the men's room, changing into the ratty clothes Randolph had provided for him. Kaileigh was doing the same thing on the other side of the cinder block wall. When he emerged from the washroom, his eyes drifted right past her on his first glance: she'd sprayed something into her red hair, making it look more brown and dirty; she wore a tight shirt—ripped at the shoulder—and another shirt beneath that, and still some other piece of clothing beneath the two. The shirts were soiled and torn, just like the tight blue jeans she wore with the knee torn out.

"Jeez!" he said, approaching her.

"You look like a cockroach," she said.

"I'll take that as a compliment." He'd smeared black and brown creams onto his face, arms, and hands, had mussed up his hair and parted it in the opposite direction. He'd smeared his eyebrows as well so they matched the soiled clothes he wore. The pants smelled sour, and the shirt was so foul that he winced as he caught a sniff of himself.

"I don't know what roaches smell like, but I think I *smell* like one too," he said.

They both carried backpacks that Randolph had warned might be searched. For this reason they divided fifty dollars between them, keeping it on their persons. Steel slipped thirty between his ankle and sock, and Kaileigh tucked the remaining twenty into the waistband of her pants.

"Your feet stink," she said.

"Yeah? Well you're no prize either. Let's go," he said. "That is, if you're ready, Your Highness?"

"Loser," she said.

He walked quickly, making sure she would follow him, not the other way around. He turned left out the door, able to visualize the map in his head. Kaileigh was about to challenge his sense of direction when she reconsidered. She hurried to catch up to him.

Some things were worth waiting for.

32.
ALL WELCOME

Steel stopped beneath the small sign that read: THE PA_L REVERE SHE_TER—AL_ WELCO_E.

He glanced over at Kaileigh. A light drizzle had been falling for the past ten minutes. She looked like a wet rat, her hair matted and tangled, her mouth turned down at the corners, her eyes sad. Her shirts were wet at the shoulders, and because of a misstep into a puddle, her sandals squeaked.

"You okay?" he asked.

"Hey, I'm terrific," she said, laden with sarcasm. "Don't I look it?"

"Brother and sister," he said.

"Don't remind me. I know this stuff so well I'm dreaming it."

"Okay, then." He pulled open the door. The first

thing that hit him was the smell of the place: a hint of lemon disinfectant mixed with the sweetness of cinnamon rolls and the animal-fat odor of gravy.

"Lovely," Kaileigh said. "Now I'm going to smell like you."

The room was big and noisy, with a wood floor and walls with old paint bearing poster art in wooden frames screwed into decaying plaster walls. A stack of folded cots crowded along the left wall while a dozen recycled-plastic picnic tables currently occupied the center of the room. A cafeteria counter had been erected against the far wall. A sad excuse for a television hung high in the corner and was tuned to a soap opera, the sound off.

A few dozen men and woman of all ages occupied fiberglass chairs at the picnic tables. Some were reading. Others played cards or board games, or dozed and snored. Not one of them looked up as Steel and Kaileigh entered. A handful of very young kids played with plastic toys under a sign that read, KIDDIE CORNER. The floor tiles in front of the men's and women's rooms showed signs of wear. It looked as if there was a second room filled with more cots.

"May I help you?" a tall thin man asked. He wore a ratty sweater and his face held kindness and concern, though it struck Steel as a practiced expression.

"Steven," Steel said.

"Kaileigh."

The man shook hands with them. "Welcome," he said. "I'm Gary. Are you hungry?"

"Always," Steven said.

"Not really," Kaileigh answered.

Gary motioned Steel toward the counter. "We serve snacks until seven. Dinner's at seven. We ask that all of our guests wash up before meals. There's no smoking, no gum chewing, no spitting or swearing or lewd behavior."

Neither said a thing.

"How old are you?" Gary asked.

Here came the tricky part. Randolph had been adamant about how to answer this. The thing was, Kaileigh could easily pass for several years older; Steel had a boyish face and was less confident about the lie. Randolph had explained that the lie would work in Steel's favor—the director of the shelter would want to keep the population down.

"Sixteen in February," he said, exactly as Randolph had told him to do. Boys liked to make themselves older.

"Seventeen," Kaileigh said. "I'm the older sister."

She smiled. "Though he doesn't like to admit it."

The brightness in the man's face dimmed. "Oh . . . I see."

"Is there a problem?" Kaileigh said.

"Well, yes, actually, there is. It's not my idea, believe me, but I'm afraid the state sets the maximum age limit at city shelters like ours at fifteen."

"But they're grown-ups," Steel said, indicating those at the picnic tables.

"They are. And it's a bit of a Catch-22," he said, checking their faces to see if they understood the reference, which neither did. "A contradiction," he said, "an oxymoron. We accept guests under fifteen when accompanied by a parent or guardian, and over eighteen—anyone over eighteen. But we're not a shelter for—"

"Teenage runaways," Steel said.

The man scrunched up his face and looked away from Kaileigh and Steel. "The state views transient adolescents as at-risk juveniles. You'll find this is true in thirty-eight of the fifty states. You are obviously new to our system, or, quite frankly, you wouldn't have come in here."

"What's it mean?" Steel asked, knowing what Randolph had told him. So far, the teacher had predicted things exactly as they'd happened.

"It means," Kaileigh said, "that Gary is going to report us."

"Is that true?" Steven said.

Gary made that adult face that said he was about to lie or exaggerate. Steel had learned to recognize the expression in his mother; his father was more difficult to read.

"It's a state law that children your age attend school. I'm sure you're aware of that. The state of Massachusetts has provided institutions to accommodate people your age to ensure that they receive the opportunity to continue their education."

"Juvenile detention," Kaileigh said.

"Not exactly." He was lying.

"You're going to report us?" Steel said.

"I'm required to file a report—a list of our guests—every forty-eight hours."

The truth! Steel had been warned to expect anything but.

"So we can spend the night?" Kaileigh asked.

"Certainly. Two nights. And get a few good meals in you." He viewed Steel. "And a shower." He eyed them curiously. "We can get you some clean clothes from Goodwill. We can even help you get in touch with your family."

"That's not going to happen," Steel said.

Gary nodded. He'd heard this enough times before. "The offer stands. Free phone calls to anywhere in the country. You just say the word."

"What does it cost?" Kaileigh asked, sounding as innocent as possible. "To stay here?"

The man's face glowed. "No, no, no. No charge!"

Kaileigh and Steel did their best to look surprised. Their efforts were convincing. Gary toured them around the shelter, orienting them: the bathrooms had showers, the second room with cots was the women's dormitory, meal times. He offered a few warnings, including to not try too hard to make conversation with the adult male guests—some could occasionally be violent.

"This is not a country club," Gary said. "You'll want to keep to yourselves for the most part, and watch each other's back. My advice is to trust no one, no matter how nice they may seem. People on the street . . . well, they learn all sorts of tricks to survive, and the young people, like yourselves, present particularly easy targets. It's one of the reasons special facilities are provided for our transient teens."

"Reform schools," Kaileigh said.

"No, actually," Gary replied, "not exactly. Minimum security juvenile facilities are designated solely for the criminally prosecuted. They're not bad at all, our juvie lockups. It's our transients—runaways—that present the state with a more difficult challenge."

"State custody," Kaileigh said.

"Social services," Steel added.

Gary looked at them gravely. He seemed to be warning them that if they stayed too long they would be swallowed up by a system ill prepared to deal with them.

"Don't hesitate to contact me if you need anything or have any questions. You're welcome here, but do be careful."

Steel felt a chill. Gary left them by the restrooms. Steel was eager to clean up. An hour of smelling bad and wearing filthy clothes had proved too much.

Kaileigh spoke in a whisper. "Mr. Randolph could have written that guy's lines. That went about exactly as he said it would."

"Yeah, kind of creepy." In fact Steel wondered how Randolph could have possibly gotten it so right. Was Gary some kind of ally of Randolph's? he wondered.

"Clean-up time?" she asked, indicating her disgusting clothes.

"Yeah, definitely."

When Steel got out of the shower, he found a pile of clean clothes left for him, presumably by Gary. He tried them on, and they fit surprisingly well. He transferred the thirty dollars from the dirty sock into his pocket—his only belongings—and threw the dirty clothes into the trash.

Kaileigh took longer than he, but eventually came out of the women's room looking much better. Only the weird hair color remained. He couldn't believe how it so radically changed her looks.

They kept to themselves, as Gary had suggested. Steel beat her in three straight chess matches—there were few people who could beat him at chess, because he'd committed to memory the strategies and moves of the world's chess champions. He read a newspaper while she watched one of the soaps. The late day dragged on. They both kept watch for the person Randolph had told them to look for.

The later the day grew, the more convinced they became that they would fail the most important part of the assignment. Randolph had warned them about impatience, had made it clear that this was a big part of the operation, but Steel felt himself edgy and antsy by the time dinner was called.

33.
A SAFE PLACE

Dinner was ham, peas, and bread, as good or better than a Saturday night mystery meal at Wynncliff. Steel and Kaileigh ate by themselves at a small table in the corner.

"Don't look now," Kaileigh said, her attention fixed on her plate, "but everyone's staring at us."

"I noticed," Steel said.

"What's with that?"

Steel stole a few glances around the room, and finally overhead.

"Duh! We're sitting directly under the TV"

"Jeez. Talk about stupid. We're asking for it," she said.

"Just look natural."

"Yeah, right," she said. She slid the ham around the plate.

"You aren't going to eat that?"

"How can you eat? I am *way* too nervous," she said.

"Because?"

"The thirty creeps staring at us wouldn't have anything to do with it," she snapped. "Neither would the fact that we're on a mission we don't even understand, but if we don't succeed we're no longer in the Program. Maybe no longer at Wynncliff."

"Yeah, but being nervous about it isn't going to help."

"You sound like Mrs. Kay."

He noticed that Kaileigh never spoke about her parents the way other kids did. She always referred to her governess, her nanny. He felt sorry for her. Even though his father traveled a lot of the time, Steel treasured his family and his dog, Cairo, and wondered what it must be like for the men and women in this room, and even Kaileigh, to live without that. The worst part of being homeless, he decided, was not being poor, but being separated from your family.

"We ought to do something to cheer them up," Steel said.

"Yeah, right." She laid on the sarcasm.

"You think I'm kidding?"

"Note to Steel: you'd better be kidding. We're supposed to keep a low profile, remember?"

"And where's the best place to hide?"

She shook her head. "Please . . ."

"In plain sight," he said rhetorically.

"Please, do not do this." She leveled a look meant to stop him cold, but it only encouraged him further.

Steel set down his plastic fork.

"I'm begging you," she whispered.

Feeling himself the focus of attention, given his position immediately beneath the TV, and finding it impossible to determine if those in the room were staring at him or the TV, Steel stood.

"I have a proposal!" he said loudly into the room.

"Oh, gosh, no!" Kaileigh gasped under her breath.

If the group's attention had been on the TV, it was now squarely fixed on Steel.

"Would anyone here like to play a game of charades after dinner?"

The people, mostly old—at least over forty—looking tired and unkempt, with varying shades of bloodshot eyes and sallow skin, looked up at once. Steel had won their attention, though he was met with dumbstruck, confused expressions that seemed to say: Did he actually just suggest charades?

"Charades," he said, just in case anyone had missed his proposal. "We'll divide into teams."

One by one a few cautious hands went up. First, only a couple, and of those, none higher than shoulder height. But then, more and more, to where a full half of the group were willing.

"See?" Steel said under his breath to Kaileigh. "Stand up."

"What?"

"Stand up. You're a team captain."

"Am not!"

"Are too. There are four women in here. I've got a hunch I know which team they'll be on."

"This is a big mistake."

"Because."

"This is not lying low."

"Trust me," he said. He stepped behind her chair. Raising his voice, he said, "This is Kaileigh. I'm Steven. We're team captains. I'm choosing first."

And so, over the next few minutes, those in the room wanting to play were divided into two teams. They moved to opposite corners and, writing on napkins, noted the titles of books, movies, and songs intended to stump the other team from being able to act out the title.

This was where it got tricky: despite their

dogged, end-of-the-rope appearances, many in the group were obviously smart; several were well-read; more than a few knew each and every film title mentioned. And as the game began, the competition among them was unleashed. To Steel's surprise, the players rallied, jeering at the opposition when an impressive time was delivered, cheering in self-congratulations when a title was guessed correctly. Kaileigh's team, consisting of three women and five men, took the early lead and never relinquished it, but that did nothing to deter the effort of each member of Steel's team.

Somewhere in the middle of the twenty-minute competition, Steel caught a glimpse of Gary. Arms folded, he was leaning against the far wall of the room, a mixture of astonishment and appreciation on his face. He seemed to be directing this all onto Steel, silently congratulating him. Or maybe it was more a look of curiosity, or even warning. The more often Steel glanced over at the man, the more confused he felt. Gary seemed to be *studying* him, *examining* him, *evaluating* him, which only led Steel to further suspect that the shelter's director was somehow tied to Randolph. But if so, then why had he and Kaileigh lied to get inside?

With the first round going to Kaileigh's team, a

second round was proposed. Not only did all those involved elect to play again, but several of the shelter guests sitting on the sidelines joined in, bringing the teams to ten people on a side, a nearly unmanageable size. Another hour passed, as lively as the first.

It was near the end—with just two players to go, one on each team, and the scores incredibly close—that Steel caught Kaileigh making hand signals from her chair. He nearly called foul, believing she was coaching the current player, only to realize she was signaling him. She motioned to her eyes and then, screening her hand, indicated the area of the room behind her and to her left—the same place where Gary had been watching. He was about to nod, to tell her he was way ahead of her, when he bothered to actually look where she was pointing.

Gary was there, leaning against the wall, as casual as before. But there was now *a woman* there as well. Nicely dressed, with neat dark hair and a pretty face—*the exact description Randolph had provided*. She and Gary were engrossed in conversation, the way teachers sometimes talked between themselves.

Steel caught a slight shake of the head from Kaileigh, and he looked away, not wanting to be caught staring. He returned his attention back to the game, though he locked eyes briefly with Kaileigh. Their training in "urban surveillance" was about to be tested.

The game of charades came to a close. Steel had lost track and wasn't even sure who'd won. A few of the homeless guys patted him on the back. A couple others suggested they play again the following night, an idea that was roundly supported. Steel and Kaileigh had made friends of themselves. Even those who hadn't actually played the game had most definitely taken notice of its two organizers. Sentiment seemed generally supportive, but there were also evil-eye looks of disapproval and outright suspicion and contempt. "How dare you challenge the routine of this place," several seemed to be saying.

"Okay," said Gary, moving into the center of the room. "We're going to put a movie on for anyone who wants it."

The sound of a single person clapping came from the dark corner over by the entrance to the men's room. It was slow, heavy-handed clapping, sarcastic and attention-getting.

The person responsible was a man roughly the size of a refrigerator. He wore a shirt with no sleeves, his arms covered in tattoos, a soiled bandana around his head, and a peevish look of disgust on his face.

He was looking at Steel—maybe had been for some time.

"On with the flick," he said. "Enough with the babysitters' club."

"Lyle!" Gary said, admonishing him. "Cool it."

Lyle and Steel shared a silent moment. It was clear he'd made himself an enemy—a big enemy, at that. Randolph had warned him to lie low, and now he thought he knew why.

Shelter curfew was 12:00 a.m. Past midnight, you were refused admission and on the streets for the night, this to discourage drunks and druggies from overrunning the place. A new world for Steel.

His chest tightened as he considered all that had to be done over the next several hours: follow the woman, identify any kids associated with her, attend the Halloween party, steal their way into the hotel suite. Did Randolph really expect them to pull this off? Maybe it was all a lie: some kind of test. Could they make it back to the shelter by midnight, or did that no longer matter? Steel was supposed to call Randolph once safely inside the suite. No plans had been made for what he and Kaileigh were supposed to do after the phone call.

Steel suddenly wondered: *Why not?*

34.
PURSUIT

Steel and Kaileigh took advantage of a particularly compelling scene in the movie to sign out, grab their backpacks, and leave the shelter. They'd been taught to get ahead of their surveillance subject so it didn't seem as if they were following the person. With two of them, they could split up into two different taxis, playing lead-and-chase the way they'd been instructed.

Steel was to commit the license plate of the woman's car to memory. If they lost the car—a Volvo, they were told—they were to phone or text Randolph the plate number and await instructions.

At the moment, the plan didn't matter: the traffic outside the shelter was bumper to bumper, and there wasn't a taxi in sight. They moved away from the shelter's entrance, stopping at a storefront long since boarded shut.

"Never seen so many cars," Steel said.

"We could walk faster than they're moving."

"Then that's what we'll do," Steel said, agreeing. "And if you see a cab, take it. We'll split up at the next intersection."

"GPS tracking would be easier." The boy's voice came from behind them.

They spun around on the balls of their feet.

"Penny?" they both exclaimed nearly simultaneously.

Pennington Cardwell III bowed from the waist. "At your service."

"But we said—"

"Not to bother you," Penny finished for Steel. "You know how tempting it is when someone says something like that? You think I could possibly *help myself*?"

The two kids were speechless.

"Now, I'm assuming from what I just overheard that following some car is part of your hazing," Penny said. "Correct?"

"I . . . ah . . . we . . . The thing is . . ." Kaileigh stammered, trying to think of what to say.

"Yeah. A woman," Steel explained. "Probably some

upperclassman's mother . . . but that's the drill."

"It's kind of . . . well . . . it's like a treasure hunt or scavenger hunt," Kaileigh added clumsily. "She works with these kids, and we have to take pictures of the kids. Depending how soon we do it, we get more—"

"Points," Steel said.

"Points," she echoed.

"It's a bunch of places and people and stuff," Steel said, continuing the lie.

"And if we get it right," Kaileigh continued, "then we have a chance to join the group we told you about."

"And you can recommend your friends," Penny said, for this had been a major part of their story.

"Absolutely!"

"How did you find us, anyway?" Steel asked, though his accusing tone bordered on rudeness.

Penny pointed to his head, suggesting his smarts. He then pointed over his shoulder, indicating his backpack. "Listen, dude, I've got enough gear in here to . . . well, like I said . . . to do *anything*. How 'bout I slip a little GPS transmitter on your friend's car, and you can follow it all night long?"

Steel and Kaileigh conferred with a glance. Kaileigh shrugged.

"Rules are we have to do this by ourselves," Steel said. "Maybe another time, man."

"Rules are made to be broken, dude. I can make this like, way easier on you."

"Sorry," Steel said. "Can't do it."

"How does it work?" Kaileigh asked Penny, winning an angry look from Steel.

"It's a Web-based GPS tracking system," Penny said. "What kind of cell phone do you have?"

"An iPhone," she said.

Steel nodded. "Me too," he said.

"So I put this box on the lady's car and give you the URL—the Web link—and she'll show up on a moving map."

"No way!" Kaileigh said.

"Way. Simple as that," Penny said. "I don't have to be part of the picture."

"And you would do this because . . . ?" Steel said.

"Because I want you to recommend me to this secret society. I help you, you help me."

Kaileigh looked seriously tempted.

"We're supposed to do it a different way," Steel said.

"But we could use Penny's thing as backup, couldn't we? No one said anything about backup." Kaileigh arched her eyebrows.

"It's yours if you want it," Penny said. He slipped the backpack off his shoulders and rummaged inside, past a laptop and a dozen other devices all tangled in a million wires.

"It's not like there are a lot of empty taxis around," she said, accepting a small gray box from Penny. She turned it over, examining it.

"It's magnetic. It'll stick most anyplace on a car." He scribbled out a Web address, tore off a piece of notebook paper, and handed it to Kaileigh.

"I have the bus routes memorized," Steel said. "Maybe we can follow her using the buses."

"Dude," Penny said, trying to sound cool, which wasn't an option. "That is so random. Use the GPS, I'm telling you."

The shelter's front door swung open, a half block away.

The three kids immediately jumped into shadow. Steel peered around the edge of a shop window and then felt Penny coming up over his back, also trying to get a look. Steel elbowed Penny in the gut, trying to let him know whose assignment this was.

The woman walked briskly away from them, down the sidewalk. She stopped alongside a car.

A Volvo, four-door sedan, silver. The model number was on the trunk: *S40.* The car's taillights blinked twice as she unlocked the car with a remote. Steel memorized the plate number.

There was no time for discussion. The Volvo poked its front wheels out into traffic, but the other cars remained tightly grouped, not allowing it in. Vehicles jockeyed for position amid the swirling sour exhaust and a cacophony of car horns.

"Okay," Steel said, grabbing the gray box from Kaileigh, "I'm going to get this onto the car somehow while you switch to the other side of the road and get as far out in front of the Volvo as possible. There's a bus stop"—he paused, squinting—"two blocks up."

They all tracked the Volvo as it finally found its way into the clog of traffic.

"There's no way she's going straight at the next light," Penny said. "She's going to turn right. Kaileigh will need a different bus line." Steel was about to challenge him, but Penny said, "This is my town."

Steel squinted. "Okay. Go right. The bus stop is three blocks ahead."

"Key in the URL," Penny instructed. "Call Steel when you see it's working." He reached across and into Steel's hands, and he pushed a button on the box.

"Go!" Steel said.

Kaileigh took off across the street.

Steel hurried up the street, keeping to the shadows, and got five stopped cars ahead of the Volvo. He ducked down and waited and, as the Volvo pulled past and stopped again, scooted behind it, ducking to avoid the car's mirrors. The driver behind the Volvo honked loudly at Steel, but Steel dropped out of sight, reaching under the car and feeling the box take hold. He stole through the opposite row of cars and stayed down until the Volvo was well past.

When he stood, he looked across for Penny.

The boy was gone.

His phone rang, and he swung his backpack off and answered his cell.

"It's working!" Kaileigh said excitedly. "There's this dot moving on the map."

"Penny vanished," Steel said.

"You may not see him, but he's probably there somewhere," she said.

"That's what I'm afraid of."

Kaileigh passed the URL on to Steel, and the two of them followed the car for the next twelve minutes, with Steel using the city bus map in his head, to keep them both within distance of the Volvo.

Steel ran two full city blocks at an all-out sprint and boarded his third bus, eastbound on Commonwealth Avenue, a large street that paralleled the Charles River. He looked to the back of the bus, and there, as expected, was Kaileigh smiling back at him. Reuniting with her felt particularly satisfying, and confirmed the importance of everything Randolph had made him memorize.

A quarter mile later, out ahead, the Volvo turned into a driveway and disappeared behind an old building. Kaileigh and Steel disembarked from the bus two long blocks later and returned on foot.

Steel's phone rang, and he answered, half expecting it to be Randolph congratulating them. He half expected that this was some sort of test, not an operation at all.

"Steel!" Penny's voice. "A big guy? Tattoos? Scarf on his head?"

Steel cupped the phone. "It's Penny. He's asking about that guy Lyle."

Kaileigh clearly couldn't place the name.

"Lyle!" said Mr. Memory. "The big guy at the shelter?"

Kaileigh looked panic struck.

"What about him?" Steel asked into the phone.

"He came out of that place like his pants were on fire. He got on a motorcycle and took off."

"Penny, exactly how would you know this?"

"I said I wouldn't bother you two, not that I wouldn't check stuff out."

"Penny . . . if we get caught, none of us will get into this secret society."

"Understood," he said. "Which is why I thought you might want to know about the dude on the motorcycle."

"Yeah . . . okay . . ." Steel didn't have a smart retort for him. "Listen, we appreciate the GPS thing, but—"

"Yeah, yeah," Penny said. "I get it." He hung up.

"Lyle may be following us. Or trying to," Steel told Kaileigh, correcting himself.

"What do we do?"

"Stay ahead," Steel said. "How else do you win?"

A dead and unkempt lawn spread out in front of the rundown building, offering few places for them to hide.

"We need to get a closer look," he said.

"Let's not do anything stupid," Kaileigh said.

"It's a little late for that."

35.
ONE OF THE GOOD DAYS

Taddler, sprawled across the SUV bench that was pushed up against the wall, used a blue marking pen to effect deep semicircles under both eyes of the white hockey goalie mask. He held the mask out at arm's length and examined his work approvingly.

"Come on!" said Johnny, dressed as a Harry Potter schoolboy in a black robe, looking a lot like Draco Malfoy, with a Quidditch broom, white hair, and sullen eyes.

"Cool it," Taddler said, working with a black marker to enhance a scar on the mask. "It's got to look right. We can't all be altar boys."

"I'm not an altar boy. Shut up."

"Boys! You must hurry," said Mrs. D., rebuking Johnny for his pestering. "The traffic is horrible."

Taddler couldn't believe Mrs. D. was actually going to give them a ride in her car. It was a first for the Corinthians, and one he was proud to have been chosen for. The other boys were envious, which was all that mattered. The competition within the boathouse was for Mrs. D.'s attention, and little else.

The arrangements for her to drive them had been hastily put together—she'd arrived only minutes before to tell them of the change in plans—a water main break had closed the bus line west on Commonwealth. Taddler, who'd waited until the last minute to prepare his costume, found himself caught off guard. A Halloween costume shouldn't be rushed. He didn't appreciate being hurried. He too donned a robe, and thought it amazing that, although he and Johnny shared the robes as part of their look, Johnny came off as a choirboy, while the disturbing hockey mask turned Taddler into a homicidal maniac.

"Your tickets," Mrs. D. said, handing them to the two boys. Several boys were missing. Taddler assumed they were already at the Armstrad Hotel; Mrs. D. had said that one way or another, all the boys would be involved with this job.

3rd Annual Halloween Charity Event for Autism!
Tenright, Templeton & Lawrence read the ticket. A law

firm was sponsoring the event, and Mrs. D. had apparently donated the $75.00 per ticket. Three hundred kids at a Halloween "extravaganza" at the Armstrad. There were supposed to be gift bags, candy, and games for the kids, and a silent auction for the adults. It sounded stupid to Taddler—*boring*—but the point wasn't the fundraiser; it was the job once they were inside. Mrs. D. had obviously gone to a good deal of trouble, so Taddler put down the markers and paid attention.

"You look wonderful," she said. "That is," she corrected herself, seeing Taddler's disappointed face, "appropriate to the occasion. We mustn't be late. Your marks—the boy and girl—will likely be some of the last to arrive, but no use taking chances." She checked her watch and gasped. "Let's get a move on."

She took in the remaining four boys. "You will prepare the river escape as planned. . . ." Taddler had heard nothing about any such plan. "And keep your ears to the ground. If you hear from me, it can mean only one thing."

"Yes, ma'am," a boy said.

"And those of you standing guard, you're to stay on heightened alert."

"Yes, Mrs. D.," said another.

She motioned to Taddler and Johnny, and they stepped in behind her and followed her out of the building through a labyrinth of hallways and into air the color of charcoal. Johnny squared his shoulders, proud to be one of two boys allowed to ride in her car.

He sighed happily. This was one of the good days.

36.
A BOOST UP

Steel and Kaileigh had just sneaked up to the side of the old crumbling boathouse when the driveway was washed in glare from head and taillights.

"Car!" Kaileigh said, pointing.

They were trapped in the driveway. Too far from the street to make it there without being seen. Nowhere to hide.

Steel didn't have to look up: he already had an image of the building filed in his head: five recessed windows and, above those, another three on the top floor. A slate stone roof. Three chimneys. An old television antenna, looking prehistoric. Some of the glass panes in the windows had been replaced by pieces of plywood.

"Lose the backpack and give me your foot," he

said, dumping his own backpack behind a rusted trash can.

"What?"

"Your foot!" he whispered sharply, stepping forward with cradled hands.

He stripped Kaileigh of her backpack and hoisted her. She pulled herself up, surprisingly gracefully, and scrambled onto the window ledge. He wedged the toe of his running shoe into a crack between stones and made three tries to catch hold of the ledge. Finally he pulled himself up, though the effort was anything but graceful.

"Just in time!" Kaileigh whispered, the taillights now snaking down the drive.

The same Volvo backed past. Steel leaned out to see the driver—quite possibly the woman—one boy in the front seat, and a shadow of one in the back.

He turned around to look through a grimy window, into the boathouse. "What is this place?"

"What *was* this place?" Kaileigh asked. "A theater or something? I think the windows are all painted on the inside."

Some of the paint on the glass had cracked and peeled and flaked, creating peepholes through which they could see.

"Looks like a church," he said, "not a theater."

"It's old enough."

"And falling apart."

"But isn't that . . . ?"

"Light!" Steel said. "Yes! It is!"

Steel tried to force his fingers into a seam between the wrought iron. "I need a thin piece of . . . metal, or a knife . . . or something."

Kaileigh reached up into her hair and produced a hair clip. "Like this?"

He accepted the curved metal clip, impressed by how quickly she'd produced it. He slipped the clip into the window frame and moved it straight up, hearing a click. The window came open with a dull shudder of rusted hinges.

Kaileigh gasped, "Oh, no . . . you are not going in there!"

"Oh, yes," Steel answered. "Most definitely yes."

37.
THE BEST PLACE
TO HIDE

The air inside the boathouse was heavy with mildew. The bottom of the windowsill was six feet off the floor. Steel allowed his eyes to adjust, his mind snapping up images and storing them.

"Get back out here!" Kaileigh hissed. "This has *nothing* to do with the operation. We were told to—"

"Get a look at whoever's connected with the woman," Steel reminded.

"Meaning the two in the car with her."

"We don't know that." He snapped his head back into the darkness, then whispered at her. "Keep it down. I think I can hear people talking."

"I'm not going in there," she hissed. She crossed her arms in defiance but, by doing so, threw herself off balance. Steel grabbed her by the shirt just as she was about to fall off the ledge. He strained to hold her. She caught hold of the window frame and steadied herself.

"Nice move," he said.

"Shut up."

"And here I was thinking you might thank me."

"Don't hold your breath."

"There's some furniture stacked along the wall beneath me. I'm going to climb down. Are you sure you're not coming?"

She tried to peer inside. Then she looked behind into the dark yard. "Positive."

"Suit yourself."

"Help me down," she said. "I'm out of here."

"Don't go! I may need you. If you have to, you can jump."

"It's like a mile down there."

"Ten feet, tops. I'll tell you what: only jump if you hear me screaming."

"This is *not* part of the operation."

"Of course it is. The woman led us here, just as Randolph said. We need to know who's in here and get pictures if possible." He patted his pocket, indicating his iPhone and its camera.

"We were supposed to follow her."

"We have Penny's GPS thing. No worries. We can track her."

"I'm not hanging around."

"Don't go anywhere. Do not desert me."

"And what about Lyle? What if he shows up? What then?"

Steel didn't want to think about Lyle.

"If you go inside, and he shows up . . ." she said, "I'm jumping. I'm out of here."

Steel felt tempted to follow through with his plan, to show her that he knew what he was doing. The problem was that her reasoning made too much sense. Being right wasn't nearly as important as *doing* right, and he had a feeling she was right.

"Okay," he said. "We'll follow the car."

Kaileigh swelled with pride.

But just then, something moved deep inside the room. Steel pressed his finger to Kaileigh's lips to silence her as a faint shadow spread along the far wall, and the silhouettes of two boys appeared in the hall.

"It's not fair, her leaving us here," a boy's voice said. It was lower than Steel's—the boy was older by at least a year or two. Steel couldn't see their faces, and there wasn't enough light for the phone's camera.

"Who cares? Johnny and Taddler are the ones

gonna get busted if something goes bad. Not us. Doesn't bother me."

Johnny and Taddler, Steel noted. *The boys in the car?* The reference to getting busted could mean the fundraiser Steel and Kaileigh were supposed to attend.

"Yeah, but have you seen that place? I scouted it last week. Going to a party there? I'd do that."

Steel sensed the bigger of the two boys turning before he actually did. He wasn't sure if this was a result of his ga-ga training, or a sixth sense, or just blind luck. But a fraction of a second before the boy turned, Steel instinctively stepped back deeper into shadow to avoid being seen. As he did, his shoe crunched down on a piece of broken glass, and the sound echoed through the room.

Both boys turned toward the windows. His adrenaline pumping, Steel reached through the window and grabbed Kaileigh's arm and gave a subtle push, signaling her to jump.

She sprang from the ledge, and he heard her thud to the ground. She groaned as if she'd hurt herself.

"Hey!" one of the boys shouted.

Steel stepped through the window and onto the ledge, and eased the window shut, wondering if there'd been enough light for them to see him.

"Clear!" Kaileigh hissed.

He jumped and rolled and came to his feet. Kaileigh tossed him his backpack and they took off running, she with a slight limp.

"They'll come after us," he warned.

"I know."

"We need to follow the Volvo."

"Duh! Never heard that before!"

They'd put fifty yards between themselves and the boathouse, but looking back, Steel saw several boys coming after them.

"I count four," he said to Kaileigh.

"Do we split up?" she gasped between breaths.

Randolph had instructed them: *Establish a rendezvous. Divide the pursuit.* Steel didn't like the thought of separating from Kaileigh, of risking her being caught by the boys behind them. But her bad ankle was slowing them down.

"The river," he said. He could make out a running path down the sloping lawn, like a ribbon along the edge of the water. There were dozens, maybe a hundred or more people walking in both directions, jogging, Rollerblading beneath the lamps that lined the path. Another two people mixed in would be difficult to spot. The string of boathouses, for there were five or six in a row, offered possible places for them to hide, but Steel thought it wise to keep moving. Again, he looked back. One of the boys was exceptionally fast and had gained on them.

"At the next building," he said breathlessly, "you keep going toward the running path. I'm going to peel off."

"No."

"Do it! Trust me."

They reached a line of big old trees, leaves crunching beneath their shoes.

"I'll catch up," he said, sliding like a baseball player into home plate directly behind the next tree trunk. He listened carefully, awaiting the crush of leaves as his signal.

One . . . Two . . .

He dove out from behind the tree, caught the approaching boy's legs, and tackled him. The two rolled, and Steel recovered, immediately springing to his feet and taking off. The tackled boy was not nearly as fast getting up—stunned by the surprise of the attack, and sprawled out on the lawn. Steel took off at a sprint, hoping he'd bought himself and Kaileigh a few extra seconds.

"Over here! This way!" he heard the fallen boy call out.

Steel reached the path, and a quick glance told

him he'd succeeded—no one was behind him. He ran down the path, dodging his way between the late-evening strollers, amazed by the number of people. Thirty seconds later he caught up to Kaileigh.

Up the path, another boathouse was all lit up, its barnlike doors hanging open. There were people gathered outside—a team of oarsmen tidying up.

"There!" he said. "Past that boathouse we'll cut back up the hill."

"You sure?"

"Yes."

"We won't make it," she said. "They'll see us."

"And you have a better idea?"

"I do," she said. "Where's the best place to hide?"

"Out in the open," he replied.

"I've been telling you this for . . . like . . . forever. The next bench. Right up there."

"What about it?"

She reached down and took his hand, slowed—the limp more apparent—and pulled him to the open bench with her. She pulled him close to her, pressing her body against his and directing his arm around her shoulder, and behind her neck.

"There's no faking this," she whispered, panting from the running.

She placed her lips to his and she kissed him, the

two of them gasping for breath in between the soft contact.

He'd passed other couples on benches, and some on the grass in the gray light of evening, wrapped up in a lovers' embrace. He hadn't given it a second thought. But he also hadn't seen himself as *one of them*.

The stampede of pursuing boys approached. Three of them, and a fourth trailing. Kaileigh tensed and clung to him even tighter, continuing the kiss.

Steel wanted to focus, wanted to remember things about the boys for Randolph, but the only thing he was going to remember was the light-headed feeling and warm sensation that overwhelmed him, the tingling of his lips and the sweet smell of Kaileigh's breath.

The boys ran past. Kaileigh kept kissing him, but began to laugh as the boys passed, and soon the two of them were hugging and laughing aloud, no one giving them a second thought—boyfriend and girlfriend on a park bench in Boston.

"You're . . . that was . . ." He pulled away, though reluctantly. His heart was about to explode.

Her eyes sparkled in the light off the water. Her lips twisted into a grin. He'd never seen her smile like that—like there was something amusing she wasn't about to share. She chuckled, but it was self-amusement, not meant for him. He had no tools with which to interpret it.

"You don't get it, do you?" she asked.

He stared at her, not knowing what to say.

"You really don't get it?" she said, amused all the more.

"Get what?"

She stood from the bench.

"We'd better hurry," she said. "Before they figure out they've lost us."

"Get what?" he repeated, still sitting on the bench.

She reached out her hand and pulled him off the bench. "Come on," she said.

They walked up the hill, hand in hand. He didn't know if they were still acting or not.

"What was I supposed to get?" he said. "Back there? What was so funny."

"Forget it," she said.

No way, he thought. He would never forget *that*. "As if," he said. "But what am I supposed to forget?"

"Oh, yeah. I forgot that you don't forget." She chuckled to herself again and hung her head, her chin to her chest. "Don't worry: you'll figure it out."

38.
STANDOFF AT THE STANDISH

Kaileigh and Steel walked on back streets, staying off Commonwealth, where a water main break had attracted a road crew. Steel kept watch for a motor-cycle's headlight, concerned that Lyle might be after them, but never saw one. He tried calling Penny, but got the boy's voice mail. He and Kaileigh rode a series of city buses, keeping an eye on the moving dot on their phones that represented the Volvo. Their destination was the party at the Armstrad Hotel, made all the more urgent when Steel realized the Volvo had stopped there—at least ten minutes ahead of them.

The two shared side-by-side seats, Steel feeling a need to fill the awkward silence that had settled between them. The kiss had changed everything.

"At least we know there are kids in the building," he said.

"Duh!" She sounded exactly the same. The same Kaileigh. But he was not the same Steel, and that seemed . . . unfair.

"The two guys I saw, they mentioned someone named Taddler and another named Johnny, so we've got two of their names. That's something."

"We're supposed to have their pictures. We're supposed to give DesConte and Reddie Long a way to spot them at the party." She couldn't take her eyes off the phone's moving map.

"When we get there," he said, "maybe we'll be able to spot them."

"How?"

"I got a look at the one in the front seat."

"How does that help DesConte?"

"How should I know?" he said, turning his head to avoid looking at her.

A motorcycle pulled up alongside the bus. The bus windows were coated with one-way advertisements; Steel could see out, but no one could see in.

"Cripes!" he said. "It's him!"

Kaileigh scrambled to lean across him. Steel leaned back, but the contact made his head spin once again.

"How could he have followed us?" she said, apparently not noticing she was lying on him.

"Not important," he said, reverting to Randolph's training. "We need to lose him. We can't let him follow us to the hotel. I'll keep the moving map going. You Google Boston hotels and find one near the Armstrad."

"Because?" she said as she sat back up. She sounded condescending, but her fingers were already busy with her phone.

"Because I have a plan," he said. "An *exit strategy*."

"And do you *plan* to share it with me?"

"We need a place to change into our costumes, and we need Lyle . . . detained. Delayed. *Whatever*. You find me a hotel near the Armstrad and—"

"The Standish," she said, showing him her phone. "Less than a block away."

"Perfect."

"Thank you."

He accepted her phone, read the address, and then, using his recall, determined where to get off the bus.

"This is going to work," he said.

"Note to Steel," Kaileigh said. "The Standish is a nice hotel. Four stars, it says here. You and I look like Goodwill models."

"We have our invitations to the Armstrad that Randolph gave us. That's all we need." He added, "That, and a little fast talking."

"That would be my department."

"That would be correct," he said. Having counted the blocks, he reached up and tripped the cord that signaled the driver to stop at the next stop.

"It might help if I knew what we were doing."

"We're going to run to the front door," he informed her. "And you're going to be winded, and you're going to explain that some creep has been following us. We've made a mistake and we're at the wrong hotel. You'll show him the invitations. We need a place to change, and we need someone to take care of the creep."

The bus slowed and pulled over to the curb, half a block from The Standish Hotel.

Beneath the bus interior's odd-colored tube lighting, Kaileigh looked at Steel with something bordering on respect. "That's good," she said. "That's *real good.*"

"No charge," he said. He pressed his face to the

glass. "Lyle pulled over at the corner. He must know we're in here."

"I'm scared," she said, grabbing his hand.

"Stay close," Steel said. "We can do this."

The bus doors swung open. Together they took off at a run, Kaileigh limping slightly. As they neared the front of the hotel, the doorman sized them up and apparently didn't like what he saw. He stepped in front of them.

"May I help you?"

"We're here for the Halloween party," she said, thrusting the invitations into the doorman's gloved hands and speaking absurdly fast. "There's some guy following us. A creepy guy on a motorcycle. You've got to help us, please! We've got our costumes."

"This is The Standish!" the doorman said. "You want the Armstrad."

"There's the guy," Steel said, pointing back down the sidewalk.

Lyle saw him and turned around and started walking away from the hotel.

The doorman was puzzled.

Kaileigh said, "Could we maybe change into our costumes here, and you could maybe keep that creep out?"

"I don't know, miss."

"Please," Steel said. "We'll go straight to the Armstrad the minute we're changed."

"Thing is," the man said, "you're not allowed in The Standish without a key card, a reservation, or in your case, an adult. Hotels have been having trouble with kids. You want me to call our security guys, I will." He seemed to be offering them a chance to change their minds.

". . . *trouble with kids*," Steel heard ringing in his head. What, if anything, did that have to do with this operation? he wondered.

"Please," Steel said. "By all means call security. Maybe they can help with this creep."

The doorman used a radio clipped to his belt. "Randy, front. Security to the entrance, please."

Randy the red-coated doorman led them inside. The lobby was marble and red velvet and there was a chandelier the size of a car hanging from the thirty-foot ceiling.

An older guy wearing a suit approached and conferred with the doorman.

"I'm sorry," the man said, moving to Kaileigh. "We have established rules for the admittance of minors. I'm sure you understand?"

"And if this creep following us, gets her?" Steel said. "That'll make some kind of news story."

"I'd like to help you—"

"But you think it's a scam," Steel said.

The man's face reflected that Steel wasn't far from the truth.

"You can have someone guard the girls' room. You can watch me change, for all I care. Once we're in our costumes, we'll leave, I promise. But if one of your guys goes outside, you will see the biker dude. We're not making this up, I promise. Check out our backpacks—the costumes are in there."

"I'm sure the Armstrad will accommodate your change of clothes. I'm sorry, but you have to leave."

"That's him!" Kaileigh whispered, spinning away from the entrance.

The security guy spotted Lyle. He reached for his radio.

Steel said, "How 'bout Randy at least lets us use a back door or something?"

The security guy eyed the kids suspiciously. He barked a code into the radio, and a man came from behind the registration desk, toward the front doors.

He nodded at Randy. "Take them out through the arcade. But make sure they're out, and that they don't return."

"Thank you," Steel said.

Lyle was stopped the moment he entered. He and Steel made eye contact across the vast lobby, and Steel felt a chill down to his toes.

"Follow me," Randy said.

39.
A PAIR OF FREAKS

Kaileigh and Steel, wearing their Goodwill outfits, approached the entrance to the Armstrad Hotel amid a dozen other kids arriving in full Halloween costumes. They coat-checked their backpacks, presented their invitations, and were admitted into a dimly lit mezzanine ballroom decked out like a haunted mansion. There were crazy mirrors, crystal balls, projected ghosts flying across the tray ceiling, orange-and-black streamers, and a full complement of party favors on every table. Two hundred people, mostly kids, milled about the ballroom, moving between amusement booths, fortune-telling and balloon tying.

Steel took in every costume, committing each and the person wearing it to memory, and hoping to see past the masks in an effort to identify the boy he'd seen riding in the Volvo's front seat. He'd had only a quick glimpse, and that glimpse a profile, so he wandered through the crowd trying to see people from the side, an effort often comical.

"Any luck?"

"Not so far."

"You realize," Kaileigh said, "that everyone's staring at us, wondering why we aren't in costume, and that if we are in costume, then we're the lamest effort of the night and probably stand a chance at getting 'worst dressed' or some similar honor we really do not want given to us since it'll only bring us attention that we also don't want."

"Yeah, I think I got that."

"Hey!" she said, grabbing his arm in a death grip with one hand while pointing with the other. "Isn't that . . . ?" Her voice trailed off.

"Who? What?"

"Never mind. I lost her. Too far away to tell. Couldn't possibly be anyway."

"Who?" he repeated.

"My bad," she said, refusing to tell him.

"A girl," he said, knowing this would explain her refusal to discuss it.

"Find the guy, Steel. Focus on finding the guy—that's what's important."

"Don't you think I know that?" he snapped defensively.

Kaileigh checked her watch, and then double-checked it against the time on her iPhone. "Our friends are going to make their grand entrance in about ten minutes."

"Don't do that: don't call them *our friends*."

"You'd prefer"—she lowered her voice—"*spies? Couriers? Operatives?*"

"*Friends* will do," he said, hating giving in to her.

"Thank you."

Hated her rubbing it in.

"Wait a second," he said as they approached the food and drink corner, an area of the ballroom packed as tightly as a rush hour subway car. Steel had caught the faintest of glimpses, but a glimpse nonetheless, of a boy who looked like the guy in the Volvo. Steel had had only a fraction of a second, spotting him deep in the crowd, shoved up against the food table. But he'd caught him in profile, where he could see what was behind the hockey mask. He could now cut and paste his own mental images and lay them side by side and, having done so, could see that it had to be the same guy.

"It's him," he said, "The kid from the Volvo."

"You sure?" Kaileigh sounded disappointed, or scared, or both.

"Positive? No. He's got a mask on. But if I can just . . ." He fumbled with the contents of his pocket, mumbling, "Camera . . . phone . . ." and, pulling out the iPhone, stepped deeper into the crowd. Kaileigh kept at his side, her phone now in hand as well, and she with the good sense to use it, taking random photographs of the various costumes. But Steel didn't think to create a cover for himself the way Kaileigh did, instead pushing his way toward the food table, raising the phone at the last minute, and snapping a shot of a big kid with a hockey mask—supposedly Jason Voorhees from the Friday the 13th horror movies. The mask was up, and the kid was stuffing his face with a green brownie. It was the lifting of the mask that allowed Steel a good look at the boy's face, and he no longer had any doubts.

Steel got off the shot, and another of the Hogwarts Quidditch kid standing with Jason. Checking both shots, and seeing they were good ones, he busied himself, head down, immediately e-mailing them to DesConte, as planned, painfully aware that he was late in doing so.

"Earth to Steel," Kaileigh said, elbowing him.

She continued taking pictures of the crowd.

Steel lifted his head, only to see the bruiser in the hockey mask coming toward him. His Hogwarts friend didn't stop eating for a second, unperturbed.

"What-a-ya doing?" Jason said, towering over Steel. The kid was as wide-shouldered as a doorway, tall and big-boned, reminding Steel of a lineman—Scott Tucker—from the Wynncliff football team.

"Excuse me?" Steel said.

"No pictures," growled the kid. "Mind your own business."

"I just like the costume," Steel said.

"Yeah?" The boy flipped down the mask, leaning toward Steel in a menacing pitch. "How 'bout now?" came his muffled voice. He hoisted a knife—plastic, hopefully—its ten-inch blade blackened with blood. Steel backed up and stumbled, and nearly went down.

The big kid laughed in a sinister way that sounded authentic.

"Stay away from me," he said. "And no more friggin' pictures!"

"Hey, leave him alone!" said Kaileigh, stepping between the two. "We're taking pictures for a school assignment."

"Yeah? Well, take them with you on your way

out," Jason Voorhees said. "I'll give you five minutes to get lost."

Kaileigh hooked Steel by the arm and led him away.

"Nice costume, by the way," the huge guy called after her. "Let me guess: Little Orphan Annie? You look more like a farm worker."

Kaileigh had a hand gesture that came to mind, but as she lifted her arm to deliver it, Steel caught her and pulled her arm down.

"I got the shots," he said.

"What a butt wipe," Kaileigh said, in a rare display of temper.

Steel wrestled free, worked the phone, and declared, "There! Got them both off to DesConte and Reddie."

"You suppose they're here somewhere?" she asked.

"I suppose," Steel said, looking around. "Thing is, we'd never know it."

Many of the costumes involved masks. Others hid their faces beneath face paint or makeup or fake facial hair.

"The sooner we change into our costumes, the better," Kaileigh said. "At least that way he won't recognize us."

"But not until we meet the marks," Steel said,

keeping his voice low. "You need to hear her talk, right?"

"Duh! I can't impersonate her without hearing her. I thought that was kind of obvious."

"What gave you the wedgie?" he asked. "Chill, dude."

"Sorry," she said. "That guy just bugged me."

"That guy works with the lady. He's the enemy. He's supposed to bug you. But you're not supposed—"

"*To show it.* I know. *To let it get to me.* I went through the same training as you, remember? But of course you remember, because you're you." She sounded disgusted with him, and he wasn't sure what he'd done to deserve it.

"Hey! Hey!" Steel said, under his breath. "Jasmine and Aladdin, two o'clock."

She wrenched her head to the right. "Finally," she said. "Okay, I do this alone. Give me two minutes."

"Showtime," he said.

She worked with her phone to activate RECORD. She slipped the phone into her shirt pocket but apparently didn't like the way it sagged, and took it back in hand. Then she headed off toward the two late arrivals, but stopped and turned back to Steel at the last second.

"The person I thought I saw," she said. "If you see her, you stay away. There's no reason for her to be here. It can only mean trouble. Tell me you'll stay away."

"What are you talking about?" he asked. "Who was it?"

"You'll know if you see her. Just stay away."

His curiosity provoked, Steel raised on tiptoe and began searching the room, looking for a girl—or had Kaileigh seen the woman from the shelter? That made more sense: they would definitely not want her to see them, in case she might remember them from earlier. But why had Kaileigh been so obtuse about it? Why not just tell him? Why was she suddenly playing games with him—and did the kiss have anything to do with her change in attitude?

His breath caught as a long aisle suddenly opened in the crowd, like the Red Sea parting for Moses. And there at the end of the aisle, in the midst of all the guests, on the far side of the room, appeared a pair of red-and-black running shoes—Wynncliff's colors—and white ankle socks that, when combined, added up to only one person: *Penny*. Never mind he wore some Zorro mask and a black cape, and was therefore difficult to recognize. Never mind the bandana tied over his head, hiding his hair, making it

360

all the more difficult to identify him. The shoes gave him away. Steel knew they were Penny's, and the discovery caused a flood of questions: What was he doing here? How had he gotten an invitation? How had he known about the party? Had he followed Steel and Kaileigh, or was he looking for them? Did Steel dare reveal himself to Penny, or should he hide? How to warn Kaileigh, who, with every step toward Jasmine and Aladdin, was now a step closer to Pennington Cardwell III?

Kaileigh reached the marks—the boy and girl dressed in Disney outfits—and started talking. Steel was glad to see this part of the operation progressing in spite of his discovery of Penny. He kept his head down and moved back into the tangle of guests to screen himself from Penny; maybe Penny hadn't spotted him or Kaileigh yet. That might work to my advantage, he thought.

Kaileigh turned and worked through the crowd to find him. Before he had a chance to speak, she was already talking.

"We got interrupted. I didn't get enough time."

"Penny's here," he said.

Kaileigh looked stunned. "What's that supposed to mean?"

"It means Penny's here."

"Duh! But *why?*"

"No clue."

"You think he followed us?"

"And just happened to have a Zorro costume in his backpack? No, I don't think so. I don't know."

"So what do we do?" she asked.

"I think this is what Randolph meant by 'a fluid situation.' I think it's like that: random."

"First Nell, then Penny."

"Nell!?" Steel barked too loudly.

"Hush! Yes, that's who I saw. Nell Campbell. She's dressed like Hope Solo, and she has an American flag painted on her face, but I'm pretty sure it's her."

"This is getting weirder by the minute. Has to be Randolph, right? His spies."

"Penny?"

"No, not Penny, but Nell for sure. She did everything but tell me she was part of all this." He thought it through. "Penny . . . I've got a feeling he's just tagging along thinking he might get invited into our secret society."

"Jason—Mr. Hockey Mask—gave us five minutes," Kaileigh reminded. "Time's running out. And somehow, a guy like that? I think he meant it."

"Of course he did," Steel said. "He's here to steal

the . . . you know," he said, aware of people all around them. "He doesn't want anyone like me around, who saw him with his mask up, saw his face."

"Have you seen DesConte or Reddie?"

"No, but if Nell and Penny are here, they can't be far away."

"This is a lot more crazy than Randolph said it would be," she complained.

"No kidding."

"Listen, if I'm going to imitate the girl, impersonate her, I need to hear her talk more. The guy did most of the talking. We need to go back together, and you've got to keep the guy busy while I talk to her."

"Ah . . . I'm not exactly the best talker."

"Yes you are."

"I am?"

"What's with you?" she said.

The kiss, he wanted to answer. One stupid kiss had totally messed him up, and he found himself doublethinking everything she said and did.

"Okay, so let's go talk to those two before we lose them," Steel said. "Then we can change into our costumes and head upstairs, and we'll be off the big dude's radar."

"Yeah, but think about it," she said. "He's here to steal the thumb drive, so he's watching those two, same as we are."

"But there's no choice," Steel said. "So we might as well get going before he screws everything up."

"I suppose."

Together they headed back toward Jasmine and Aladdin. As they drew closer, it was obvious Randolph had chosen them both in part for their height. Kaileigh matched evenly with the girl; Steel was only slightly shorter than the Russian boy.

Steel introduced himself to the boy and asked if he was from Boston. Kaileigh went to work on the girl, starting up a conversation about how much she loved Disney. The Iranian girl spoke with a thick accent but had a good command of English. She told Kaileigh she'd always wanted to go to Walt Disney World, and then peppered Kaileigh with questions when she found out Kaileigh had been there several times.

The Russian boy didn't speak as well. He asked if Steel followed the World Cup, and said he was bugging his father to take him to the competition in South Africa this summer. Steel tried to describe ga-ga, but he failed miserably. The boy evidently thought he was talking about babies.

Everything seemed to be going fairly well until Steel caught sight of Victor DesConte and Reddie Long—both choirboys, wearing the deep red robes from the chapel, and carrying choir books under their arms. No two boys could look any less like choirboys than these two.

DesConte moved stiffly, as if in a hurry, drawing Steel's attention somewhat to the right, where he picked up Jason Voorhees making a beeline toward him and Kaileigh. DesConte had spotted him too, and was running interference, trying to cut off the kid in the hockey mask before he reached Steel and rearranged his face for staying overtime.

"Peter, is that you?" DesConte said, striking Jason in both shoulders like two football players celebrating a touchdown. Steel didn't actually hear this; he read DesConte's lips—the movement of the human mouth long since committed to memory—and it was as if he could hear the conversation between the two.

The blow knocked Jason back a step. "What the . . . ?"

"North Atlantic hockey tournament?" DesConte said. "We played you guys in the third round."

"Wrong guy, choirboy." Jason Voorhees took a step forward. DesConte tried to block his way. Until that moment, Steel had considered DesConte to be the son of the Incredible Hulk, but the way Jason bumped him aside made him look like a wimp.

Steel saw Jason coming, and wasn't sure what to say. A second later, the boy blindsided them. He bumped into the Russian kid, stumbled, and pushed Jasmine into Kaileigh and, as he apologized to both, shot Steel a look that needed no translation: Steel was going to die for overstaying his welcome.

Kaileigh signaled Steel with her eyes, and the two said their good-byes and moved toward the front, where they'd checked their bags.

"Did you get enough?" Steel asked.

Kaileigh looked around to make sure no one was within earshot and, lowering her own voice, spoke in Jasmine's broken English, then in Farsi. If Steel hadn't seen the words coming out of Kaileigh's mouth, he would have sworn she'd tricked him by playing back what she'd captured with the recorder.

"That is freaky," he said.

"You're hardly one to talk," she said.

"So we're a pair of freaks."

She grinned at him. He liked that. Truth be told, right now he liked everything about her.

40.

MALFOY AND THE
PUNCH BOWL

Now filled to capacity, the party had escalated from a hum to a buzz. Taddler returned to the punch bowl, where Johnny continued to eat his way through everything the caterers put out. Johnny's lack of focus bothered Taddler; he seemed more interested in girls and food than the assignment.

Taddler grabbed his cape from behind and dragged him away from the food table.

"Hey! What the—"

"You're off-mission, dude," he whispered through his hockey mask.

"No I'm not, I'm . . . scouting. So . . . are we outta here?"

"No. They didn't have it on them."

"But I thought—"

"So did I," Taddler said, "but Mrs. D. was wrong, or the pass hasn't happened yet. I frisked them both. Nothing. So stop stuffing your face and keep your eyes on the two of them, because that's your job."

"Who put you in charge?"

"You have other ideas?"

"I'm just saying . . ." But Johnny got a look through the hockey mask at the beady eyes, and he cut himself off. "We're cool," he said.

"We are so *not* cool," Taddler said. "We're going to have to follow them, and I'm going to have bump them again, and that makes twice, which means they're going to be suspicious. So once it goes down, we're going to have to move fast. Mrs. D. wanted us out the front door, but now it's probably going to be the staircase drop."

"We practiced that. I'm cool with it."

"Stop saying that, would you? You are not cool with anything. It's tricky dropping that thing, and you gotta be there to catch it, and if we screw up and it bounces off the railing or something, then one of us has to go find it, and that's probably going to be you."

"Okay."

"We've got to know where everybody is, 'specially

any security guys, and that's your job, and I don't see you doing it."

"Lose the rash, dude. We're fine."

"I'm going upstairs now."

"I know . . . I know . . ."

"I've got the phone." Taddler was proud that they'd been given the phones, and was hoping to actually use them.

"I've got mine too." Johnny patted his pocket. But then, finally doing his job, he took a look around the big room, his eyes quickly lighting upon a familiar woman near the entrance, wearing a Buffy the Vampire Slayer costume. She wore a headband that held back her long hair, and she was talking to a tough guy in an old suit, who Johnny knew, absolutely knew, had to be a cop. She was pointing at him and Taddler.

"Dude, you'd . . . better . . . get . . . going." He hadn't meant for his voice to quaver, but there was no taking it back now.

Taddler followed Johnny's paralyzed stare, and recognized the woman from the giant tarot card on the outside of her store.

"The fortune-teller," he said.

Johnny's astonishment that Taddler could possibly know the woman registered as a wide-eyed gawk. "Dude?"

"I saw you," Taddler explained. "Tell me you didn't tell her about this job."

"I wanted to know if I was going to be one of the two picked by Mrs. D."

"You *told* her?"

"Only that I had a job to do and that it was kinda dangerous and—" But as Johnny heard his own words he realized how lame he'd been. "Oh, man . . . I didn't mean to."

"That's a cop she's with."

"Oh, *man*," Johnny moaned.

"You screwed us. You . . . totally screwed us!"

"You get gone," Johnny said. "I can lose the cop."

"I need someone to catch the thing when I drop it. I need *you*."

"I'm cool," he said. "Seriously, I'll be there."

"You are so not cool. If you cost me this chance, Johnny, you'd better not ever show your face at the boathouse again."

"I can do this," Johnny insisted.

"You'd better."

41.
IDENTICAL TWINS

By the time the elevator stopped on the fourteenth floor and the doors slid open, revealing the hallway, with its dark wood paneling, a lead cut mirror in a gilded frame looming above an antique side table that held a giant bouquet of fresh flowers, Steel's throat felt choked, and he found himself unable to speak. Although he'd practiced wearing the pigmented contact lenses, his eyes stung. The makeup he'd used to look more like Aladdin (and less like himself) made his face feel puckered. To make matters worse, he wore a gold turban, a vest over a baggy shirt, and puffy-legged pants, with faux-leather pointy-toed slippers that were supposed to look like genie shoes. But it wasn't the costume he found suffocating, it was their situation.

The hallway looked about a mile long. Halfway between the elevators and an exit at the far end stood two men in black suits, their backs to the wall on either side of a hotel room door. With each step, Steel and Kaileigh grew farther from the safety of the elevators and closer to the danger of the men, for, according to Randolph, these two were professional bodyguards whose job it was to keep the ambassador and his family safe. The ambassador's family included his daughter, and Kaileigh was now going to try to impersonate her—someone these two men probably knew well. The more Steel thought about it, the more foolish it seemed. Maybe he and Kaileigh were nothing but sacrificial lambs; maybe Randolph had other plans.

The problem, if there was one, wouldn't be a matter of disguise. Like the Iranian girl downstairs, Kaileigh wore a piece of brown silk pulled across to hide her face—with only her brown contact lenses showing. She wore a Jasmine wig, a Jasmine blouse, and Jasmine pants that puffed out like Steel's. At first glance, there was no telling the two apart.

Together, he thought, he and Kaileigh looked ridiculous, a situation that might play in their favor: it would be hard for the bodyguards to take them seriously. Maybe they wouldn't look very closely.

Kaileigh played it cool, offering a slight wave to the bodyguards. She kept her head down—her face covered by the gauze—as she rattled off something in Farsi, pointing to Steel's Aladdin. She'd introduced him. The two men smiled and nodded. Kaileigh and Steel stood there in front of the door. No one moved. It seemed to last a minute. Then one of the guards said something, and Kaileigh's dark contact lenses flashed at Steel as she began patting her costume.

The key. The guard had politely told her to use her card—a room key she didn't possess.

She said something back to him, throwing up her arms.

The guard nodded, reached into his pocket, and unlocked the door for them. He said something to Kaileigh as they entered, and she said something back, and the guard pulled the door closed. It clicked shut.

She called out "Hello?" in Farsi and waited for an answer.

Four doors led off the living room: a small bathroom and presumably three bedrooms. Randolph's intel had been good: they were alone in a luxurious living room with a gorgeous view of the city lights. A grand piano stood in the corner, accompanied by twin sofas, four comfortable-looking chairs, and enough potted plants to make a small jungle.

A giant flat-panel television on the far wall ran CNN. It sounded like another television was playing nearby.

"The safe!" Steel whispered, knowing there would be one in each of the hotel bedroom closets. They split up, Steel taking one of the bedrooms to the right, Kaileigh to the left.

"Over here," she called out only seconds later. She'd located a bedroom with a king-size bed and a man's dark suits hanging in the closet—the ambassador's bedroom. She pointed out the safe below a stack of folded shirts.

Steel had memorized birth dates, phone numbers, the numbers from national identification cards, and even driver's licenses for the ambassador and all his family. The safe used a four-digit combination, and Randolph had advised Steel to start with the month and date of family birthdays and eventually graduate to four-digit groupings of the ambassador's Iranian identification card.

He entered a variety of different combinations. The safe continued to beep at him, displaying: IMPROPER CODE . . . PLEASE TRY AGAIN.

The flat-panel TV was tuned to a financial

channel. The woman on the show was throwing out a series of numbers, confusing Steel.

"Mute that thing, would you?" Steel asked. Kaileigh found the wand and silenced the television.

The bedside phone rang, along with every phone in the suite. They stared at it, but did not answer. Steel turned back to the safe.

On his sixth try—the last four digits of the ambassador's identification card—the safe opened. Inside were passports, some cash, jewelry, and a gray thumb drive.

"Got it," Steel said, emerging from the bedroom. "Computer?"

"In here," Kaileigh said, having found and started up a laptop in the kids' bedroom. The TV was tuned to the Disney Channel.

The thumb drive was highly encrypted—requiring six groups of four combinations of letters and numbers, like software registration codes—but Steel had been told to expect this, and went about inputting the first of six possible code keys that Randolph had explained they'd intercepted in the string of e-mails that had put them on to the exchange in the first place. The first two failed, but the third took, and the thumb drive's directory appeared.

Less than a minute later, Steel's eyes were trained

on the laptop screen as he scrolled down one page at a time, information captured in his brain like taking a series of photographs. Page by page he stored the data, moving remarkably quickly through the first two sizable files.

Six files to go . . .

He felt the clock ticking, the passing time working against him.

"Steel?" Kaileigh said, her voice a combination of demand and insecurity.

"Not now."

"Yes . . . now," she said, moving to the bedside end table and grabbing the television wand.

Steel mentally marked where he'd left off and turned to face her.

A face looked back from the TV screen. It was Penny's.

She punched the mute button, and they caught him midsentence.

". . . my suite friends. I tried calling you . . ."

Steel patted his pocket, as did Kaileigh. Steel had brought his cell phone with him because he was supposed to call Randolph, but he had it on vibrate and had somehow missed it ringing.

"He means the hotel room," she whispered. "That was *him*, just now."

"Hopefully you can hear me. If you can, you know that only I could figure out to hijack the hotel's TV system, so you'd better trust me. Just trust me, okay? I'm on your side. There was a scene down here. Your *magical friends*," he said with emphasis, "are heading your way. So is Mr. Motorcycle. You have like, three minutes. Do not, repeat, do not, use the elevators." His image jerked, and Penny said, "A little gift for you."

"Our side?" she said, as the screen changed to a four-way display, divided into quarters.

"Yeah, I caught that too, believe me."

It took them both several seconds to understand that Penny was showing them views from various security cameras. The upper left revealed the real Aladdin and Jasmine riding in an elevator. The upper right showed Jason Voorhees and Malfoy in another elevator. Upper right showed . . .

The choirboys, DesConte and Reddie, *also* in an elevator.

The screen's lower left frame displayed a long view of the fourteenth-floor hallway shot from the direction of the elevators and, next to it, a shot looking at the hallway from the other direction: toward the elevators.

The bodyguards stood by the living room door.

"They're on the sixth floor . . . seventh . . . We've got to go," she said, her voice rising in terror.

"No. I'm going to try to finish up here." He fished out his phone and handed it to her. "Quick: call Randolph! Tell him it's thrust technology detailed on the thumb drive and ask him what we're supposed to do."

"It's *what*?"

"Thrust technology. Just tell him. Now!" Steel turned back to the screen and began scrolling again. Kaileigh made the call, but Steel paid little attention.

His eyes shifted from the laptop to the TV, where he saw the elevator information overlaid: the costumed kids were on the ninth floor. The doors opened, and no one boarded. Jason Voorhees, on the adjacent screen, also stopped; again, no one boarded his elevator car—currently on the third floor.

Penny was somehow overriding the elevators and causing them to stop on every floor to buy Steel time.

Steel sped up the pagination, careful to advance to the next screen only once he was certain he'd seen enough to memorize. The third file was short, and he got through it quickly. The fourth file was a PDF document of engineering plans—nozzle specifications. He had to view these a few seconds longer in order to catch every detail, but there were far fewer of them and he was into the fifth, and then the sixth file before Kaileigh returned to the room.

She waited for Steel to acknowledge her.

"He said to flush the thumb drive down the toilet," she said.

"What?"

"I know. We weren't supposed to take anything—to *steal* anything—and I started to say something about it, and he said how making something go away and taking it are different. He said to 'crush it and flush it.'"

"He said that?"

"Those words: 'crush it and flush it.'"

"Well . . . I suppose . . . if it's actually secret stuff and it gets lost, it's different than us stealing it. But I don't know . . ."

"We are stealing it," she said. "It's in your head."

Steel turned back to the laptop and committed the last few pages of data to memory. "It is now . . ." he said.

On the television, the Iranian girl and the Russian boy reached the fourteenth floor and stepped into the hallway, showing up on both the lower quadrants. They walked steadily toward the guards.

"Okay . . ." Steel said, "now we're cooked."

"We are so dead," she said.

Steel took in the television and tried to concentrate.

"We're trapped!" Kaileigh said, her fear turning to panic.

"No . . ." Steel ejected the thumb drive and removed it. It sat in his hand—so tiny and almost insignificant that it was difficult to see it as something important to the government. He knew that in the real world there were spies, and despite the fact that his father fought a kind of war against them, and who knows what Kaileigh's parents did, Steel didn't see himself as one.

"Penny made it so we can time it," he said, indicating the room's door. Each room in the suite had its own door leading into the hallway; the bodyguards were positioned at the central main door, outside the living room.

Predetermine your exit strategies. Always have more than one.

He recalled the hotel blueprints without so much as a second thought. "West stairway exit is twenty feet to the left of this door," he said. "There's another to the right, maybe thirty yards, but that's past the bodyguards and past the elevators. We go together."

He jumped up from the chair, hurried to the

bathroom, smashed the thumb drive and flushed it, and joined Kaileigh, who stood at the door.

"I don't get it," she said.

"Watch the TV," he said. The costumed kids came down the hall, and the girl clearly greeted one of the bodyguards. There was confusion and discussion, and Steel could hear muted voices through the living room door.

"We're going to time it," he said.

"We're what?"

On screen, Jasmine talked to the guard and opened the door.

"Get ready," he said, pointing to the television screen. "We time it so as they come in, we go out," he instructed. "Stairway is to the left."

"Okay."

He'd seen Kaileigh nervous before—in Washington, D.C. they'd taken some big risks—so he knew she was terrified now; he tried not to show his own fear. If they were caught he had no idea what might happen to them; Randolph had convinced them to break into a hotel room; there had to be laws against that.

As the other Aladdin, Jasmine, and the two guards charged *into* the living room, Steel and Kaileigh slipped out into the hall and turned left.

The emergency exit door at the end of the hall opened, and Jason Voorhees and Malfoy stepped through.

"Back!" Steel said, turning quickly around, now facing an impossibly long hallway.

"You left the party!" Taddler—dressed as Jason—called out.

"Ignore them," Steel whispered. But Kaileigh glanced over her shoulder. "They're coming fast!"

Steel had nowhere to go: every door was locked, the elevators might take a minute or more to arrive, and the far exit suddenly felt like it was in another zip code.

The elevator door sounded, and out stepped Victor DesConte and Reddie Long dressed as choirboys. Concurrently, the other Jasmine and Aladdin and the two security guards rushed out of the suite, bumping into Steel and Kaileigh.

Steel knew immediately what to do: he grabbed Kaileigh's hand and swung her into the other Aladdin, knocking the boy into the other Jasmine, making sure that he and Kaileigh tangled with them.

The confusion stopped Taddler and Johnny in their tracks.

"I'm seeing double," Taddler said.

"What the heck?" Johnny gasped.

"You!" one of the bodyguards hollered, grabbing an Aladdin by the scruff of the neck. The boy spouted Russian, crying out.

At Randolph's instructions, Steel had learned a total of six full sentences in Russian, all with a decent accent: three had to do with politely asking someone to open a door; two involved conversational introductions; and one roughly translated to "I need help." This was the first, and only, of the sentences that popped into his head as the other Aladdin cried out.

Steel shouted, "I need help!" quickly and loudly, accomplishing his goal of further confusing the bodyguard. If both boys spoke Russian, who was the real Aladdin?

The girls struggled off the floor. One of them called out in Farsi, followed by the other girl saying the *exact same thing in the exact same voice.* Two voices, two girls, sounding perfectly alike, stunned both guards, who were responsible for defending *one of them.*

Taddler stepped forward as if to help one of the girls, when his sole intention was to pick her pockets. The bodyguard stepped to block Taddler. But as he did, Steel saw the man's eyes go wide, and now

Steel saw why: Lyle had arrived in the hallway through the same exit door Taddler and Johnny had used. A big man and heavily muscled, he was moving fast, right for the guard.

The guard's reaction was too late. Lyle threw him against the wall and raised his arms to fend off a blow from the man's partner. While Lyle fought the second guard, Taddler, a.k.a. Jason Voorhees, shouted something incoherent and went for body contact with the nearest Jasmine. He'd just gotten his hand on her when DesConte caught him with a flying elbow to the hockey mask. Taddler staggered back. Reddie Long dived for Johnny, who had crept behind the fight between Lyle and the bodyguard, and tackled Steel, frisking him in the process. Reddie caught Johnny by the cape, spun him around, and kicked out, knocking him down.

Steel came to his feet, facing the two Jasmines. Kaileigh might have sounded Iranian, and might have been able, by keeping her head down, to avoid being spotted as a fake by the two bodyguards, but the two girls looked nothing alike. He grabbed her by the hand for a second time and dragged her with him, saying, "We're out of here!"

He took two steps and fell flat on his face. The Russian Aladdin had tackled him. Crawling up

Steel's legs and punching him in the stomach, the boy was saying in passable English, "Thief! Thief! Give it back!"

Kaileigh grabbed the kid and tried to drag him off, at which point she flew sideways, struck in a flying body ram by the Jasmine counterpart, the Iranian girl.

Lyle subdued the second bodyguard, but failed to account for the first, and was caught from behind. The fight between the three lasted only a matter of seconds; the bodyguards were well trained, and without the element of surprise in his favor, Lyle was quickly overwhelmed.

Likewise, DesConte and Reddie Long were no match for the street-smart Taddler and Johnny. It was barely a fight at all, despite DesConte throwing a few wrestling moves that managed to delay Taddler's victory. But in only a few seconds, Taddler had knocked the wind out of DesConte, leaving him gasping for air and doubled up on Reddie, knocking his legs out and sending the choirboy sprawling.

Steel rolled, breaking the grip of the Russian. As the boy came for him a second time, Steel realized he already knew the way the boy favored his left foot as he struck with his right. Two months earlier, his incredible memory wouldn't have helped him one bit with this, but now, thanks to ga-ga, he saw a person's movements in a new way, each action connected to the next in what was instantly a predictable string. He spun to his left, counterclockwise, arriving to a point two feet from where Aladdin expected him, just as he might have to avoid a well-thrown ball in a match. The Russian kid not only missed him completely, but fell off balance in the process. Steel pushed him from behind, shoving him to the wall.

"Steel!" It was Kaileigh, who had also managed to get herself free.

They ran for the bank of elevators, two of which came open at the exact same moment.

In the elevator to their left stood Mr. Randolph. To the right, Benny the Bulb Morgan.

As if choreographed, both teachers stepped out of the elevators but held the automatic doors with a trailing arm.

The two teachers saw each other and barely reacted.

"Mr. Trapp!" Randolph reached out his free hand. "Hurry!"

"DO NOT TAKE ANOTHER STEP!" Benny shouted, catching both kids and managing to stop them. Steel and Kaileigh stood frozen. "He's a fraud!"

Randolph responded. "Me? Pay no attention to him, Mr. Trapp! Mr. Morgan is the enemy."

The others down the hall moved toward them, the bodyguards in the lead.

"Stop!" one called out.

DesConte and Reddie Long came to their feet and ran for the far elevator, disappearing through it.

Predetermine your exit strategies, Steel thought.

Benny said, "Steel, you have to ask yourself how Pennington got control of the hotel's television system, and how he always seemed to be where you needed him to be at the right time. Get in this elevator right now. There are police in the lobby."

"Don't listen to him!" Randolph called out from his elevator. "Hurry!"

Steel took another step in Randolph's direction, but Kaileigh, still holding his hand, held him back.

"This hallway has been seen by every television in this hotel," Benny called out. "You must come now or risk arrest!"

"Don't be a fool!" Randolph called. "He's the enemy, Mr. Trapp. Beware the enemy."

Lyle came to his feet, drawing the interest and attention of the bodyguards.

"Lyle's ours," Benny said. "Part of the Program," he whispered, running shivers up Steel's spine.

"Get in this elevator RIGHT NOW!" thundered Randolph.

"Just as your father was," Benny said. "I graduated a year behind him."

The door alarms to both elevators began sounding their obnoxious beeps.

Steel looked down the hall in both directions. He looked at Randolph, then Mr. Morgan. The distant exit was unblocked—but only for a moment. A winded Nell Campbell stepped into the hallway.

"Nell tried to warn you," Benny said. "Now you must heed that warning."

Randolph lunged for Steel, giving up holding the elevator. But Kaileigh saw the attack and spun around Steel, putting herself in the way.

"Go!" she shouted, pushing Steel at the same time toward Benny.

Steel stumbled forward and into Benny the Bulb's elevator, calling out, "Kai!" Benny stepped back and the doors closed.

The last Steel saw of Kaileigh, Nell Campbell was running toward her and Randolph with a look of fire in her eyes.

"Ms. Augustine will be fine, I promise you,"

Benny said calmly. "We'll see her at the safe house."

"The what?" Steel said. The elevator was heading *up*. It had taken Steel a moment to feel its direction. "Where are you taking me?" He panicked that he'd made the wrong choice.

"Quite enough excitement for one night, wouldn't you say?"

Steel saw a gold card stuck into a slot in the elevator's control panel. The last light, floor thirty-seven, lit up and then went dark, and the elevator continued to ascend. Steel's stomach felt it as the car slowed.

The elevator doors opened right into an enormous living room that made the ambassador's residence look second class.

Benny motioned for Steel, but the boy didn't move, sensing a trap. Benny waved a second time. Still, Steel didn't move. Benny stepped out, holding the door, saying, "Who but the federal government— your government—could arrange the Penthouse Terrace Suite at the Armstrad on a moment's notice? Take that into account, Mr. Trapp, and then come and enjoy the surroundings. This may be the only night of your life you'll ever experience something like this." Steel remained unable to move. "And in case you're wondering: there are four bedrooms, six televisions, and Ms. Augustine and Ms. Campbell will be up shortly to join you. Ms. Campbell knows the drill."

"Who *are* you?" Steel choked out.

"Haven't you figured it out?" Benny asked. "I'm your future."

42.
DOWNLOAD

Kaileigh and Steel, swallowed by a couch, faced Benny the Bulb Morgan, while Nell Campbell occupied a chair at the dining table, working at a laptop. Penny sat in a chair to Mr. Morgan's left.

"So," Benny said, addressing Penny, "where should I start? Do you want to explain what you can?"

"I'm *in* the Program," Penny told them.

"One of only a few Fourth Form students ever invited," Benny said. "You two will be the first Third Form students."

Penny said, "I caught the two of you snooping around campus by monitoring the school security cameras, one of my jobs for the Program."

"And you were assigned to keep an eye on us," Steel answered.

Penny nodded. "Yeah. Sorry about that, but I wasn't allowed to tell."

"And our friendship?" Kaileigh asked, clearly wounded.

Penny shrugged. "Don't get me wrong, I'm glad we're friends."

"But it started out as an assignment," Steel said.

Penny nodded.

"My doing, I'm afraid," Benny said. "He was only following the assignment. When a secret has been well kept for over fifty years, you hate to have it broken on your watch."

"Fifty years?" Steel said.

"The modern program, yes. The Program itself is nearly as old as Wynncliff. It's compartmentalized, meaning no one really knows what anyone else is doing. It was ramped up in the 1960s, but it was going strong back during the Second World War, and possibly before that. No one knows exactly how long."

"Some of us," Penny said, "like me, are analysts."

"Some are operatives," Benny said.

Nell Campbell turned to look in their direction.

"And of course," Benny said, "some of the faculty are training instructors."

"Like Randolph," Steel supplied.

Benny grimaced. "Not exactly. We've suspected for some time that Mr. Randolph was running a rogue operation—training students to work for him while telling them they were working for the Program. He suffered a great loss when his wife died, and I'm afraid the temptation of money, or maybe some combination of grief and regret, along with greed, overcame him."

"We suspected that Mr. DesConte, Mr. Long, and certain other students had been unwittingly recruited," Mr. Morgan said. "That is, believed they were working for the good of the country and all, until—"

"We came along," Kaileigh said.

"Just so," Mr. Morgan said. "When you discovered their use of the tunnels, and reported to Mr. Cardwell, we thought we had our proof. From then on your actions were monitored closely."

"And Lyle?" Steel asked.

"Lyle's an independent contractor," Benny said. "He works for me, in recruitment. More on that later, or not, depending where we all end up."

Steel said, "The woman we were told to follow. She's part of the recruitment? Lyle spots kids arriving at the shelter, and the woman's called. She scouts them, maybe makes friends and offers them a place to stay at the boathouse."

"Mrs. DeWulf?" Benny said. "A little more complicated than that, but you've got the general idea."

"Those boys are operatives," Kaileigh said. "The big guy in the hockey mask . . ."

"You might call us allies," Mr. Morgan said. "The way France and England work together, or the U.S. and Israel. Mrs. D.'s recruits are of age. If they are runaways, we attempt to reunite them with their families. If the situation is abusive, we take counter measures."

"But they're operatives," Kaileigh said, pushing him.

Mr. Morgan appraised her. "Let me just say that her boys can take certain risks that ours cannot, and never will. They provide a necessary function. Fill a missing gap."

"Are you telling me," Steel said, "that we were all on the same side down there?"

"When we determined your operation, thanks in no small part to Mr. Cardwell, I should add, we determined support was needed. Ms. Campbell and Mr. Cardwell were part of that support. I knew Mrs. D. had operatives at the function. I had hoped to allow them to do what it is they do so well, but Mr. Randolph had other ideas, and you interfered. He apparently discovered that Mrs. D. intended to visit the shelter earlier tonight—the shelter had a function in the conveyance of the recovered thumb drive . . . had it been recovered. That's as much as I can tell you. I imagine Mr. Randolph sent Mr. DesConte and Mr. Long to the fund-raiser as backup for you, for surely he suspected Mrs. D. would have her own people on the ground. We may never know everything about Mr. Randolph's intentions." He sounded gravely disappointed.

Steel felt a tightness in his chest. He'd been lied to repeatedly. He had a hard time knowing who was on his side.

"And now, if you will, Mr. Steel . . . or you, Ms. Augustine . . ." Mr. Morgan held out his hand. "The thumb drive."

Kaileigh and Steel looked at each other blankly.

Mr. Morgan shook his hand. "I assure you, you want to turn it over to me. Possession of that drive is a federal offense."

"We destroyed it," Steel said.

Mr. Morgan's lower lip twitched. "He told you to say that. Am I correct? This is something Mr. Randolph prepared you for—a debriefing like this—and you're having second thoughts? I promise you I—"

"Steel stepped on it," Kaileigh said, "and he flushed it down the toilet."

"Good . . . *God*." If a man could have died from being told something, Mr. Morgan just had.

Steel and Kaileigh met eyes. Hers pushed him. His refused.

Mr. Morgan caught the exchange. "What's going on here?" His voice had lost its friendly tone, turning hard and critical.

"I think I know," Penny said.

Mr. Morgan never took his eyes off Steel. "Very well, Mr. Cardwell?"

"Steel memorized it."

"Say again?"

"He memorized it. The contents of the thumb drive."

"Nice try. That thumb drive," Mr. Morgan said, "is believed to contain specific scientific information—equations mostly, some comparisons, and fifty to a hundred pages of diagrams—"

"Eighty-seven," Steel said.

"I beg your pardon?"

"There were eighty-seven pages of diagrams. A hundred and sixteen pages of equations in the first file. There's a nine-page letter addressed to someone named Illavich Vladikovski, and some kind of essay, forty-three pages, like from college or something."

"And you destroyed it!" Mr. Morgan's face shone redder than a sunset.

"The drive, yes," Steel said.

"But he memorized the contents," Kaileigh said. "The safest thing to do is get him to that computer Nell's on and have him start typing. It's a lot of information. It's going to take a while."

It took three days. Men and women, most wearing uniforms, some in dark suits, came and supervised Steel's "downloading," as Mr. Morgan called it. Steel typed some of it, read back a great deal of it into a voice recorder, and delivered some of it into the waiting lens of a video camera. Nell and Kaileigh and Mr. Morgan remained with him for the three days, taking wonderful room service meals at the suite's dining table, writing reports, talking to people, and signing dozens of forms.

At night the girls watched DVDs while Steel continued to pour out the information. He noted more than once that it took a lot longer to get it out than it had to get in, and said how he wasn't sure he liked this part of the Program.

Mr. Morgan didn't miss a second of the procedure, clearly astonished at the depth of Steel's memory. He took meetings with some military types, and Steel was pretty sure they were discussing him. They were behaving as if they'd discovered a secret weapon, and he was it.

Kaileigh spent time in one of the bedrooms, also being recorded on video. Steel heard her speaking in Farsi several times during the process, and again the military people were involved—this time women.

More than once, Mr. Morgan mumbled something about "a bright future," but kept it shrouded in so much mystery, Steel didn't know what to make of it.

Finally it all came to an end. Steel and Kaileigh, Mr. Morgan, Nell, and Penny rode in a stretch limousine—Steel's first time in such a vehicle—from Boston back to Wynncliff Academy. Steel and Kaileigh had signed a dozen papers promising to keep everything secret. The "cover story" for their Halloween weekend was a visit to Penny's house, with a trip down to Cape Cod. The details of that make-believe weekend had been carefully spelled out; Steel only had to hear them once.

Returning back to the school proved a bit of a letdown. Steel and Kaileigh stood on the lawn outside the dorms, realizing—or so it felt to him—that they had to split up now.

"So," he said.

"Yeah, I know," Kaileigh answered.

"Well it's kind of cool we're both thinking the same thing."

"Yes, it is," she agreed. "Should I thank you? Because I want to."

"Other way around," he said. "I know this sounds ridiculous coming from me, but I'm never going to forget this weekend."

She laughed, reached down, and her fingers brushed his. He left his hand there, hoping she might take it, but she didn't.

"All I can say," she said in a voice so soft that it was barely audible, "is that if I'm ever asked to do something like this again, I hope it's with you."

"Ditto."

"Well . . . later, I guess."

"Yeah," he said, flexing his fingers and trying to touch hers. But he missed.

He walked to his dorm with a knot in his throat and a sick feeling in his gut, and he thought maybe he felt better than he had in his whole life. If this was growing up, he wanted more of it. If this was school, he never wanted to leave.

43.
IMPOSSIBLE TO FORGET

On a crisp autumn day in the first week of November, the air was so pure it tasted like snow. It smelled of fallen leaves and pine. Winter hid around the corner like an unwelcome guest. The school—the entire school, it seemed—was gathered around the ga-ga pit for the final outdoor competition of the term. The contest pitted the Spartans against the Argives, and there was a definite buzz in the air.

Currently, the play had gone for nearly an hour—an impossibly long and equal game where, due mainly to exhaustion, attrition had finally begun to claim players. First one, then another, and now, impossible as it seemed, it was down to just DesConte and Steel, face-to-face, sweat dripping off their faces.

Chants carried out through the stands and beyond, some for the champion Argives, some for the upstart Spartans. The ball rebounded off the octagon. Steel jumped, landed, and deflected it. DesConte was too fast to be caught. He slid out of the way and made a miraculous one-handed strike in the process.

The crowd cheered.

Steel sensed a person's presence. It wasn't Kaileigh, as he'd expected; he knew where she was sitting—next to Nell Campbell—and he heard her voice carry through all others. Penny sat to her left, their cheers for him rising together.

But this other sensation felt both foreign and familiar.

He caught an image out of the corner of his eye, and his curiosity was satisfied.

His father stood alongside the bleachers, Mr. Morgan at his side.

They had talked by phone the past week in a roundabout way, where Steel never violated his vow of secrecy, nor had his father asked him to. But his father knew, in the way a father knows. They shared something now that they'd never shared before.

He wasn't there to push for details, he was there to watch the ga-ga tournament. After years of Steel not knowing much about his father, of not seeing him much, he suddenly felt as if he knew him a whole lot better.

DesConte's next shot almost struck the thoughtful Steel, nearly ending the game, but Steel leaped at the last possible second, spun, and slapped the ball for the near wall. It was a brilliant use of angles, and might have hit DesConte, but the boy slipped and fell, and the ball passed within a fraction of an inch of him, but missed.

The crowd released a collective sigh.

Steel got out of the way of his own rebound. DesConte sent the ball flying, and Steel dodged it yet again. He slapped it back, and DesConte artfully moved out of the way.

It was a chess match. A stalemate. No simple move was going to win the game; neither would be caught by a standard attack.

DesConte bent down and struck the ball backward between his legs—the same shot that had ended their previous one-on-one. But Steel had seen it before, and wasn't going to be caught.

He jumped high, landed hard, and lay flat on his back, so the rebounding ball flew directly over him—feet to head. The crowd oohed and groaned. Some thought he had been hit, but the referee's flag remained at his side.

As the ball flew past his head, Steel diverted it, slapping it with a hard spin so that as it struck the near wall, it bounced off in a reverse angle.

DesConte saw it coming—and was well prepared to strike, but he never predicted that Steel would do a back somersault, spin, and hit the ball with both hands, directly at him.

The spud didn't merely graze DesConte. It struck him so hard in the legs he went over backward.

The crowd exploded into cheers.

It took Steel a second to comprehend that he'd won. He stepped forward and offered DesConte a hand, and the boy took it and allowed Steel to pull him up, and the crowd cheered even louder. The boys threw an arm around one another and made a slight bow.

DesConte spoke into Steel's ear above another roar.

"Welcome to Wynncliff, Trapp. Next time, you lose."

DesConte trundled off, greeted by Reddie Long and others.

Steel, left alone in the pit, caught sight of Hinchman, who gave Steel an enthusiastic thumbs-up.

He rose on his toes, searching for his father, but

he was nowhere to be seen. Checking left and right, into the bleachers and in the crowds around them, he searched, his confidence in his memory skills challenged—had he imagined him there? Invented him out of thin air?

A hand landed firmly on his shoulder, and Steel knew. He pivoted to see his father wearing a broad smile.

44.
FOOD FOR
THOUGHT

That evening Mr. Trapp took Steel and Kaileigh out
to dinner at a roadside tavern, The Ale House, which
had been in operation since 1796. It was dark and
smelled sweetly of smoke.

They ate a fine meal—Steel consumed two
entrees. They talked about ordinary things, and his
father replayed the ga-ga game nearly shot for shot.

Then dessert came around, and in the middle of
apple pie, his father lowered his voice and addressed
them both. "I've been caught up by Ben . . . Mr.
Morgan . . . on your Boston trip."

"DesConte and Reddie Long?"

"Will be . . . *fraternity* brothers of yours . . . by
Christmas break. Yes," his father said. He meant the
Program.

"Mr. Randolph?"

"Some things you can't be told."

Steel nodded, accepting his new role.

"There will be overseas travel involved," his father said.

"No way!" Steel said.

"Your particular skill sets—*both* of you," he added for Kaileigh's benefit, "are of particular use in these interesting times. There are places you can help, and though you are incredibly young, I sense not so young as I might think."

"Help how?" Steel said.

"That kind of detail is better left to Ben."

"And you'd let me do this?" Steel asked. "I mean, I'm not complaining . . ."

"With certain safeguards and covers. There's much to be discussed at many levels."

"Overseas, where?" Kaileigh asked. "When?"

"There's talk of something before Fifth Form— your junior year—which is unusual."

"That's *next* year," Steel said.

"Let's not get ahead of ourselves."

"Any place in particular?" Kaileigh pressed.

"China was mentioned."

For a moment, all Steel heard was the pounding of blood in his ears.

"Awe . . . some," Kaileigh said, drawing it out.

"Nothing's definite."

Steel beamed.

"And there's something else." Steel's dad eyed them both thoughtfully. "The woman you followed?"

"Yes?"

"You were told about her."

"Yes."

"Well, following Thanksgiving break there will be two new students attending Wynncliff. I want you to be civil to them, to welcome them, and show them the way. Treat them right. It's not easy coming into a school midsemester. With any luck, by Easter they may be part of the Program."

He removed two photographs from his pocket and laid them on the table.

Kaileigh gasped.

Steel reeled. "No way!" he said.

"These are the boys. Yes. Do you know them?"

Kaileigh laughed so hard she nearly tipped over her chair.

Steel joined in.

The pictures were of Jason Voorhees and Malfoy from the fund-raiser.

Not understanding, Mr. Trapp continued being

Mr. Trapp. "Well, if you know them, I suppose it's all the better. Easier to make them both feel at home. You must understand the undue hardship such boys have suffered. They have lived on the street. They are without families. It hasn't been easy—far, far from it. The transition will be difficult. Such attempts have failed as often as succeeded. They will need support. Friends. People to treat them decently and help them along. Wynncliff will be their home."

"Home," whispered Kaileigh, regaining her composure. She seemed to be savoring the word as if carefully sucking on a sweet.

Steel reached under the table and touched hands with her, the warmth of her like touching a live wire.

That sensation remained for the duration of the drive back to school, like some kind of burn; it lingered there like memories boiling inside him.

Like the kiss, impossible to forget.

FIC PEA
Pearson, Ridley
   Steel Trapp : the academy
T 37071

DATE DUE

8-19-11			

Demco, Inc. 38-293